W9-CRY-917

## "What kind of 'protection' did you really provide?

"We lived in fear for my father's life every day, of his being found and killed. And for what? Because he testified in a federal trial to get *you* a conviction."

"Not my conviction," he said. "The government's. Look," he said. "I could have sent another agent here. Instead, I came to see you because I thought familiarity—"

"Breeds contempt?" Cameron walked toward the door. "Thank you for coming, Deputy Marshal Ransom. If there's nothing else—"

"I'm not finished. Sit down," he said.

Cameron knew she was close to losing the last of her control. She didn't want Ransom to know how shaken she'd felt tonight. Didn't want to hear what else he'd come to say...

"I think you're in danger," Ransom said, holding her gaze. "I think you're next."

Dear Harlequin Intrigue Reader,

We have another month of spine-tingling romantic thrillers lined up for you—starting with the much anticipated second book in Joanna Wayne's tantalizing miniseries duo, HIDDEN PASSIONS: FULL MOON MADNESS. In *Just Before Dawn,* a reclusive mountain man vows to get to the bottom of a single mother's terrifying nightmares before darkness closes in.

Award-winning author Leigh Riker makes an exciting debut in the Harlequin Intrigue line this May with *Double Take.* Next, pulses race out of control in *Mask of a Hunter* by Sylvie Kurtz—the second installment in THE SEEKERS—when a tough operative's cover story as doting lover to a pretty librarian threatens to blow up.

Be there from the beginning of our brand-new in-line continuity, SHOTGUN SALLYS! In this exciting trilogy, three young women friends uncover a scandal in the town of Mustang Valley, Texas, that puts their lives—and the lives of the men they love—on the line. Don't miss *Out for Justice* by Susan Kearney.

To wrap up a month of can't-miss romantic suspense, Doreen Roberts debuts in the Harlequin Intrigue line with *Official Duty,* the next title in our COWBOY COPS thematic promotion. It's a double-murder investigation that forces a woman out of hiding to face her perilous past…and her pent-up feelings for the sexy sheriff who still has her heart in custody. Last but certainly not least, *Emergency Contact* by Susan Peterson—part of our DEAD BOLT promotion—is an edgy psychological thriller about a traumatized amnesiac who may have been brainwashed to do the unthinkable….

Enjoy all our selections this month!

Sincerely,

Denise O'Sullivan
Senior Editor,
Harlequin Intrigue

# DOUBLE TAKE
## LEIGH RIKER

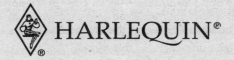

# HARLEQUIN®

TORONTO • NEW YORK • LONDON
AMSTERDAM • PARIS • SYDNEY • HAMBURG
STOCKHOLM • ATHENS • TOKYO • MILAN • MADRID
PRAGUE • WARSAW • BUDAPEST • AUCKLAND

If you purchased this book without a cover you should be aware
that this book is stolen property. It was reported as "unsold and
destroyed" to the publisher, and neither the author nor the
publisher has received any payment for this "stripped book."

ISBN 0-373-22772-8

DOUBLE TAKE

Copyright © 2004 by Leigh Riker

All rights reserved. Except for use in any review, the reproduction or
utilization of this work in whole or in part in any form by any electronic,
mechanical or other means, now known or hereafter invented, including
xerography, photocopying and recording, or in any information storage
or retrieval system, is forbidden without the written permission of the
publisher, Harlequin Enterprises Limited, 225 Duncan Mill Road,
Don Mills, Ontario, Canada M3B 3K9.

All characters in this book have no existence outside the imagination of
the author and have no relation whatsoever to anyone bearing the same
name or names. They are not even distantly inspired by any individual
known or unknown to the author, and all incidents are pure invention.

This edition published by arrangement with Harlequin Books S.A.

® and TM are trademarks of the publisher. Trademarks indicated with
® are registered in the United States Patent and Trademark Office, the
Canadian Trade Marks Office and in other countries.

www.eHarlequin.com

**Printed in U.S.A.**

# ABOUT THE AUTHOR

Like many readers and writers, Leigh Riker grew up with her nose in a book—still the best activity, in her opinion, on a hot summer afternoon or a cold winter night. To this day, she can't imagine a better combination than suspense and romance.

The award-winning author of ten previous novels, she confesses she doesn't like the sight of blood yet is a real fan of TV's many forensics shows—a vicarious "walk on the wild side," not to mention great research for her own novels. And when romance heats up the mix? It doesn't get any better than that.

Born in Ohio, this former creative-writing instructor has lived in various parts of the U.S. She is now, with her husband, at home on a mountain in Tennessee with an inspiring view from her office of three states. She loves to hear from readers! Write to Leigh at P.O. Box 250, Soddy Daisy, TN 37384, or visit her Web site www.eclectics.com/authorsgalore/leighriker.

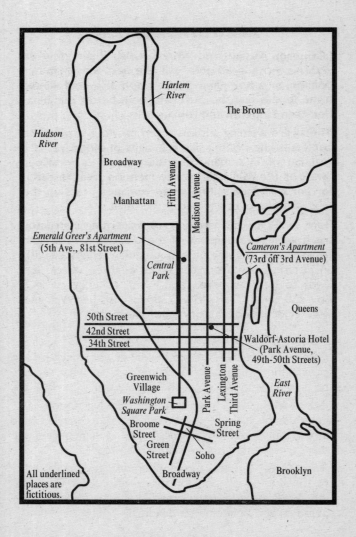

Harlem
River

The Bronx

Hudson
River

Broadway

Fifth Avenue

Manhattan

Madison Avenue

Emerald Greer's Apartment
(5th Ave., 81st Street)

Cameron's Apartment
(73rd off 3rd Avenue)

Central
Park

Queens

50th Street
42nd Street
34th Street

Waldorf-Astoria Hotel
(Park Avenue,
49th-50th Streets)

Park Avenue

Lexington

Third Avenue

Greenwich
Village

East
River

Washington
Square Park

Broome
Street
Green
Street

Spring
Street

Soho

All underlined
places are
fictitious.

Broadway

Brooklyn

# CAST OF CHARACTERS

*Cameron McKenzie*—After growing up in Witness Protection, this celebrity chef craves a normal life. When her reluctant protector, J. C. Ransom, shows up, Cameron doesn't want to believe she holds the key to her father's unsolved case—or that she is now the target of a killer.

*J. C. Ransom*—The U.S. Marshal responsible for a federal witness—Cameron's father—thinks he failed to do his job. Now James McKenzie is dead and his killer is on the loose. Cameron may be next...

*James McKenzie*—His testimony sent a vicious crime boss to jail. Was Cameron's beloved father the victim of revenge?

*Kyle McKenzie*—Estranged from Cameron for many years, he wants to reconcile with his sister. Could he be harboring a deadly secret?

*Venuto Destina*—His stint in federal prison—and now-failing health—have weakened but not vanquished the deadly crime kingpin.

*Emerald Greer*—About to make her comeback on the courts, the temperamental tennis star has what seems to be a perfect life—until she disappears.

*Grace Miller*—As an assistant to the ill-tempered Emerald, this plain Jane's coveted job is no picnic. Could a resentful Grace have orchestrated a kidnapping—and murder—to snuff out her famous employer?

*Ron Davis*—Emerald's hunky personal trainer would restore her to full glory on the tennis courts. That's his job. But Ron's interest in Emerald may be far more personal and sinister, even deadly....

For Dianne Kruetzkamp, for friendship, support and all those mutual brainstorming sessions. Thanks so much. And for Jasmine, the best little kitty on earth.

# Prologue

*Denver, Colorado*

The man was almost dead.

J.C. watched the life slip out of him, but no matter how he tried, J.C. couldn't stop the slow, inexorable march of death.

*My fault.*

Jordan Christopher Ransom, Deputy U.S. Marshal. It was his mission, for God's sake, to protect...to safeguard his charge.

J.C.'s mouth twisted at the thought. Sitting on the cold ground in January with James McKenzie in his arms, he cursed himself for not figuring things out in time, not getting here faster, not being able to prevent what had finally come down in this grim, dark alley. And instead of hearing the whistle of the wind all around, he heard the utter silence that follows violence. After the gunshots, the running feet. The shouts.

Some of them had been his own.

No matter.

James was still lying here, his eyes on J.C., pleading as he slowly bled to death. His stomach knotting, J.C. worked his fingers deeper into the hole in McKenzie's neck, but he knew his efforts to stanch the blood flow from a major vessel, no matter how hard he pressed, would do no good.

It was a killer wound.

From the cold-blooded bastard who had vowed revenge.

And achieved his goal after all.

Or so it seemed.

J.C.'s jaw tightened. In the darkness he heard the wailing of sirens coming closer. He'd called for help on his cell phone moments before.

"They're on the way," he told McKenzie, sounding desperate with relief, but the other man's eyes didn't change. "We'll get you somewhere safe."

His job. But he had failed.

McKenzie's mouth opened then closed, as if the attempt to speak was simply too much. And of course it would be.

"Hang in there," J.C. muttered.

The advice proved futile. His own heart thumped against the inside of his coat, against the blue steel semiautomatic in his shoulder holster. No reason to have it out now. They were alone. The coward had gone. He tightened his grip around McKenzie in cold comfort. It was the last the man would feel in this lifetime, and whether or not J.C. had ever believed McKenzie was innocent, he tried to provide solace.

It was the least he could do.

*Because of me you're lying here in a pool of your own blood.*

McKenzie clutched at his coat sleeve, his voice weaker now.

"Cameron…" Then in a final gasp, another name. "Ven."

Her name went through J.C. not like a sweet reprieve but like the bullets James had taken for J.C.'s brutal error, and he wondered for a moment if his own blood had spilled on the ground. The place smelled of rotting garbage, but of stale whiskey, too, and now of death.

He didn't trust McKenzie, not one bit more than he'd trusted his own father. Even McKenzie's name, his real name before the many aliases he'd used, was only a point of reference now for J.C.

But that didn't mean he wanted him dead either.

A chill raced along J.C.'s veins, like guilt. His fingers clenched around McKenzie's shoulders, then moved up to his throat.

And he realized he felt nothing. Nothing.

That last faint beat of blood was gone, like the assassin who had struck Cameron's father. All that remained was the ever-closer scream of the sirens that shattered silence. The sirens, and now his own fear.

The body slumped against him. J.C. looked down into blank, staring eyes. James McKenzie was dead. All he'd left behind was a daughter and those last few words.

The cops and the ambulance shrieked to a halt at the entrance to the alley. But J.C. didn't move.

*This isn't over yet,* he kept thinking, and the words kept echoing inside.

# Chapter One

New York City

Her father had been dead for nearly a year. Venuto Destina had been out of prison for a week. And Cameron McKenzie was still looking over her shoulder.

Now she felt the back of her neck prickle, and the too-familiar thought shot through her brain. *I'm being followed.* Unable to fight the lifelong urge, she glanced behind her again along the dark Manhattan street but the footsteps she imagined hearing had died.

She saw no one.

Relief swept through her, canceling the swift rush of adrenaline, and for a moment she felt her heartbeat begin to slow. She often worked late—how else could The Unlimited Chef, Cameron's cooking business for celebrities, show more than a small profit?—but she never liked walking home by herself.

It was necessary, of course, for her own peace of mind. Yet on this cold December night—the week after Thanksgiving—with light snow falling, she liked it even less. As if to acknowledge a threat, fewer people seemed to be out. Only a handful dotted the normally crowded sidewalks and several restaurants had closed early tonight. On this side street in the Seventies off Third Avenue, where Christmas lights already twinkled in almost every window, she felt utterly alone.

She strode briskly toward her apartment, arms wrapped around her too-thin coat trying to keep warm, but the chill seemed to penetrate her very bones. Just a few more blocks, she told herself. Then she'd feel safe.

Suddenly, her pulse hitched again. Her heart took up a noisy pounding.

Was that another footstep behind her? The sound of a man's shoes muffled by the lightly falling snow? She would *not* look.

Then the blare of a passing taxi's horn sent a shock blast through her body, and she struggled against panic. Now she heard nothing. The danger she had lived with for most of her life was gone, like those imagined footsteps. *Safe,* she tried to think.

Only the past lurked behind her now, not some assailant or unseen threat that seemed to hover in the cold air like a hand about to snuff out her breath.

Cameron silently scolded herself. This unfounded paranoia was why she forced herself to walk home each night rather than hail a cab or hop a city bus and bathe herself in its harsh interior light. She wouldn't take the easy way out.

"I am going to lead a normal life," she said aloud.

*Even without Dad.*

At the thought of James McKenzie, she pressed her lips tight.

She missed him. Oh God, how she missed him.

But he, of all people, wouldn't want her cowering behind closed doors. Wouldn't want her shivering in terror because Destina was free.

With one ear still tuned to any sound behind her, she picked up her pace.

She would go home, fix a cup of hot chocolate, open her mail...

Normal things. Everyday things.

She had yearned for them too long. Now, most of the time, she had them.

Yet the vague feeling of impending doom stalked her every step and Cameron finally surrendered again to the heart-thumping need to look over her shoulder. One more time. Just to be sure...

Seeing nothing, she felt in a pocket for her key then clutched it tight, ready to strike out at some attacker's eyes. Frowning, she swept into the lighted lobby of her high-rise apartment building. There, too, the lobby was already decked out with wreaths and a huge tree. Normally, the sight would cheer her.

"'Evening, Fred," she greeted the elderly doorman. And checked the sidewalk outside, reflected in the mirrored glass of the elevator bank, while she waited for the car.

"A cold one," he said, clearly relishing the overheated lobby.

She shivered. "I'm glad to be home."

"This is New York, not Arizona. You need a warmer coat."

"Or thicker blood." Leaving his laugh behind, she stepped into the elevator.

Blood. There must have been so much blood when her father...

Cameron blinked and stared up at the floor indicator. Two, three, four...at number eight the doors glided open. Cameron knew she was being silly, but she held them back anyway—and peered out into the long hall. Looking left then right, she confirmed that it, like the street downstairs, remained empty.

With her key gripped tight in a fist, she hurried to her own door. Her sensible shoes sank into the dense plush of the hallway carpet. She couldn't afford this address, but she needed it. Image was everything.

After all, she had been forced to reinvent herself. More than once.

Turning her back on the hall, she slipped the key into her lock.

Startled by a slight sound from behind, she froze. Alarm flashed through her body like a scream. Dread pooled in her veins and her pulse beat thundered again. *I was right, I was right, dammit.* Before she could spin around, she felt someone at her back. She sensed the hard male body inches from her spine, watched the large, callused hand cover hers on the key. Her nose picked up his scent, but the lone word didn't calm her.

"Relax."

That harsh male voice, deep and low, sent her crashing back into the nightmare. That scent he carried, so uniquely his...she'd hoped never to smell it again. A hint of outdoors, of musk, of heat. Even a frigid December in New York couldn't protect her.

Maybe, Cameron thought, there was no escape.

HE SHOULD LET HER GO. Now.

Yet he couldn't seem to move and J.C. silently cursed himself again.

He knew better than to come up behind a solitary woman in a dimly lit hall—especially an edgy woman like this— just as he'd known not to follow her home, or to accost her downstairs in the building lobby.

Frankly, there didn't seem to be an optimum place to confront her.

Just as there would be no easy way to tell her what he'd come to say.

In the past week everything had changed.

J.C. kept his mouth shut. His professional training hadn't

covered these bases, no way, but he'd done enough damage, especially with James McKenzie. From the race of the
pulse at Cameron's slender wrist, he guessed she wouldn't
relax until next week. If then.

Fresh guilt swamped him. Nothing new, but for the past
year he'd devoted his every waking moment to official routine, official protocol, to one careful bureaucratic step at a
time. It hadn't helped. He didn't sleep much and when he
did, he dreamed of death and destruction and his own
deadly error in that Denver alley.

*Cameron... Ven...*

Then there were the shakes, the sweats.

No wonder he'd finally been relieved of his duties.

Unfortunately, a medical leave of absence wouldn't close
this case.

Now, not unlike J.C., he could see that Cameron Mc-
Kenzie was no more than a breath away from hyperventi-
lating—his fault all over again—and he couldn't seem to
let go of her hand, or to block out the feel of her so near,
or even to remember who he was and how to do his job.
Unofficially this time.

Never mind business. Cameron made his head swim. Her
strong yet delicate-feeling bones beneath his harder grip
sent a swift rush of desire through his own body, and he
had to remind himself why he had tracked her down. When
he inhaled the fresh smells of shampoo and clean female
skin, mixed with the faintest hint of some tempting spice—
perhaps from her dinner—he felt his heart beat faster. J.C.
fought the urge to lean even closer, to touch her.

She always had that effect on him.

That, and more.

For an instant, J.C. felt grateful. He could almost stop
obsessing about the night in the alley, about James. And
his latest suspicion. He could almost believe panic wouldn't

overtake him again. He could almost hope that he affected her the same way she always got to him.

Talk about wishful thinking.

No wonder she hated him, J.C. thought. Certainly she wouldn't have opened her door to him tonight. So here they were, standing in the hall of her expensive apartment building—which didn't strike him right—and Cameron, all five feet four inches of her, with her medium-length flow of dark hair and stiffened shoulders and taut, willowy frame, appeared about to faint.

When he gave her the latest bad news, she probably would.

Because J.C. had been thinking. He'd gone over—obsessed over—every detail in the Destina files. And he'd altered his view. Destina hadn't gotten his revenge—not all of it anyway—and maybe James hadn't said his daughter's name at the end of his life merely as a goodbye. In the past days since Destina's release from prison, someone had been making inquiries, not about James but about the big chunk of money that remained missing twenty-five years after Destina's trial.

J.C. was convinced Destina had a new target.

"Let's go inside," he muttered, his cheek a fraction of an inch away from the softness of her silky hair. Her skin would feel equally slick, he imagined. For an instant J.C. allowed himself to envision Cameron in his bed, her hair spread out across his pillow, his fingers tangled in its rich, warm depths. Her wide hazel eyes would look up into his and her smile would light his weary spirit just before his mouth covered hers. As the kiss deepened, his hand would drift between them to seek her perfect breast, then the nip of her narrow waist, the modest swell of her hips, and he would hear Cameron moan.

The imaginary sound made J.C. straighten. If he didn't

step back, in the next few seconds she would realize exactly what effect she had on him.

On the other hand, her obvious impression of him came as no surprise. She pushed back, dislodging his hand from hers on the key then whirling around. He gazed down into her hazel eyes and saw the dislike he expected. Her voice dripped with it, along with the remnants of stark fear.

"J. C. Ransom. What the hell are you doing here?"

EVERY TIME CAMERON saw a U.S. Marshal, it meant trouble.

Despite that, she couldn't help noticing that J. C. Ransom was one intriguing hunk of obviously red-blooded male.

Her senses clanged like a five-alarm fire bell as she took him in.

Tall, lean, broad-shouldered and sleekly muscled, he sure fit the Marshals' service profile. His sun-streaked hair, on the other hand, didn't. He could never blend into the background. Thick and silky, his hair always drew her gaze first, gleaming like a California surfer boy's. But the lethal-looking gun he carried under his jacket ruined the effect. As did the hard metal badge clipped to his belt that glinted in the hall light. Just when she thought she had control of the situation, she made the mistake of gazing into his eyes.

*Oh, God.*

She shouldn't have looked. Dark, enigmatic, almost navy blue, they wore that intense look of purpose that Cameron identified with him. The look that had always meant he'd be whisking her off to another relocation, another move away from new friends and treasured new belongings. Another escape under darkness to somewhere else, to somewhere safe. Where did he get such eyes? Were they military—or no, U.S. Department of Justice—issue?

That blue gaze could burn a hole through titanium, but the most Ransom had ever gotten from her in return was a heartfelt glare of rebuke for destroying her security, her life, again. Carefully chosen from her repertoire of careful looks. Nobody saw anything in Cameron McKenzie that she didn't want them to see.

She'd learned that when she was three years old.

Yet at twenty-eight, a woman not a child, she saw the world through newly changed lenses. Those blue eyes looked different now, not only his usual sexy as sin but…haunted. Yes, that was it. And that was new.

"What happened to you?" was the next thing she managed to say.

Ransom's gaze had settled on her lips, watching her speak, watching her react to his stare with a quick dart of her tongue over her lower lip that turned his dark eyes to midnight blue.

She hadn't seen *that* look before.

Not willing to explain her observation, or to ponder his, she busied herself opening the lock with shaking fingers, hoping to slip inside and shut the door in his face.

Ransom was everything she hated, everything that reminded her of being afraid.

Her ploy didn't work. He straight-armed the steel door panel and followed her inside, so close behind her that she could feel his body heat. Had his footsteps been the ones on the street behind her?

In the foyer Cameron whirled to face him.

"I suppose you have some reason for scaring me half to death."

"Maybe you'd better sit down."

"I'm fine standing up." She wasn't on a level with him—Ransom stood just over six feet—but she managed to meet his gaze squarely, hoping he wouldn't hear the pounding of her heart. "Make it quick. I'm tired. I'd like to go to bed."

"So would I," he murmured.

Cameron blinked under his steady regard. He couldn't mean that the way it sounded in that husky tone, but his eyes held hers and it wasn't his official, government-agent gaze she saw. Those blue eyes had warmed with what Cameron recognized as desire. Her pulse pounded harder. Now there was another twist.

A dozen images of him flashed through her memory.

Maybe, until her last years in the program, she had simply repressed that hot, dark look. And before that…

"I've known you since I was thirteen," she said. "I never heard you crack a dirty joke, even with your buddies. So I assume…"

"This isn't a joke. I need to tell you something."

His gaze had cooled and he was back to business again. The way she knew him best. And liked him least. Cameron tossed her coat over a chair in the living room—her only real furniture. She wouldn't invite him any farther into her sanctuary. Her first home of her own. This U.S. Marshal had no right to violate her privacy here. He had no right to stun her with his masculine good looks, either. But his statement had drawn her attention.

Straightening, she turned back to him. "Well?"

"It's about your father."

"God. I should have known." Cameron cast a quick glance toward the fireplace mantel—and the copper urn that held her father's ashes. Then she sank onto the arm of the chair, her legs suddenly weak. "You've never minced words before. Why start now?"

"Look, I'm sorry, Cameron. I don't know how to tell you this except to just say it." He stepped closer to her and she tilted her head to look up at him. "You know Destina was released from federal prison last week?"

"Yes. I did read the papers." To be honest, she'd stayed glued to CNN for days, hoping for any scrap of information, any statement from Destina that would allay the last of her fears. She'd seen a glimpse of his son at the prison gates, but only the briefest flash of the camera's eye on Destina himself, and then later, outside his rural Connecticut compound. "There wasn't much reported. What they didn't tell me was *why*."

"Supposedly he earned an early parole for health reasons. Compassionate release." Scoffing at the very label, Ransom took a seat across from her on the folding chair she kept for rare guests in her sparsely furnished living room. "Nobody believes that," he said, "but it's the official word."

"That means he's ill?"

"Usually means it's terminal."

"My father is already dead. Destina killed him." He'd always said he would.

Ransom lifted his eyebrows. "There's no physical evidence, but I agree with you. Destina may have been in prison at the time, but he has a long reach. His organization employed any number of assassins when James testified against him."

She couldn't keep the reminder to herself. Her voice shook. "And Destina vowed revenge because my father spoke the truth."

"That truth—if it was the whole truth—put Destina behind bars."

She sighed. "Now he's out. And presumably sick."

"Either that or his lawyers are more clever than they were years ago. The assassins, too. All I know is, your father died in Denver and you're in New York." He hesitated, as if he had decided to keep something more to himself. "That's why I'm here."

Her mouth thinned with disapproval. "The U.S. Marshals to the rescue?"

"I know you don't like that—or me—but it's necessary. Just as you know James was in WITSEC when he died."

It was the official name for the more familiar Witness Protection program. "That made him our responsibility."

"Looks like you did a lousy job."

He flinched and Cameron cautioned herself to hold her temper. Ransom knew how she felt, but he was no longer *her* keeper. Twenty-two years in WP had been that many years too long. Now he had no jurisdiction over her.

Cameron tried to forget looking over her shoulder on the way home.

His mouth tightened. "James was secure in Denver for—"

"Three years. Since you brought me the happy news in Phoenix that my family would have to relocate *again*."

"Because *you* had decided to leave. When your brother left WP, we couldn't risk him inadvertently leading someone else—Destina—to James, your mother, or you."

"How many times did we relocate, Ransom? Five? *Fifteen?*" A flash of guilt about Phoenix went through her, but she knew, of course. They were all losses, engraved on her heart like her father's murder. "I left in Phoenix because what was the point, after all? Maybe my brother was right to leave, too. He just realized it first." She didn't know where Kyle—at least, that had been his WP name the last time she saw him—was living now, and the knowledge pained Cameron, but she felt too angry to stop. "If you people were doing what the taxpayers of this country hired you to do, my father wouldn't be dead!"

The edges of his mouth had turned white. "I admit that we—"

"What kind of 'protection' did *you* really provide?"

This time he said nothing. His whole face had turned pale.

"News flash, Ransom. We lived in fear for my father's life every day, of his being found and killed. And for what?

Because he testified in a federal trial to get *you* a conviction.''

''Not my conviction,'' he said. ''The government's.''

''You *are* the government.'' She rose from the chair, still shaking. ''It wasn't you who spent all those years hiding behind closed blinds, afraid of every slam of a car door or backfire in the street! Afraid of telling something—anything—to a neighbor or a friend that would indicate another life.''

Ransom stood up, too. ''I know that wasn't easy. But putting that bastard behind bars, making a serious dent in Venuto Destina's multicrime organization, had to seem worth it.''

''Spoken like a man who's never lived behind closed doors.''

Ransom ran a not-quite-steady hand through his sun-streaked hair.

''Look,'' he said again. ''I could have sent another agent here. Instead, I came to see you because I thought familiarity—''

''Breeds contempt?''

He held up both hands. ''I guess so.''

Cameron walked toward the door. ''Thank you for coming, Deputy Marshal Ransom. If there's nothing else—''

''I'm not finished. Sit down,'' he said again.

''Why?'' Cameron waved a hand in dismissal. ''I have lived all over this country, in a dozen or more ratty little houses. Under a dozen or more different names, which, I might add, is why I now prefer the name I was born with. It's my father's name too—''

''The name he took back when he died,'' Ransom said.

''And that's why I gave the marshals my real name as their contact—your contact—when I left the program.'' She dragged in a breath. ''I learned very young, when I lost that name, to be careful what I did and said and who I said it to, and at this point when I no longer have to watch my tongue or hide who I really am I am extremely tempted to tell *you* to go to hell.'' She took a breath. ''However, my mother managed to instill in me a few manners. So instead of throwing you out right now, I'll listen. For two minutes.'' She paused. ''Then I'll toss you out into the hall.''

Cameron knew she was close to losing the last of her control. She didn't want Ransom to know how shaken she'd felt tonight. Didn't want to hear what else he'd come to say…

''Destina.'' The name again shot fear along her nerve ends, as it had on the darkened street earlier. ''I think you're in danger,'' Ransom said, holding her gaze. ''I think you're next.''

Cameron thought she'd heard him wrong. She hoped she had. ''*I'm* in danger? But the only reason I lived in Witness Protection was because of my father. He's dead now.'' Saying the words still hurt. ''Destina's already had his threatened revenge.''

''Has he?'' Ransom cleared his throat. ''It would help if you could tell me about the money that's still missing. Since Destina's release, someone has been sniffing around. I'm sure James knew where it is.''

''The money?'' To Cameron, it was just a shadowy mention, in hushed tones, between her parents long ago when she was a child. What did the still-missing funds in the case have to do with her? Or even her father now? The government didn't pay its witnesses well. James, her mother, Kyle and Cameron had lived in near poverty. Surely Ransom didn't think… ''Why would my father know anything about that?'' Unless he thought James was a crook, too. Which he seemed to. ''Why would I?''

''Because the one thing that kept you all sane in WP was family. Maybe that didn't mean as much to Kyle, or whatever he calls himself now, or maybe he got restless and left the program to stay sane himself. But you stayed. A lot longer.''

"I had to. I was still a kid—and then my mother was ill."

"But after she died...?" he pressed.

"My father was all alone. He needed me while he adjusted to her loss."

"See what I mean?" Ransom looked at her with raised eyebrows. "Family," he repeated. "If James knew about that money, then you know about it, too."

Cameron glared. "By what circuitous route of logic did you figure that out?"

"You love your father. He loved you. He'd tell you everything. No secrets."

"He didn't tell me about any money," she said, her jaw tense, "because he... didn't...know...about...it...himself." She spaced the words so he'd understand.

Ransom looked around, as if he'd just now noticed her apartment. "I'd say you've already spent some of it." He gestured at the room. "Look at this place. Fancy address, fancy building. Marble lobby. A doorman. You're on a relatively high floor—with a good view, I bet—and in New York. Even I know this rent must be well into four figures. You're what?" he said. "A cook?"

She stiffened. "A celebrity chef."

"You feed other people. How much does that pay?"

"Not enough right now." With the admission, she seemed to have walked into his trap again. "That doesn't mean I steal. Don't pat yourself on the back too hard, Marshal. You might fall on your face."

"Deputy Marshal." Giving her a look, Ransom strolled through the living room.

Her sparse living room.

Cameron watched him take in the old chair she'd bought at a flea market in SoHo, the bare windows. She wasn't sure she'd ever buy draperies, because she couldn't bear to shut out the light, the world outside. But she had plans, eventually, to furnish the place. To sink roots at last, for herself.

"It's an investment," she said, seeing his appraisal of the barren surroundings. "I need the good address. It gives me an air of respectability, of prosperity. I doubt the kind of clients I solicit—celebrities—would sign on with someone who worked out of a slum, which is more like what I can actually afford." She hesitated, knowing she was again playing to his preconceived opinion of her. "I assure you, I do earn enough to pay the rent. That's about all, but for now it has to do."

Ransom remained silent.

"You don't believe me."

"I'm closer," he admitted, "but not there yet."

His steady gaze made Cameron's eyes lower. Her pulse drummed with tension, and something more. She didn't want to acknowledge the effect that blue gaze was having on her, yet his hot, hungry stare made her tremble inside. Desire flowed, thick and heavy, in her veins before Cameron pushed the response aside like an unwanted thought. This was Ransom. If he chose to believe she and her father were thieves like Destina, she couldn't prevent it. She didn't need to like him for it, though. She didn't need to feel tainted herself.

Wasn't it enough for him, for the U.S. Marshals, that in the end her father had given his life for justice? To accuse him now, when he could no longer defend himself, of stealing…to accuse her…

"Tell me one thing, Deputy Marshal. How did Destina's men find my father in Denver?"

"I couldn't say." He frowned, his blue eyes turning even darker. "Unless you tipped someone off."

Fresh anger boiled inside her. "There is no way I would lead anyone—most of all, Destina or his men—to my father. We had an elaborate system for communication, which we used as seldom as possible and always with extreme caution. It was foolproof."

"Apparently not."

"How dare you—" Unable to go on, she paced the room. "As for the missing money, I know nothing about it."

"Destina must think you do."

"And so do you," she said to him.

Not answering, he studied the living room again. "Your decor doesn't look too comfortable. Is there a spare bed I can borrow for the night?"

Cameron's heart lurched. She had only one bed—actually, a new mattress but on the floor. Next payday she'd buy the frame, then, eventually, a headboard. In the meantime she'd lived too much of her life under the U.S. Marshals. Now, she was done with that.

"Forget it. You're not staying here."

"How about a sleeping bag?" He tested the carpet's softness with a foot.

"I don't have one." Cameron flung open the door and pointed a finger. "Out."

Ransom didn't budge. "Look, until we can build a case against Destina and he's back behind bars, I'm going to protect you. Like it or not." He stared at her. "Until that money is entered as evidence."

That evidence—which Ransom thought she was part of—seemed more important to him than it did to Cameron, who despised Destina with her very soul. He had ruined her childhood, destroyed her family, shattered her father and caused her mother's death from overwork and a broken heart. That didn't mean she believed Ransom.

"Do you have a court order?"

"Do I need one?"

"Definitely. Yes." Cameron urged him into the hall. "Otherwise, I'm finished with government protection." *And you.* "If you remember, the last time we talked was by phone after Dad died. I wanted it to be the last time. Thanks—again—for your condolences."

Again, he hesitated then apparently changed his mind. His tone gentled. "I told you then I was with James when he died. And I've been thinking about what he said. I've decided that with his last words he was warning me—warning *you*."

Cameron's mouth trembled. *Oh God, Dad.* None of what Ransom had said thus far could be true. James wasn't a thief. She wasn't in danger.

"He said your name," Ransom reminded her, his haunted blue eyes on hers. "And something else." He paused, as if he didn't want to finish. "He said 'Ven.'"

"Meaning Destina?" Her blood chilled.

"Think about it."

But to her surprise, Ransom didn't argue about staying. He took out a small pad, scribbled on it, then tore off the sheet and handed it to her.

"My cell phone number," he said, "and the place where I'm staying—with a friend from the NYPD." Then he stepped into the elevator and, with the closing doors, disappeared—as if he, not Cameron, had vanished into Witness Protection.

Slowly, she crumpled the piece of paper.

She had the uneasy feeling she hadn't seen the last of him.

## Chapter Two

Blood dripped from her fingers.

The room spun around her and Cameron stared down at the knife she'd dropped on the counter. Her new employer's personal assistant looked at the accident scene. And swallowed.

"I can't believe I was that stupid," Cameron said, her assurance seeming to come from a distance. This was all Ransom's fault, she wanted to think. *Ven… I've decided he was…warning you.* She hadn't slept at all last night after Ransom left but had startled awake at every sound. It was only the afternoon but she felt bone-tired. "You'd think I never attended culinary school, or learned how to cut an onion without dicing my own finger."

Grace Jennings paled another shade. She wrung her hands. "Should I call 911?"

"No, of course not."

"Then let me get the first-aid kit."

While she was gone, Cameron grabbed a towel. Her heart was thumping, but she breathed deeply to get it under control. It wasn't only Ransom who troubled her. She couldn't seem to do her job today without thinking about her father.

After holding the two fingers that she'd clipped with the sharp blade under cold running water, she accepted a pair of bandages from Grace, who still looked as if she was about to faint.

Cameron hoped she wouldn't pass out herself. She hadn't seen Grace leave the kitchen of Emerald Greer's large co-op apartment, hadn't heard her come back. Grace moved like a ghost. Or Cameron felt too shocked by her own negligence on top of her anger at Ransom to register anything but pain. Her fingers began to pulse with it.

"Hand me that bowl of zucchini, please." She was still shaking but hoped Grace didn't notice, Emerald Greer either if she happened to appear at just the wrong moment. Cameron shot a glance at the kitchen doorway but with relief found it empty. She added green squash to the other fresh vegetables sautéing on the industrial-style range, and another enticing aroma wafted upward into the warm, moist air.

Maybe she shouldn't have tried to work. But activity seemed preferable to pacing her apartment all day, fretting. Or remembering Ransom.

He wasn't easy to forget. Or to ignore, for that matter. She tried to think objectively. Broad shoulders, lean build, long legs, well-muscled arms and strong hands…he had a powerful physique, but so did other men. Ransom's masculine appeal didn't stop there. Her first sight of him last night might have stolen her breath, not to mention her will. His sensual mouth and piercing blue eyes could melt any woman's defenses. But Cameron didn't intend to let him— or his masculinity—slip under her guard.

With swift, abrupt motions she stirred the mixture in the pan. "If this doesn't tempt the boss from her exercise room, I don't know what will."

"Emerald hates vegetables."

"I'll change her mind. Ratatouille Provençal has never failed me before."

Brave words. Cameron wasn't that sure about Emerald. Neither was Grace.

"She'll change your mind first," Grace said.

Cameron's hand throbbed. She didn't exactly regret her decision to work for Emerald Greer. Time in the celebrated but injured tennis star's kitchen bought Cameron a valuable client—and time she hadn't expected to need to calm her nerves about Ransom.

To her fury, he hadn't given up as easily as she thought last night. He'd obviously followed her to work this morning, his footsteps echoing hers. Briefly at first, she had let her paranoia kick in again until she realized—this time— who walked behind her. A couple of weeks in this well-appointed setting couldn't hurt, the money either, but Cameron refused to call it hiding out.

*The money.*

Ransom was wrong. Let him dog her trail if he liked. No one but him was after her.

"Now the yellow squash," she said, tipping pieces into the pan. Fresh garlic had gone in first with salt and pepper then a splash of red wine. She added the onions that had led to her accident.

"How did your other clients go today?" From her perch on a stool at the center island, Grace brushed wispy brown bangs from her forehead. "Two, you said," clearly trying to distract them both.

"A psychiatrist on West End Avenue and that dress designer in the Village. I saved time by making both of them similar menus. Did all my shopping at once—" She broke off. "Don't let me bore you with Fulton Market. But that veal saltimbocca…"

"You leave everything in the refrigerator when you're done?"

"For some clients, a week at a time. Three meals per day, seven days." It usually took Cameron six hours at each of their apartments to cook and fill the containers. Today, she'd taken only four and hurried to leave time for Emerald. "I put their prepared foods in the fridge or the freezer. I don't usually cook in-house for someone like Emerald and stay to serve." She was being well paid to do so, however, and then there was Emerald's upcoming wedding, a top story in all the newspapers. She stifled a yawn. "The doc wanted a huge fruit salad, the designer likes pasta. Everyone has favorites."

Grace looked wistful. "Wish I could afford your services."

"It's not expensive. You'd be surprised. You *will* be surprised when I give you my bill for Emerald." She stirred the vegetable mixture then added a waiting bowl of quartered tomatoes. Cameron would catch up on her sleep later, and the pay she earned was only part of her concerns. "After I cook for my clients, I clean their kitchens. That's the worst part." She held up her chapped hands. "If you can recommend a good dishwashing liquid, let me know. I do all the pots by hand. Are you staying for dinner, Grace?"

Sometimes she did, Cameron had discovered, sometimes not. It depended on the workload Emerald gave her, Grace claimed, but Cameron suspected the decision depended more on Emerald's mood. Cameron had quickly learned that her newest client was not only a celebrity, she was a very difficult woman.

Before Grace could answer, Emerald entered the kitchen, still sweating from her workout with Ron, her personal trainer. Cameron's exercise program consisted of her nightly walk home. Emerald wore hot-pink tights and a crop top today. Oh, and a frown. When the front door closed in the distance, Cameron remembered hearing raised voices earlier from the fitness room. So Ron wasn't staying. Emerald cast a glance at the sink where the bloodstained towel lay.

"What happened in here?" She turned to Grace. "Attacking our new chef? What did she suggest—skim milk and dry toast?"

Despite Grace's obvious embarrassment, which made Cameron uncomfortable, too, she decided the high color in Grace's cheeks improved her looks. With her mousy brown hair and almost colorless eyes, she normally appeared bland, even invisible. Grace seemed to define the old term *spinster,* and even the little mole beside her mouth had more color than her drab beige clothes, which failed to hide Grace's plump yet small-boned figure.

Cameron's heart went out to her. She checked the pan of salmon fillets poaching on another burner. "It was my fault. I honed my knife too sharp."

Grace looked thankful for Cameron's intervention, but Emerald quickly dismissed the incident in favor of her own problems. She seemed to be Grace's opposite, a classic blue-eyed blonde in contrast to Grace's brown on brown, always outspoken compared to Grace's softer tones. In the overhead light a huge diamond flashed on Emerald's hand.

And a collage of recent media coverage went through Cameron's mind.

Emerald was engaged to Theodore Kayne, a Wall Street success story who'd made his fortune buying up midsized companies then turning them into giants in their consumer specialties. *Rich* wasn't the word for him.

"We're still waiting to hear from that French bakery?" Emerald asked Grace as if she couldn't wait another second for the answer. She slid onto the stool beside her. "Their quotes for the wedding cake and the groom's cake were both too high. They promised to refigure by today."

"They'll call first thing tomorrow morning."

Cameron smiled, hoping to lighten the mood.

"Piece of...cake. I could bake for you, Miss Greer, if you'd like me to."

She was already handling the rehearsal dinner. What was another task? More income, she thought. She would use fresh edible flowers on the cake, purple and yellow and white pansies, maybe a few marigolds for trim… ⸗

"We'll see." Emerald shrugged. "Gracie, go home. I'm too tired to work tonight. Ron forced me to a near cardiac arrest today. Pure torture. He'll have my biceps looking like Arnold Schwarzenegger's before he's done. I'll be too muscle-bound to hold a racket. And my poor knee so soon after surgery…that man is a sadist." She went to the refrigerator to get a soda. "Did Ted call?"

"Mr. Kayne's assistant said he has meetings all evening. He'll phone tomorrow."

Emerald looked displeased with her fiancé. "What about the Zeus reception?"

Grace's gaze flickered. With irritation?

That surprised Cameron. She didn't imagine Grace had much passion. Zeus Sportswear was Emerald's latest sponsor and Kayne's newest acquisition. With Emerald as celebrity spokesperson for the company, he intended Zeus to move from its present middle-of-the-pack position to a dominant market share of the industry.

"Eight o'clock tomorrow night," Grace told Emerald. "The limo will pick you up at seven-thirty." She stopped. "Will you need me then?"

Emerald smirked. "I never need you, dearest. I keep you around for amusement." She grabbed a carrot then slid off the stool, her assistant apparently forgotten. "Do I have time for a shower before dinner?"

Cameron sent Grace a look of commiseration.

"A half hour," Cameron said. "I need to finish the endive salad, too."

"I don't need salad. I need fat, protein and cholesterol."

Cameron forced the smile this time. "That's not why you hired me."

Without answering, Emerald stalked from the kitchen, limping a little every few paces, letting the door swing shut behind her. Cameron stirred the vegetable ratatouille, trying not to see Grace's glare for her employer.

"She didn't mean that," Cameron murmured. "About you—or dinner."

"You don't know her. Yes. She did."

"She's a champion," Cameron pointed out. "Temperamental."

Which had a benefit for Cameron. Whether she wanted to admit it or not, Emerald's rudeness had made her forget Ransom, at least for now.

Grace scoffed, "She's worried about her career. You should have been here right after her knee surgery. The first time Ron worked with her, she turned the air blue." Grace shrugged. "Wonder how Ted Kayne will deal with her."

For the second time, Cameron saw that look of resentment.

"Everything comes easy to her," Grace complained. "Too bad she doesn't appreciate it." She rose from the stool at the counter as if she knew she'd said too much. "With the 'champ's' permission, I'm off."

"Have a good night, Grace. Don't worry about a thing."

"The only thing I worry about is Emerald Greer living to be a hundred."

Her words lingered in the fragrant kitchen and Cameron stared after her. Like Cameron, she supposed Grace was too well paid to quit her job.

If Cameron did her own job here, did it well, she might even keep from going mad over her father's death. She might be able to overlook Ransom and the traitorous desire he aroused in her.

Still, working for Emerald wasn't easy. *If I didn't need the money…*

The thought died before it had formed, to be replaced by another.

*Tell me about the money.*

Cameron pushed aside Ransom's words, too. She couldn't afford to indulge him or to antagonize Emerald Greer.

In a best-case scenario, if Cameron's wedding reception for her was a success, Emerald might recommend her to her friends, assuming she had any.

WHILE EMERALD ATE DINNER alone that night, Cameron took an hour off. The click of silver on china from the dining room had set her nerves on edge. So did the empty echo of each movement in the silent apartment. So did Ransom's visit last night. She needed a break. She would wash the pots and pans later.

Outside, after taking a breath of air, she refused to check the street for any sign of her unneeded "protector." Keeping her gaze straight ahead, she stopped first at a nearby pharmacy to buy emery boards and nail polish. In her line of work, her hands suffered every day. Then at the corner banking center she deposited her last week's receipts. The mundane tasks should have calmed her, eased the pulse of blood in her cut fingers. But they didn't. Cameron felt the back of her neck tingle again.

When she turned from the automatic teller, Ransom stood there.

Frowning at her. Wouldn't you know.

Cameron's heart whapped against the lining of her coat. She shivered, feeling cold.

His deep blue eyes regarded her in the darkness, and then the ATM. "Did you know that's one of the most dangerous things you can do?"

"What?"

"Stick a bank card in a machine on the street. With your back turned to anyone who might approach."

Cameron eyed him without apparent interest. "I don't need a keeper, Ransom. Quit following me. The only one after me is you. I'm perfectly safe."

He hitched his chin at the line of stores across the street. "There's a suspicious character over there by the tobacco shop."

She barely glanced in that direction. "He's just a homeless guy. The city is filled with them, sad to say."

If she could afford to do so, Cameron would start her own soup kitchen. But she didn't even have a day off lately—for which she was actually grateful, because that meant business was getting better—and at least for now, she couldn't afford to donate her services. Yet she knew exactly how it felt to be without a home, or roots.

"Don't be naive," Ransom said. "He could be a druggie. Insane. Violent…"

Cameron studied his grim expression. Even that couldn't disguise his beautiful eyes. "It must be even sadder to feel so jaded about mankind."

"I'm surprised you don't. Considering how you grew up."

"Thanks for the reminder, Ransom." She started off down the street. He followed her again. "I never did like the U.S. Marshals. I haven't changed my mind." She went fifty feet before she spun around again. The whole day was getting to her. His reminder of James's death. The money, and Destina. No sleep. Three clients today, one of them too demanding to make even the money that appealing. Cutting her hand had topped off the day, not to mention Ransom, stalking her like a madman himself. "Will you stop? I don't need protection."

"That's for me to decide."

"Oh," she said, "just doing your job?"

"More or less." He lifted a broad shoulder, defined by his wool coat. "I'm on leave of absence," he admitted. "Burnout," though that didn't seem to be the full explanation. "Too much, too long on the Destina case. Guess I should have mentioned that last night." His breath frosted in the chill air, reminding Cameron that she felt colder by the minute. When he didn't go on, she started marching down the sidewalk toward Emerald's building, its cheerful Christmas lights and welcome heat.

Ransom trailed two paces behind.

"You work late," he said, but Cameron wouldn't look at him.

"That's how I build my business. Emerald Greer is my most important client to date."

"Talk about a tough case."

"You know her? Not just from the TV news?" Surprised, she couldn't keep from asking. Ransom was at her shoulder now, inches away, his stride matched to hers. Cameron felt her blood beat faster, warming her from the inside.

"I know of her. She had a nut, a guy named Edgar Mills, harassing her on the circuit a while back. A friend of mine—the guy I'm staying with—works the stalker unit here in New York. Said he had to sympathize with the stalker."

"Did your friend arrest him?"

"Gabe never had enough to make it stick."

She missed another step. "So Edgar Mills is still on the loose."

She could sense his smile in the dark. "And I suppose you're Emerald Greer's new best friend. You always did want connections."

"I always wanted to get out of some crummy, run-down house in some crummy, run-down neighborhood—"

"In some crummy, run-down town," he finished for her. "I can't blame you."

"Well, I'm out now. I'm making a new life—for myself. Friends are going to be part of that." As soon as she had time. She had reached the entrance to Emerald's building, and Cameron stopped with one foot on the first step to the lobby. "So is walking to the corner bank without a shadow."

She felt him shrug again. His shoulder brushed hers and a slow trickle of heat crept down Cameron's spine like the prickle of awareness last night at her door. She didn't have to think hard to realize she'd almost prefer having to look over her shoulder for an assailant than feel any attraction to Ransom.

"Disagree if you want," he said. "That's your right. It doesn't change anything. I won't have you end up like your father."

When he reached for her hand, alarm jerked along her nerve ends. Ransom held it up between them and Cameron's twin white bandages gleamed in the dark. "How the hell did this happen?"

"Nothing sinister. I got careless with a knife."

Cameron's heartbeat slammed. His nearness surrounded her, seemed to smother her like that attacker from behind. Or a lover? By the time Ransom released her, she no longer felt chilled. She was sweating.

"Be more careful," he said, his eyes dark and hot.

Hoping to comfort herself, she turned and went up the steps. The lighted lobby, with its Christmas tree, beckoned her. She saw Emerald's doorman step out from behind his podium. "I can take care of myself," she said like a litany.

"With my help," Ransom added. Then he faded again into the night.

She had no doubt he would be waiting for her when she left Emerald's apartment later. Waiting, in the dark.

EMERALD GREER DIDN'T SEEM to have any friends.

No one came to see her that evening. At midnight she summoned Cameron into the den just as Cameron prepared to leave for the day, and a sense of utter loneliness seemed to hang in the air. More than that, so did some undefined tension.

Cameron stepped across the threshold into the discreetly lighted room all done in white: ceiling, walls, carpet, deep-cushioned chairs and sofas. It was so totally different from her own nearly barren apartment that immediately she felt out of place.

Emerald looked edgy. Perhaps Cameron was about to be fired.

In that case, never mind her employer's lack of friends or her own hope for more clients like Emerald. How would Cameron pay her rent?

Emerald flicked a glance at the phone then went to the bar. "Drink?"

"No, thank you." It didn't seem wise to try being cozy with her boss.

"Your back must be aching by now. Your hands look raw."

She did hurt—her cut fingers, too—but Cameron managed a smile. "The pots are clean. And breakfast for tomorrow is in the fridge."

Lifting her glass of wine, Emerald made a gesture with her free hand.

"Sit down. You work too hard."

"I don't mind. I have to."

Emerald studied her. "I suspect you always will push yourself. Even when there's no need. You and I are alike in that."

So true. And they shared other similarities. Their builds, for instance, if not their opposite coloring. Although Emerald's slightly heavier frame supported more muscle, they were the same height and nearly the same weight, Cameron guessed. Yet this very apartment pointed up their differences. It was a far cry from the program, when Cameron had lived simply, and even at first her father's modest monthly government stipend didn't buy luxuries. At times even food and clothing had been hard to come by. Sadly, her mother had borne the brunt of responsibility to support the family. And finally it had killed her. Cameron wouldn't forget that soon. She needed to take care of herself.

"I've worked in restaurants since I was sixteen," she said. "After I finished culinary school in Arizona, I became sous chef in a local spot, later moved to several other places—" she had never mentioned specifics before, and only now because her father was gone "—then became head chef at a golf club before I moved to New York, where I hope to stay."

"You lived in Scottsdale? Phoenix?"

The two resort communities were loaded with golf courses, but Cameron raised an eyebrow, not answering directly.

"I left home to play tennis at nine," Emerald said. "Thank fortune—and my lethal serve—I've never been back. That little upstate town was a nowhere place."

Surprised by the confidence, which only confirmed her suspicion that Emerald was essentially a solitary person despite her celebrity, Cameron relaxed into her chair. Where was this late-night girlie session leading? She watched Emerald pour more wine, rattling the glass with a none-too-steady hand as she detailed her own unhappy childhood before tennis. Finally, she sighed.

"But enough of that. I'm pleased with your work, by the way."

Hope flared inside her. Maybe this wasn't bad news then. If it was, why would Emerald open up to her? Cameron felt obligated to offer something, too. She wouldn't hide the truth. She straightened—then told Emerald about her life in Witness Protection. It was the first time in three years that she'd told anyone.

To her surprise, Emerald didn't judge her. "That was your father, not you. Whatever his problem, you and I are self-made women. I like that."

Neither of them had led normal lives, Cameron realized. Could she form a personal bond with Emerald? Having admitted to her own past, Cameron seized the opportunity she'd been given. "Ms. Greer, I'd welcome the chance to continue working for you. If you have colleagues who need someone like me…"

She smiled. "I'm also a selfish woman. I like the notion of exclusivity."

Cameron frowned. "I couldn't afford just one client, if that's what you mean."

"We'll see." She fidgeted with her glass and Cameron again thought she seemed nervous, not about letting Cameron go, but as if she was filling the silent air with conversation while she waited for something, someone.

*She had a nut harassing her…*

A clock ticked on the mantel. Twelve-fifteen. Emerald's second sharp glance at the phone beside Cameron made Ransom's words seem more immediate. Or perhaps Emerald simply expected her fiancé to call. But no, Grace had said tomorrow.

Cameron's frown deepened. She really should go. It was late, and after last night she needed sleep. Obviously, she wasn't about to be fired…but what was going on here?

If Cameron hadn't wanted to avoid Ransom as long as possible, she would have left much sooner. And found him waiting downstairs, no doubt, to walk her home in the dark. When the telephone shrilled next to her, Cameron jumped as if he'd suddenly appeared from nowhere.

At the next ring, her gaze darted to the phone. Emerald startled, too, then froze. Her carefully made-up face paled.

"Please. Answer."

On the third ring Cameron caught up the receiver, feeling even more uneasy when the caller spoke. His vicious tone made her pulse lurch, her stomach tighten.

"Listen, bitch. I've had enough. You tell me what I want to hear, or else... I'm coming after you. Understand?"

He hung up before Cameron could hand the phone to Emerald.

Stunned by the violence in the man's gravelly voice, which sounded mechanically altered, she slowly replaced the receiver then turned to Emerald. For an instant, Cameron had feared the call might be for her. But who would call her here? Unless Ransom wanted to frighten her into accepting his unnecessary protection.

Emerald asked, "What did he say this time?"

By the shocked look on her face and her words, she had heard from this man before. Edgar Mills?

Cameron repeated the message then watched Emerald's face turn even whiter.

"He's phoned every night for the past week. I can't imagine why, except that my engagement to Ted was made public right before the calls began."

"Did you tell the police?"

Emerald moved stiffly toward the bar again. She filled her glass and drank half the wine down in a single swallow then topped off the glass. And confirmed what Ransom had said earlier.

"I've told them. It never helped."

"But surely if you—"

"I am not phoning the police. They'll say the same thing they did before—that unless the man physically confronts me, which they consider 'unlikely,' there's little they can do. And they're probably right. I already have a restraining order.''

Cameron's pulse was still racing, hard. Now she understood why Emerald would stay home alone at night, why she didn't appear to have friends. Maybe she never knew who to trust, a familiar feeling for Cameron, too. Emerald tried again to defuse the call's importance.

"The man is a rabid fan…one of the type that always feel they own you. It's possible my coming marriage has upset him."

"And he wants you to say the engagement is off."

But then, why such threatening words—even though he hadn't mentioned murder? Emerald finished her wine. She had more color in her face now, but the topic was obviously closed. "Thank you for staying, for talking."

"I can stay longer if you like. Or call Grace for you. And Ron."

"No, I'm fine. It's foolish to allow someone like that to upset me."

Forcing a smile, she walked to the door of the den, and taking her cue that it was time to leave, Cameron followed her. She hesitated then reached out to touch Emerald's forearm in comfort. She felt hard muscle under quivering flesh.

"You're sure…?"

Emerald didn't answer. She pulled away.

"I'll see you tomorrow."

Ah, she was being dismissed—and put back in her place.

But Cameron couldn't as easily ignore the threat she'd heard.

*I'm coming after you…*

A fan—perhaps Edgar Mills again—who had become unhinged but posed no real danger to Emerald?

Cameron didn't know.

But all the way down in the elevator to the street, the

words reminded her of Venuto Destina's vow of revenge. Of her father. And of Ransom's caution.

With her heart still in her throat, she walked out into the night.

*You're in danger. You're next.*

She couldn't shake the feeling. If Ransom had been right, which she doubted, it seemed she wasn't alone.

Emerald Greer didn't have friends. But she did have enemies.

THE DARKNESS SWALLOWED Cameron up. The feeling of menace followed her home.

Even the blast of taxi horns, of people laughing in the doorways of restaurants and bars, made her skin twitch and her senses buzz. If Ransom was behind her, somewhere in the darkness, he was a darn good tail. She couldn't see him. Couldn't hear him. Couldn't even smell that subtle scent of his aftershave.

If he was there, as she assumed, maybe it wasn't such a terrible thing tonight.

Should she stop, turn around, tell Ransom about Emerald's caller?

No, that was a matter for the NYPD. And his friend Gabe.

She didn't want Ransom trailing her, she reminded herself. She didn't want him in her life, except to find James's killer.

As for the missing money and Emerald's telephone threat...

None of that related to Cameron.

Why feel so spooked, then?

It was Ransom's fault, she decided, key clutched tightly out of habit in her hand when she left the blackness of night and prepared to step out of the shadows near her building. Just a few paces more and she'd be in the light. Inside, with her doors locked and the dead bolt thrown. Maybe she'd toss the covers over her head tonight.

Suddenly, from the corner of her eye, she sensed movement.

"*Ransom!*" she cried out.

That quickly, a hand had touched her shoulder. She froze, heart lurching into high gear, as if it would reach a thousand beats per minute, her pulse throbbing in her injured fingers.

Cameron tried to wrench away. But in the next second, she learned it wasn't Ransom.

The man behind her tightened his grip on her shoulder and she screamed.

# Chapter Three

"Hey," the man growled, "take it easy."

That first voice in the darkness had barely spoken, his mouth close to her ear, before a second, deeper voice shattered the still night. "Let her go, dammit!"

Ransom barged out of the shadows, hauled the other man's grip from her shoulder and then spun him around.

Cocking one fist, he slammed it into her assailant's jaw. Cameron heard the sickening sound of flesh hitting bone. The small package the other man had been carrying dropped to the pavement. And her gaze jerked upward.

In the darkness she made out a set of features that set her pulse skittering: a square jaw, a generous mouth, shadowed eyes glittering with anger. She saw a mop of dark hair above a wide forehead. He reeled back, staggering, a hand to his head.

He had a wide forehead, like her father's.

Cameron froze in shock. *It couldn't be...*

When his fist balled for a retaliatory blow at Ransom, she quickly stepped between the two men.

"Wait!" She shoved at Ransom's chest. It felt like granite under her hands. "Stand back and listen. Both of you." She glared into his heated dark gaze, shielding the man behind her, as if she could. He'd always been bigger than she was, and he towered over her now. But Cameron had no doubts. "This is my brother," she said, slowly and carefully so Ransom would understand through the red haze of his own fury. Then she turned. Blood trickled from the corner of the other man's mouth.

"Kyle, you're bleeding."

Even bloodied, he looked good to her. She'd never thought to see him again. For a second, his betrayal of her family years ago—their family—flashed through her mind. The attempts she'd made to find him when James died had proved futile. Cameron gave him a curious look.

"I'm all right," he said. "And yes, it's Kyle—the name I was using when I left WP. Nothing like a souvenir, huh? Call me sentimental." He moved his jaw, experimenting, she supposed, to see if it was broken. "I went back to McKenzie for my last name. Might as well," he added. "Preserve the family heritage, you know."

Cameron continued to study him. Did he know, somehow, that their father was dead? Whatever he had done, Kyle had a right to know. He deserved her loyalty—at least until they were alone.

She spun around on Ransom. "You are out of your mind."

His jaw set. "Some guy pounces on you in the middle of the night, and I'm not supposed to react?" He shook his head, obviously disgusted. "You are an accident waiting to happen."

"If so, it's my accident. I didn't ask you to be my bloodhound."

"I'm a trained bloodhound. The habit's hard to break."

Cameron turned back to her brother, who was blotting his mouth with a handkerchief. The simple motion touched her. James had always carried one and Kyle had learned the habit from him at an early age. Taking over the job, she *tsk*ed at the amount of blood she saw oozing from his cut lip. "He didn't break anything, did he?"

"Teeth all here. My jaw still works," he muttered behind the linen, which smelled of James's favored aftershave, too. She stooped down to retrieve his package and handed it back to him.

"Come inside. I need to see you in the light."

She didn't mean only to clean his wound. Before she opened the door to the lobby that was decorated for Christmas, Ransom reached out to do it for her then ushered them inside. Cameron balked.

"Where do you think you're going?"

"Upstairs. With you." Nodding to the doorman, who stepped back at the look in his eyes, he punched the elevator button. "I'm hoping he'll listen to sense, since it's clear you won't."

"What's this all about, Cam?"

At Kyle's shortened version of her name—older brother to kid sister—she felt her resistance to him weaken. Kyle was five years older than Cameron. No matter what he'd done long ago, he was still family, and for the first time since their father's murder, she wanted to collapse in grief, surrender to it at last. Feel safe in Kyle's arms. Or could she? Cameron glanced into her brother's brown eyes.

"Let's go upstairs," she agreed with Ransom.

If Kyle didn't know about their father, she wanted him to hear it now from her. But she also wanted his presence to protect her—from Ransom.

IN HER LIVING ROOM, perched on the chair arm while Kyle told her about his life since she'd last seen him, Cameron helped him pat disinfectant over his bruised jaw. The skin was already beginning to turn a dark, mottled purple and she could almost see the imprint of Ransom's knuckles. He packed a mean punch. All that training, she supposed. From the look of him, he spent time in a gym, too, and she'd felt all that hard muscle and powerful strength up close, against her, at her door only last night. Now Cameron refused to glance his way. Despite her snarled feelings about her estranged brother, Kyle was more welcome in her home than any government agent.

She still couldn't believe Kyle had just stepped out of the dark—out of her past—like this. After her unsuccessful search to find him, she'd given up. By then, James was gone and his ashes were in the copper urn on her mantel. What was the point? The crisis, she decided, had passed. If Kyle didn't locate her one day, he would have to remain a shadowy part of her childhood.

Cameron glanced at the mantel. If they did reconnect and she forgave him, she and Kyle would scatter their father's remains—together—near their family's original home. Near their mother's final resting place, too.

Now he had found her, but seeing him again continued to unsettle her. He hadn't reacted much to the news of their father's death. But then he and Kyle had been poles apart for so long, she admitted. One minute she wanted to lash out, to punish him for leaving years ago, for not being there when James died. In the next…should she climb onto his lap, as she had at the age of five, or hug him as she had at twelve, the night he left their family? Any comfort seemed better than none at all.

Kyle winced then set the peroxide bottle on the crate Cameron used for an end table. "I'm sorry as hell, Cam. About Dad, too. But I only discovered where you were— where you are—a few days ago. When I got to New York, I looked in the phone book, then called Information." He held her gaze, as if fearing she would send him away. "I do that everywhere I go. I check every name of yours that I remember from the program, plus your real name. I'm glad you returned to that when you left the program. Glad you didn't invent an entirely new one."

"I've changed names too many times in my life. I don't need another." Her forceful tone was meant for Ransom.

"Yeah," Kyle said, "I know how that was."

Ransom shot her a look and Cameron stilled. There was another reason she'd taken back her own name, and after all this time she finally recognized it. "I...guess I wanted you to be able to find me. If I used another name—again—you never would."

Kyle agreed, then bypassed any further talk about James. Catching up, he told her about his career in the aerospace industry. He lived in Houston now—or had, until a recent job layoff caused by the loss of a government contract—but had traveled a great deal. In part on business but partly, he claimed, to be able to hunt for Cameron and, even now and then, for their father. "I wanted to make amends," he finished.

"If you were so determined to find Cameron," Ransom murmured, "why not use the Internet? You can find anybody's number there—except your father's, of course."

Kyle didn't answer, but Cameron noted he was careful not to make eye contact with Ransom. She didn't bother to hide her own disapproval. Why was Ransom hanging around? Why didn't he leave?

Ransom was roaming the small apartment like a convict on death row. Every time he met her gaze, which Cameron, too, tried to avoid, his eyes seemed to darken another shade. His barely leashed intensity bounced off the walls. They were beginning to close in on Cameron, too. Like Ransom. She didn't have to look at him to feel that slow heat inside, to sense his nearness.

"I'm sorry about your job troubles," she told Kyle, redirecting her own thoughts, "and just before Christmas, too."

He dismissed his business failure. "I'll get another. In the meantime, I have interviews—some here—plus unemployment benefits.'' He moved his package aside on the chair cushion. Even those small gestures were her father's, too. Maybe the years apart no longer mattered. ''Of course, I also have bills to pay.''

Considering the circumstances, Cameron felt a strange sense of welcome peace wash through her. Even his total estrangement from James couldn't override her relationship with him. With Kyle she wasn't alone in this…whatever it was.

She didn't buy Ransom's theories about Destina. But Kyle, it turned out, wasn't as sure. While Ransom filled him in on his version of Destina, he listened intently.

''So you think Venuto is responsible for our father's death?'' he asked Ransom. ''And Cameron may be his target, too?''

Cameron clenched her teeth. She wouldn't say a word. Let Kyle sort this out, come to the same conclusion she had, send Ransom on his way. For that alone, she might forgive Kyle. When Ransom finished his rant about the still-open investigation, Cameron added, ''But no one has tried to reach me.'' She held both arms out. ''See? I survived last night by myself. I'd have been fine all day without you staking out my employer's apartment, watching everyone who came and went.''

''The doorman and I found a lot to talk about.''

''Revenge?'' Kyle was still working through Ransom's theory. ''After all this time? That's hard to believe—''

''Destina swore to destroy your father for his testimony. He was always a threat,'' Ransom said. ''Isn't that why your family went into the program in the first place? But apparently you didn't agree about the need to keep out of his way.''

''I left WP for reasons of my own. That's between me and my father—between Cam and me now. I didn't leave because I thought Destina posed no further danger to my family. I was just willing to take my chances in the light.''

Cameron frowned at his surprising admission. The same old sense of loss she'd experienced since Kyle left ''home'' years ago raced along her nerve ends. The last quarrel with their father, the shouted words that couldn't be taken back, words she didn't quite remember, Kyle leaving in the middle of the night...

Ransom stuck to his guns. ''Your leaving years ago doesn't mean Destina can't strike for vengeance even now. Or try for that missing money. He's still a powerful man.''

''So is his son,'' Kyle said. ''Have your people interviewed Tony Destina?''

''When he stood still long enough. Tony's been busy. Since his father's release from prison, he's had Venuto in some pricey private clinic. Right now no one seems to know where that is.''

He didn't say more, and Cameron glanced away from Ransom's dark eyes to exchange a look with Kyle. In contrast to Ransom, it was easy to read her brother's face—composed yet concerned—and she could almost hear him thinking, *I'm here for you.*

But would he stay? Cameron blinked back the tears.

*Oh, Benjamin.*

The sudden thought of his birth name, so long unused, overwhelmed her. For that single instant she had allowed herself to see him as the boy he'd been years ago, before the program, before they lived in hiding and fear, before the trial and Destina. Then in the next breath he betrayed her all over again.

''I think Ransom is right. You're in danger now, Cam.'' He still didn't look at Ransom, but Cameron did—and saw a flash of victory in his eyes. Her own brother had helped him. ''I don't like your being here alone,'' Kyle said. ''I don't like you working until all hours then walking home by yourself. You didn't even hear me coming tonight.''

*See?* Ransom's gaze echoed the statement.

Cameron looked away. She busied herself putting the disinfectant back in the first-aid kit, then neatly lined up a stack of bandages in the case.

''I can—'' she began.

''Take care of herself,'' Ransom finished for her. He prowled the other end of the living room, not far enough away from her for Cameron's taste. Why couldn't she seem to ignore him as she wanted to? Why didn't he go?

''I disagree,'' her brother said, making things worse. ''Kyle…''

''It's all very well to be independent, Cam—under normal circumstances. But obviously, this is not normal. Until Dad's killer is caught, you aren't safe either. If Destina feels you know where that money is—that damn money— he sure can't learn that from Dad. He won't stop until *you* tell him.''

Cameron shuddered. ''I don't know where it is! I can't believe this. I thought you'd be on my side.'' She turned a beseeching look on him, probably the same look he'd seen the night he left WP, left her. ''My job keeps me sane. I can't sit around here worrying. Wondering. Feeling afraid again.''

He glanced around the spare room. ''Then come with me tonight. To my hotel.''

She started to shake her head, but he took her hands and held them, searching her eyes with his. ''My place isn't fancy—'' he glanced at her living room ''—but it has furniture. The second bed's already made up. You can stay with me.''

''Until when?'' she said. ''Until you find another position in Houston, in Detroit, or Seattle?'' To her horror, her eyes filled. ''I need my space here, Kyle.''

Kyle looked toward Ransom, who was still walking her carpet. If he wore a hole in it, she'd kill him. She sure as heck wouldn't meet that heated gaze of his again. Or, at the moment, Kyle's cooler one. Why were they joining forces against her?

Kyle gripped her hands tighter. He blocked out Ransom and lowered his voice. "I don't care for the marshals any better than you do, but we need to end this thing. In the meantime, I'd feel much better with you beside me."

"I know you would."

"Yeah, yeah." He'd heard the sarcasm in her tone. "I know, I'm being the older, overly protective brother. Let me be just that, Cam. I've missed you for too many years."

True enough, on her part.

Yet, in that moment, she realized she wasn't ready to simply trust him again. Trust didn't come easily to Cameron, and Ransom had a point. Why had Kyle shown up now? she wondered. Because *he* was in trouble? She'd been in New York for almost three years.

"Too many years," she agreed. "I'm grown up now."

He smiled, his gaze running over her in approval. "No more scrawny kid with big eyes and scabs on her knees. You turned out good, Cam. Now, about tonight…"

"I'm staying right here. Alone," she emphasized. "I don't believe there's any threat to fear. Besides," she added, taking a breath before she admitted, "I'm not ready to forgive you yet."

With a sigh Kyle folded her in his arms. "I was afraid of that." She felt him look over her head at Ransom, felt the long-missed warmth of Kyle's body.

"We heard the lady," Kyle said.

Ransom crossed the room. "Then good night. I guess."

"You'll give us a heads-up on the investigation?" Kyle pressed.

Ransom didn't answer immediately. He opened the door

then turned to look back at Cameron. She had no doubt he'd stay nearby tonight, make friends with her doorman rather than Emerald's, but she wondered whether because of his medical leave he even had any official part in the investigation. It didn't seem so. Yet despite the irritation he always caused, she felt that stubborn, slow tingle of need run down her spine.

"You're okay with this?" He nodded at Cameron then at Kyle.

"I'm…okay."

He studied her for a long moment before glancing at her brother again. "Then do what he says."

"Why don't you stay awhile longer—and deputize him?"

Ransom's mouth twitched. "Cute, Cameron. Very cute."

When the door closed behind him, she leaned back in Kyle's arms. But the lingering buzz Ransom caused in her veins, through her entire body, didn't cool. "That man makes my blood steam."

Kyle surprised her by saying, "I think you make his blood steam, too."

She flushed. "I didn't mean…attraction."

He frowned. "Well, he does."

She made her voice flippant. "Oh. Is that why he stalks me everywhere?"

"From now on, kid, I'm your stalker."

She smiled up at him, but Kyle's eyes stayed serious and Cameron's niggling distrust of his surprise appearance tonight remained. "I'm not making light of Destina," she tried to assure him. "Come into the kitchen. I'll fix us both some cocoa before you go. Ransom tends to be a bit obsessed. I'd rather move on with my life. Our lives."

"It's a nice idea, Cam."

As if he didn't believe that was possible yet either.

With her confused emotions still running high, her

awareness of Ransom and the anger he made her feel and her wariness of himself on his mind, Kyle started for the kitchen. But he paused to retrieve from the chair the small package he'd brought with him.

"Here. Open this. It's for you." He urged her fingers to the string that tied it closed. "Something from another time," he added. "A peace offering."

When she pulled off the paper, tangling with the string, an object fell out and thudded to the floor. Cameron picked it up and her heart melted.

"Oh, Kyle." In a flash she recognized the soft-bodied doll from her childhood—the treasured doll she'd had to leave behind when her family entered Witness Protection. Along with everything else, her favorite toy had been abandoned. Nothing, absolutely nothing, had made that first move except her mother, her father, Kyle and Cameron.

Her throat tightened. Cameron cradled the doll, feeling a slight stiffness here and there. It must have been left in the rain at some point, then dried. The doll looked dirty and worn—apparently well loved—but its button eyes brightly stared up at her as they had done so often at night before she fell asleep. At three years old, on the verge of having her world destroyed, she'd clutched that doll for a final time like a talisman against the dark that would soon engulf her. Now she had a piece of her life back again.

"Where did you find this?"

"At Gram's." After leaving the program—before he'd vanished without a trace—Kyle had gone to live with their maternal grandmother until he finished school. Like their mother and James, Gram was dead now. But she'd saved this doll for Cameron. All those years.

Kyle had guessed at its significance to her. She didn't know what to say now except, "Thank you," which seemed so inadequate.

Kyle shrugged. "I knew you'd appreciate the memento

from our childhood. All I remember is getting uprooted and living where I didn't want to go, always lying about who I was.''

Like their names, she thought. She wasn't ready to forgive Kyle. But at least now she had the chance to rebuild what they'd lost.

''WHY WOULD YOU choose not to?'' Emerald said in a strident tone late the next afternoon. ''How could you refuse?''

She didn't mean Kyle, and Cameron felt her first reaction—a simple no—take flight. She surveyed the pile of evening gowns on Emerald's wide bed and tried not to stare. Black velvet, bronze satin, red silk…they must be worth more money than Cameron's entire wardrobe—mostly practical pants and shirts—several times over.

Emerald's hands fluttered over the obviously expensive fabrics. And again, Cameron thought how nervous she seemed. Last night's phone call must still be bothering her. Why else had she made such an outrageous suggestion?

She didn't really have a choice, Cameron realized. If she wanted to keep her job here, if she wanted to talk her way into other clients through Emerald, she would have to do as Emerald asked. No, demanded.

''Stand in for you?'' she said. ''Me?'' Determined to decide her own fate, she tried to back out. ''I realize we're the same height and build, more or less, but…''

Irritation edged Emerald's tone. ''It's only for one night.'' She ripped another dress from a hanger in her closet. Dark green watered silk flowed onto the bed and drank up the soft light from the bedside lamp. Once more she ran through the scenario. ''You'll come to the hotel just before the Zeus reception ends. We'll trade clothes there in my dressing room. Then I disappear in your jeans while you take my place in the evening dress I wore to the reception. You climb into my limousine for the ride home and wave to the press through the tinted windows. No one will actually see you except getting in and getting out of the car. You'll wear my coat, which has a hood to hide your face. Now, is that so hard?''

Emerald dashed back to the walk-in closet and came out with a suitcase. She threw in lingerie, shoes, pants and blouses. They didn't match but Emerald didn't seem to care. She seemed intent upon one thing now—leaving town.

At a sharp rap on the open door, Emerald jerked around. She clutched a pair of designer jeans in both hands, her knuckles white. Her features didn't relax but faint relief sounded in her voice when she recognized her personal trainer, a huge, barrel-chested man, lounging in the doorway.

''Ron. I thought we had finished for the day.''

''Torture's over but I wondered about my pay.''

''Grace will write a check, you know that. See her.''

Uh-oh, Cameron thought. More trouble. Ron's frown and the hard look in his eyes sent a chill down her spine. Turning her back, Emerald dropped the jeans then rearranged the gowns on the bed.

''Grace had a headache.'' Ron straightened, his gaze raking Emerald. ''Probably from one of your browbeatings. She went home.''

''Then she'll pay you tomorrow.''

''This isn't the first time I've been put off.'' He glanced at Cameron, who felt decidedly uncomfortable being in the middle of their quarrel. ''You have no idea what you're in for,'' he told her. ''Greer's up to her pretty ears in unpaid bills. Her staff's income is the last to be dealt with, which I'm sure you'll learn.''

''I will talk with you tomorrow, Ron,'' Emerald cut across his statement. ''Don't be late tonight.'' He doubled as her chauffeur, Cameron knew, and would drive her to the Zeus reception. Carrying a dress, Emerald walked toward him, clearly intent upon shutting the door behind him for now. "Thank you for the workout. I'm still perspiring. I must have lost five pounds."

"That why you're shaking now?"

Cameron had noticed, too. Emerald was not in control.

"Or is it the guy who keeps calling?" He stepped back into the hall before Emerald reached him. The muscles of his massive chest and biceps stood out when he folded his arms. Not a man to make an enemy of, Cameron thought. "Better watch it, Champ," he said. "There are a lot of nuts out there. If he takes it in mind to turn up here—"

"I'm sure you'll protect me." Emerald's voice dripped with both honey and vinegar, but her fingers twitched again on the silk in her hands.

"That's why you pay me."

His sarcastic tone served as a reminder that she owed him. As if satisfied with that for the moment, Ron gave Cameron a nod, turned and went soundlessly down the hall.

For a long moment no one spoke. Emerald threw down the silk gown.

Then she said, "Don't let his muscle-bound appearance fool you. Ron is minor league. I pulled him out of the gutter two years ago. He's not that good a driver, either. When I'm back on top in my game, and my knee is fully healed, he'll be the first to go."

"Still," Cameron mused, "I wouldn't want to cross him."

"He's a nobody. Grace undoubtedly paid him—and he simply wants more."

She turned back to the suitcase, pushed everything flat inside and closed the latches. When she faced Cameron again, she was smiling.

"Imagine being afraid of him, or that deranged man who called. They won't touch me." She waved toward the dresses on the bed. Red, green, black. "I think the bronze satin will do for you. It suits both of us." She returned to the closet then handed Cameron a sleek, long-haired object.

Cameron recoiled.

"Take it," Emerald said with a half smile. "My wig for those bad-hair days. If you're going to impersonate me tonight, you'll need to be blond."

Cameron frowned. "What if this doesn't work?"

"Of course it will work. Most people are completely unobservant. Unless you're forced to play tennis, you can easily pass for me." A pleading note had entered her voice and Cameron sank down on the bed, knowing she'd been defeated.

As far as she could tell, Emerald had plenty of colleagues and professional acquaintances—all potential clients for Cameron—but no real friends. Ron and Grace didn't appear to like her either. As for enemies, that "fan"... Cameron shuddered at the memory of his harsh voice, his threat. She knew all about that—in the past. Now she had her job to consider. Plus, she felt a connection to Emerald.

"Well, if it will help..."

Emerald headed for the bathroom to shower.

"You'll save my life," she said, sounding confident again. "I'll be at Ted's if anyone needs me. Grace has his number."

Cameron knew a look of escape when she saw it.

"I need a few days out of the limelight," Emerald said over her shoulder. "When I get back, we'll see about a reward for your service."

"Miss Greer. Emerald..."

But she was gone in a click of heels on marble tile.

HOURS LATER, Cameron gazed at herself in the mirror of Emerald's dressing room at the Waldorf-Astoria. Her heart beat a rapid tattoo beneath the low-cut neckline of the bronze satin gown.

"Well?" she said, taking care to hide her bandaged fingers in the skirt.

"Perfect." Wearing Cameron's jeans and sweater, Emerald stood behind her.

Cameron compared their images. Briefly, another wave of uncertainty about tonight darkened her eyes, but she had to admit, she didn't look half-bad. She and Emerald did resemble each other—in reverse now. Their shoulders were on a level, their heads, too, and anyone would be hard-pressed to notice the few pounds' difference between them. When Cameron put on a coat, it would be impossible to discern unless that person knew them well.

Which made her ask the question.

"What about Ron?"

"I didn't tell him. It won't matter. He's being paid—and he will be paid—to drive me to this hotel then home again. I have nothing more to say to him tonight."

Because of their earlier quarrel, that left Cameron to explain the ruse to Ron later. Emerald didn't seem to care.

So, big deal. She could play someone else—again—for one night. She'd had plenty of practice, and she had to admit, the dress was flattering. The bronze satin nipped in Cameron's waist and emphasized her smaller breasts. No jeans tonight. This might be her one chance to shine.

If she succeeded, Emerald would be grateful.

As a reward, The Unlimited Chef might benefit from her gratitude.

Cameron would be that much closer to making it on her own. Being normal.

Taking a deep breath, she willed herself to relax.

What was the harm? Even in the back seat of a darkened limousine, she would be more a part of things, out in the open and free, than in all her years in Witness Protection.

Maybe it would be fun to lead a harmless press, rather than a killer, off the track.

Emerald gathered Cameron's coat and wool hat.

Cameron reached for the blond wig. Its thick, silky strands shimmered in the light. When she put it on and adjusted the fit, Cameron gazed at a total stranger in the reflection. The wig fell in a shining cascade to her bare shoulders.

"Wow," she murmured. "I run in the wrong circles."

Emerald smiled. "Not tonight."

The shadows had left Emerald's eyes and she hurried to the door. With her hair tucked into the hat, the coat collar turned up and gloves on to hide her diamond engagement ring, no one would notice Emerald in the nondescript outfit. She left without a goodbye, or even a thank-you.

Could Cameron pull this off? Her coloring looked wrong to be a blonde and her eyes were hazel rather than Emerald's blue. Another wave of indecision swept her. Too bad she didn't have contact lenses. Yet Emerald was right. Who would see her that closely? The rest of the transformation worked. Picking up the small satin evening bag that matched the bronze gown, she tucked it under her arm. She swirled once, twice, then started for the door.

If Emerald simply wanted to spend time with her fiancé, she had it.

The explanation didn't satisfy Cameron. It seemed obvious Emerald was running scared. But what else could she do?

She had agreed to this onetime deception and it had an added benefit. One she hadn't thought of before. She'd walked to the hotel on her own tonight, the smell of snow in the air, Ransom's shadow behind her. That morning he'd followed her to work again, too, probably after spending the night lurking around her apartment. Dressed now as

Emerald, she could leave the building without Ransom seeing her at all.

Her own escape.

Under cover of the full-length dark faux mink coat keeping her warm, Cameron flipped up its deep hood and buried her hands in the pockets to hide her bandaged fingers. In disguise she rode the elevator down to the lobby and walked through the glass revolving doors. It had begun to snow, but as Emerald had promised, the black stretch limousine was waiting for her, double-parked.

Its powerful engine purred like a throaty-voiced panther.

As Emerald could predict, flashes went off from cameras nearby. Cameron blinked at a scruffy man who aimed at her again and fired off several more shots.

Harmless, she reminded herself even as her pulse hitched, but Cameron quickly bent her head. It wouldn't do for the press to see that her smile didn't match the tennis star's.

''Emerald! Emerald!'' they called.

''How's the knee?'' one reporter shouted.

Someone opened the car's rear door for her. Warmth rushed out at her, enveloping her like a cocoon, drawing her in.

''Thank you.'' Inside, with a sigh, she settled against the plush seat. Soft music played from a top-quality stereo through top-quality speakers.

Luxury. It was such an uncommon concept for Cameron that suddenly she felt exhilarated by even this too-brief ride through the streets of Manhattan.

''Ready, Miss Greer?'' the chauffeur said from the driver's seat. He flicked on bright headlights and slipped the long dark car into gear even before she answered. The windshield wipers clacked against the glass.

''Ready. Yes.''

So far, so good. Ron obviously hadn't caught on yet. Maybe she could avoid having to explain things to him.

Then Cameron's smile faded. Why did his voice sound ironic? Too familiar? A shiver of awareness ran down her spine.

Why did she feel...uneasy now? Had Ron realized who she really was after all? *Don't be silly.* Cameron studied the small side table on which a glass of sparkling champagne already sat in a recess, bubbles rising, catching the dim light from hidden bulbs along the doors.

For this one night, she would pretend this was her world, removed from the past, from Kyle. From Ransom's theory of Venuto Destina.

In the next instant the illusion shattered.

"Where to, Cinderella?"

Her gaze shot to the rearview mirror and the reflection of the chauffeur's face. Cameron groaned. The dark, haunted eyes and deep voice belonged to Ransom.

# Chapter Four

Cameron's gaze held his for a few long seconds. Then Ransom nudged the accelerator and the long car picked up speed into the snow-snarled flow of traffic on Park Avenue. In the mirror, in the darkness, all she could see was the reflection of his blue eyes. They looked black now. Like her mood.

"You are becoming a problem," she finally said. "How did you find me? I thought Emerald and I had made the switch neatly. Now, here you are again—like a bad penny. Maybe I should rent you a room in my apartment."

"Not a bad idea. You could buy furniture with my share."

She huffed out a sigh.

"This has to stop. You tell me you're not even on the case—on the job right now. Maybe instead, I should call your superiors to have you removed."

His glance flicked to hers.

"I wouldn't recommend it." He maneuvered the limo left, across the median bedecked with Christmas lights, then onto a street in the East Fifties. "But how in hell did you get pulled into this mess?"

"I work for Emerald Greer."

"You *cook* for her," he said, his gaze hot in the rearview mirror. "You're not her counselor. You're sure as hell not her troubleshooter.'' He paused. ''What triggered your little disguise tonight?''

How did he know there was trouble? ''I'm doing her a favor.''

''Why?'' he said, sliding around a stalled taxicab.

Cameron didn't answer. She leaned deeper into the plush rear-seat cushions. She felt tempted to drink the champagne still sparkling in its crystal flute, if for no reason except to calm herself, but she didn't reach for it. She needed her wits about her now. Her brief, pleasurable ride seemed to be over—as any stay in a certain place during WP had seemed to end too abruptly.

Cameron straightened. Ransom had no right to be angry with her. This wasn't his concern.

''You can let me off at home,'' she told him.

''I'm taking you to Greer's apartment.''

Cameron bolted upright. ''But I—''

''The press will expect her—that is, you—to arrive there.''

She would have objected to his making the decision for her, but then she realized he was right. For once. If she meant to honor the deception with Emerald, she had to continue this charade on her behalf awhile longer.

She subsided against the seat again. Cameron decided she'd be glad when this night ended. Why couldn't Emerald have sent her personal assistant in her place?

The answer seemed obvious. Grace didn't resemble Emerald in build, but Cameron did. Thanks to the hooded faux mink she wore, she'd already pulled off ''Emerald's'' departure from the Waldorf. Besides, she wasn't sure Grace's timidity would have allowed her to do something like this. And Grace had gone home early that afternoon with a headache. There was no need to mention that, but Cameron did feel curious about Ron Emory.

''Emerald's usual driver,'' she said. ''Where is he now?''

''Ron and I came to an agreement. I'd stick with you,

he'll make sure Emerald gets where she wants to go tonight.''

"If they don't come to blows," Cameron murmured.

Ransom flicked a glance at her. "They don't get along?"

"They had an argument this afternoon. I was supposed to explain to Ron why he found himself taking me home rather than Emerald."

"Well, I did the explaining."

Ransom had his own reason for driving Cameron to Emerald's apartment. She'd been waiting for that explanation, and now he finally exploded.

"I can't believe you risked your own safety for her!"

"This sounds interesting. How did I risk myself?" She gestured at Emerald's bronze satin gown, her coat. "I'm obviously *not* myself at the moment."

"No, you're another target."

"Hmm," she said.

"Greer didn't take off out of town just to be with her fiancé. Did she?"

That surprised Cameron. He was too perceptive. "Who told you she didn't?"

"Ron, but he didn't need to. It took me about five seconds to realize the woman in your jeans and coat wasn't Cameron McKenzie." His tone turned ironic but appreciative. "You have better legs," he said, then eased past a stalled Lexus. "I cornered Greer's chauffeur-cum-bodyguard. With persuasion, Ron gave me the limo keys."

"Your devotion touches me."

"Nice try, by the way—giving me the slip." He went on, "My guess is, Emerald's on the run from something or someone. You may as well tell me."

"I thought your concern was for me."

"It still is. Obviously, between the time I left you with Kyle and this evening, something happened…something that lit a fire in Greer. Otherwise, she'd still be around soaking up attention, posing for photos."

Good call, she acknowledged, but Cameron didn't want

to betray a confidence. Still, she and Ransom had talked about Emerald's stalker.

"A man phoned her last night. I answered. He threatened me—but of course he meant her. He must have confused our voices."

His gaze shot to hers in the mirror. "Someone she knew?"

"A fan, she said. I'm thinking it was—"

"Edgar Mills. The same guy who hounded her before."

"Yes." Cameron looked away from his eyes in the mirror. "When I relayed the message, she seemed frightened."

His tone hardened. "Tell me what he said."

Cameron hesitated then repeated the harsh words. "His voice was far from friendly. No, that's an understatement. He...frankly, he scared me, too."

She hated to admit it.

"You should be scared." If she could see his hands on the wheel, Cameron would also see white knuckles. He was holding back again—but not for much longer. "Cameron, *hell.* I cannot believe you were foolish enough to get involved with Emerald Greer's problems! Aren't you in enough danger?"

"I'm not in danger!"

He swore. Then he eased the car to the right and ground to a stop at the curb halfway to Fifth Avenue, in front of a fire hydrant. Ransom, she guessed, was beyond paying attention to the law he so revered. Before Cameron knew it, he had slammed out the driver's side of the limo and, in the steady snow, was yanking open her door.

A second later he pushed in beside her, crowding Cameron against the seat.

She tried to retreat but he wouldn't let her.

His dark presence loomed over her. His eyes snapped with temper.

And Cameron recoiled again. She wasn't afraid of him, but he radiated a danger all his own. A very personal danger. She wasn't sure she could resist him.

He was on leave, he'd told her. Medical leave. For some physical reason, she'd assumed. Burnout, he'd said. But what were his symptoms? Headaches? Stomach troubles? In the next heartbeat, she wondered if his problem could be mental. Clearly, he was losing it.

Holding her gaze, Ransom edged even closer, until Cameron's vision blurred out of focus and she could smell his special, all-male scent. His right hand tipped her chin up, then clamped tight around her lower jaw.

Cameron's pulse tripled. She couldn't seem to look away now.

But oh, she wanted to. For her own safety.

Because the look in his eyes had nothing to do with mental illness—or Edgar Mills, Emerald's caller. Or even Venuto Destina himself. That look was all heat and anger. And stark, raw desire. For her.

She took one deep breath and shut her eyes.

Talk about danger.

"Don't touch me," she said, her tone pleading, her eyes still closed.

And J.C. tried to unclench his fingers. He wanted to let her go. He really did.

Yet he'd had enough of her flippant attitude toward her own security. He'd had enough of wanting her until he felt torn inside out. He couldn't stop thinking about her, worrying about her. His already shattered nerves were shot.

· First, the night before—when Kyle McKenzie had turned up after how many years since he'd left Witness Protection? J.C. still wished he'd slammed Kyle against the side of Cameron's apartment building and shaken the truth out of him.

Why had Kyle shown up now?

Then tonight…when Cameron had vanished from the hotel, J.C.'s heart had jumped into his throat. One minute she was there in the crowd, weaving her way through the vast reception area of the Waldorf-Astoria, the next she was gone. When she reappeared, J.C. had taken one shattered breath. Then his knee-jerk relief vanished, too.

What the hell?

The woman striding down the hall was *not* Cameron McKenzie.

The clothes were hers all right, but then he'd focused on her legs. They didn't look as slender or shapely as Cameron's. The woman's well-defined calf muscles, even in jeans, could plainly be seen. Athletic calves that strained the denim—like a tennis player's. J.C. had hurried his pace to catch up with her. He had to be sure, but he never got the chance to confront her. He swung her around, took one look into her blue eyes, not hazel, and stopped dead in his tracks. The woman was trying to hide a slight limp, too, he saw. And that did it.

He left Emerald Greer behind. And went looking for her chauffeur.

"That sounds like Emerald," Ron had said, not surprised by the switch.

Surprise wasn't all J.C. felt. For years, he had done his job—until James McKenzie died in his arms. He'd be lucky to survive with his sanity intact. Now he stared into Cameron's eyes.

He had never felt so thwarted, so close—except for James—to losing someone.

Not even his own father.

"I *am* touching you," he said. "And you listen to me."

"I doubt your boss—whatever his title may be—would like to hear that you're strong-arming an innocent civilian. I'll say this once more. I have nothing to do with you—or the program. Do I make myself clear?"

She sounded convincing but her voice shook. She didn't seem as immune to him as she must want him to think. Beyond Destina, beyond the still-missing money and the danger it posed to her, lurked another even more powerful threat. Outside the limo, people walked past. A few stopped to gape, obviously wondering who the celebrity there might be. A siren shrieked down Fifth Avenue. J.C. heard the Santa on the corner ringing his bell for charity. He heard his own heart beat.

"I guess not," he said.

Cameron turned her face away. She could have escaped—in another instant he would have let her go—she could have slapped him. But then, instead, she stopped struggling, as if the effort seemed too much. The fight went out of her and she leaned back into the seat, her body going limp against the deep cushions. J.C.'s hand slipped away from her chin. His skin seemed to buzz from the lost contact.

"Please, Ransom. Leave me alone."

"Believe me. I wish I could."

J.C. braced both hands on either side of her head next to her temples, his fingers digging into the seat's thick upholstery. Outside, snow covered the windows. He looked at her for another breath or two. Then while he was telling himself that this was insane—unprofessional—even foolhardy, he lowered his head.

And kissed her.

To his utter astonishment, she didn't resist. Didn't even try. If anything, Cameron went more boneless on the seat, just inches from his body. Her mouth felt warm and soft. Heat raced through him. His lips clung to hers, his arms caught her close, his heart pounded like a pile driver. No, like a bullet to his brain.

"You scared me to death tonight," he whispered into her mouth.

"You scare me every night."

"God, I don't mean to." He caressed her back, slow and rhythmic, soothing up and down, feeling the heavy warmth of the imitation fur coat beneath his fingers. The faux mink seemed to flow around her, to be part of her. "I didn't want to frighten you when I first showed up, either. But trust me on this, Cameron. You could be in a world of hurt—"

"If I spend any more time with you, I will be."

"—or worse. You could end up...dead."

"Why? Because you have some hunch about Destina? About the money?"

He didn't answer for a moment. He nipped at her lower lip, and the heat flamed hotter inside him. How long had he wanted this? She'd been a kid when he joined the marshals. But he'd watched her grow up, from that skinny girl into this gorgeous woman. And with the years, his need of her had grown, too.

"You think that's all it is? A hunch?"

Dammit, he couldn't seem to get through to her. Couldn't seem to pull away. Last night he'd been almost glad to relinquish her to Kyle—except he didn't trust the guy. In his time as a government agent, J.C. had developed a fine sixth sense. His well-honed instincts told him to be careful. To convince Cameron to be careful, too.

But how?

Frustrated that she wouldn't take his advice, he stroked her back once more, up then down. Down, then up. He felt chilled from his brief time out in the snow, and the fluid faux mink warmed him, too. It made his fingers feel more sensitive, as if he were touching Cameron's bare skin. The coat seemed part of him as well, as if Cameron's body had joined with his and become one. His touch became a hot, sensuous sensation. When he took her mouth again, she whimpered, a very un–Cameron like sound, and J.C. half smiled against her lips. Another jolt of need flashed through him.

"Open up."

Her weak protest never came, and she did just that before she even started to speak. J.C. seized his advantage. He slipped his tongue inside her mouth, explored the slick, smooth lining—and heard himself groan. Or was it her? He couldn't believe she'd actually accepted him. His left hand was sliding up her rib cage now, under the butter-soft faux mink, inching along warm bronze satin.

"You feel..." Naked, like sin, but he didn't say it. He

skimmed over a last rib, his fingers grazing the soft under-side, toward what would surely be her even softer breast, when Cameron broke the kiss. She straightened, pushing at his chest.

"No you don't, Marshal."

Frustrated all over again, J.C. flopped back in the seat. He ran a not-quite-steady hand through his hair. He let out a shaken breath.

"Should I apologize?"

"Why?" she said. "It was my fault, too." She didn't sound happy.

"Then I won't say I'm sorry—which would be a lie. Because I'm not."

"Why doesn't that surprise me?" She frowned. "No, actually. It does surprise me. I never guessed… I never even thought…"

"You didn't notice that I'm attracted to you? Always have been."

In the dark limousine, she peered at him, curious. "Really?"

"Were you attracted to me?"

The frown deepened. "Maybe. A little. I mean, you're a good-looking man. But if I was aware, I probably assumed I had a teenage crush."

J.C. felt tempted to disabuse her of that notion. Poor excuse. Cameron had been twenty-five when he last saw her, not a kid. She'd had plenty of time in the previous twelve years—since they'd met—for her to recognize their chemistry. He suspected that most of the time, she knew her own mind. She'd shared it with him enough, about Destina. Still, J.C. was the hated U.S. Marshal. He supposed that made a sufficient obstacle.

"But back then you couldn't get past your dislike."

"My resentment. I was safer resenting you."

J.C. gently rearranged the lapels of her coat. Or rather, Emerald's. The soft, sinuous fake fur made his palms tingle again. Or was it because of Cameron? Her kiss? His body's new memory of her?

He wanted to go back for more. He wanted to drown in her.

She didn't seem to entertain the same fantasy.

"Is this how you treat all your potential suspects? Don't forget, Ransom. I'm the daughter of a thief. The woman who knows—according to you—where all that missing money is."

He studied her. "You're right. You were safer resenting me." The stream of cars and taxis glided past the dark limousine, lights arced through the tinted windows, a horn blew at the light where traffic had gridlocked. "That why you're trying to go back there now? To your comfort zone?"

She smiled a little. "Maybe."

"You know the old saying— 'You can't go home again.'"

He saw Cameron shiver despite the warmth of the mink around her. Was she feeling the same remnant of their kiss as he was, that aftershock frisson of pleasure? "I never had a home," she murmured. "I'm making one of my own."

He felt almost sympathetic. J.C. knew that life in Witness Protection could be no life at all. It sounded better, safer, than it sometimes was. How could he blame her for wanting to forget her past? Yet, if she did reject that, he could not. He wouldn't lose his chance to nail Destina.

"Cameron, you can't move on until Destina is behind bars. For good this time. If you'd cooperate—"

"This was not my doing." He wondered if she meant the kiss, too. But she'd already shared responsibility for that. "I had nothing to do with that trial or what led to it. I was a child then, only thirteen when I met you! The only thing I care about other than having my own life back—a normal life—is seeing my father's killer on death row."

She slid across the rear seat to the corner farthest from him. "Just do your job, Ransom—if you still have one. I can't help you."

CAMERON STAYED in the corner. After a few moments, she heard Ransom utter a sigh. He got out of the back, then went around to the driver's side. Unable to help herself, she watched him stand there, a hand to the back of his neck, his gaze staring down at the snow-covered pavement. Without glancing at her, he finally slipped behind the wheel, cleared the windshield, then wedged the long, black car into the ceaseless line of traffic headed for Fifth Avenue. Another few minutes and she'd be safe. Secure.

She was referring to Ransom now. His firm yet pliant mouth...

Without thinking, she put a hand to her lips. They felt swollen, warm and tender. My God, he could kiss. The instant his lips touched hers nothing else mattered, even, for those few moments, finding her father's killer. All she wanted then was the feel of him, the taste. The heat.

*You're right. You were safer.*

He wasn't talking to her any longer. Obviously, she'd wounded his male ego. He'd turned on the stereo. Low and full of bass throb, a mournful blues tune reverberated through the car. Her one limo ride in a lifetime, perhaps, and she'd gotten swept away by desire for *Ransom,* of all people.

His kiss, his concern—both seemed genuine. And that frightened her more than Destina, of being his target.

In front of Emerald's Fifth Avenue apartment building, Ransom drew up at the canopied entrance. But Cameron didn't get out. She was still wearing Emerald's bronze satin gown and had no change of clothes. What would she wear home?

"Ransom?"

"Yeah." He rammed the car into Park but didn't shut off the engine. He didn't move from the steering wheel. He couldn't wait to leave, she assumed. So, fine.

''Do me a favor.''

His shoulders stiffened. ''If I can.''

''Stop following me everywhere. Please. It's not doing either of us any good.''

''I won't touch you again,'' he said, his tone taut. ''You have my word.''

Cameron slid across to exit the car. She'd handled this poorly. She paused, one hand on the glass panel that separated her from the driver. From Ransom.

''Not okay. The other night when you tracked me on the way home—''

He jerked around. His gaze had darkened another shade.

''You think *I* followed you home?''

''The first night I saw you here. Then you came up to me at my door.''

''I didn't 'track' you, Cameron. I waited in the hall, or rather, inside the Exit stairwell. I wanted to approach without scaring you. As we both know, I didn't succeed.''

''But you must have been there, before—''

''Where?'' He seemed genuinely confused. Or suspicious.

''On the street,'' she said. ''All the way from Emerald's apartment.''

Ransom killed the engine. With a grim set to his mouth, he came around the limo before the doorman could approach and handed her out. As soon as she stood up, Cameron slipped from his grasp, but Ransom stayed right with her, guiding her to the building entrance with one hand at the small of her back.

A little shiver of desire ran through her.

She felt warm everywhere, not from the faux mink.

Cameron drew away when he spoke to the doorman.

''Have the car parked, will you?'' He slipped the man a bill, then, inside, brushed past the lobby's towering Christmas tree to punch the elevator button. Cameron didn't ask where he thought he was going. When they were inside the car, he said, "I did not follow you home. Someone else did."

"Kyle?" But her heart thumped hard. "He wasn't here until the next night."

"Maybe. Maybe not." At Emerald's floor he took the key from Cameron. In the apartment Ransom flipped on lights in the foyer and the living room. He went straight to the cart where Emerald kept her liquor and poured himself a hefty scotch. "Want one?"

"No, thanks." She paused, upset by his manner. By the whole evening. By his kiss. She changed her mind. "Well. Maybe a splash of sherry."

Glasses in hand, they stared at each other.

"I know you won't want to hear this," Ransom began. "But it's important." He urged her down onto the sofa beside him. "You talked to the man who phoned Emerald, right?"

"Yes, but what—"

He set down his glass and took her face between his hands.

"Cameron, what if that call wasn't for Emerald?"

She'd had the same reaction herself, for only a second. The harsh, guttural tone of voice had horrified her. His message... *You bitch. Tell me what I want to hear,* was the sort of call her parents had lived in terror of, the kind Cameron vowed would never be part of her life again. "You said yourself, she had a stalker."

"Years ago, but why would Edgar Mills turn up again now?" he asked.

"Emerald says he's upset about her marriage."

"Maybe. Why did you answer the call?"

"She asked me to." Still edgy after those moments in the limousine, he must be trying to rattle her, to prove his point.

"Isn't it possible that the same person who trailed you home is the same guy who phoned here? He'd know you work for Greer. He'd already followed you."

She felt her face pale. All the blood seemed to drain to her shoes. Cameron slipped them off, as if to escape the growing—unfounded—feeling of menace.

"You've been a marshal too long, Ransom. You're paranoid."

"I'm experienced. Considering Destina's release, your father's still-open murder case, the money, now Kyle..."

"Kyle has nothing to do with this!" She leaped up from the sofa. Her cordial glass tipped, spilling liquid onto the carpet. "Now look what I've done!" She fell to her knees, scrubbing at the spot with the hem of Emerald's gown. She would have to pay to have the dress cleaned and the carpet stains removed. "Are you satisfied? You've finally rattled me."

"Cameron." He pulled her to her feet, then folded her against his chest. "Don't keep fighting this. Can't you see? There is *real* danger, danger to you. It's not something I imagine in my 'paranoid' state. Or because I'm on medical leave. I haven't lost my mind—yet—and I want you to be safe."

Her voice sounded faint, even to herself. "I lived in hiding for most of my life. I won't do so again."

"Not in hiding. Just with my protection. For a little while longer."

She trembled against him. "Until when? You find evidence against *me* about the missing money? I hope you're not asking me to trust you, Ransom. Because I never did."

He frowned. "Too bad. I'm still your shadow."

Pulling away, he headed for the door. She fought an insane urge to call him back.

Heading out the door, he didn't say good-night. He didn't look at her.

Following him outside, she couldn't help taking one last look. Ransom stood in the hall near the elevators, his tall, lean form rigid.

Maybe he *was* crazy.

No, maybe she was.

"Wait," she said just before he stepped into the elevator.

He turned and raised an eyebrow. "I'll be right downstairs."

She shook her head. "I need a ride."

"No. You don't." Ransom's mouth had tightened.

"I want to go to my own apartment."

Even to herself, the statement sounded needy. But after their kisses in the limousine, that was how she felt. These weren't her clothes, this wasn't her apartment. She needed her own things, her own space.

She might not believe his theories about Destina, the money, her brother, even her father's murder. But her own desire for Ransom—his hot kisses and the feel of his body—was another matter.

She needed to be home. Needed to think.

*You have become a real problem.*

# Chapter Five

Her heart still pounded. Hard.

At her apartment door, Cameron breathed a sigh of relief. She'd had a narrow escape. In Ransom's arms earlier that night, she had lost her equilibrium. The reminder of who he was and his conviction that her father knew about the missing money, that *she* knew about it now, had caused her to pull back.

Just in time.

Then, of course, at Emerald's apartment he'd tried again to make her see his view about that disturbing call to Emerald. She refused to believe he was right. Because that would mean losing her freedom all over again.

During the tense drive home those forbidden moments in the darkened limousine had played through her mind, hummed through her body. His, too, she supposed. A frustrated man could be very surly and he was acting just that. To her surprise Ransom had left her in her building's lobby without a good-night, apparently accepting Cameron's insistence that she could see herself to her door. Fred was on duty. She didn't need Ransom's protection—although she imagined he would stay nearby tonight, too. When did the man sleep?

Still dressed in Emerald's bronze satin gown and her coat, there was one thing she couldn't deny. In the limo, his touch, his kisses, the hard weight of his body had thrilled her. Then at the last instant she'd come to her senses. She wouldn't lose them a second time. Shaking off her disturbing thoughts, she retrieved her key chain from her purse.

Her apartment key didn't fit.

The door didn't budge.

Frowning, Cameron pushed—and felt it give way. The door hung crookedly on its hinges, and when she looked closer she could see that the lock had been tampered with. Now it was useless. Someone had obviously tried to get in.

Without stopping to think how unwise the action might prove, she inched inside. Anger surged and her blood pounded. She didn't take time to feel afraid. Then her pulse leaped into her throat in shock. *My God.*

Her apartment had been trashed!

In her rational mind Cameron knew that she should run for the nearest phone to call the police. She knew she should knock on some neighbor's door, even someone she didn't know, to beg for help.

The last thing she should do was to move any farther inside.

*Who had been here?*

Her first thought, so soon after tonight's near miss in his arms, was Ransom.

But that didn't make sense. No more than her behavior with him hours ago.

Drawn by her own growing horror at the obvious violation of her personal space, Cameron tiptoed into the foyer. Was that a sound she heard from the rear of the apartment? She stepped over a mass of clothing tumbled across the parquet floor, bent down to examine the ripped panties and blouses, the torn jeans. Her favorite wool skirt had been sliced to ribbons.

Why? And what were her clothes doing in the hall? Her

heartbeat seemed to drown out any other sound, but still she listened. It was possible that someone remained in the apartment.

*Run, Cameron.*

Yet she couldn't make her feet move.

For long, palpable moments she stood there, listening, breathing, willing her pulse to settle—as if it would.

For three years she had lived in the real world again, in peace. Until James was killed last January. So close, she thought, feeling tears prick behind her eyelids. So close to being normal. Then Ransom showed up.

And now, this.

She willed herself to relax. She had been burglarized, that was all.

Happened all the time in New York, she told herself, like some rite of passage, a weird initiation to the big city. She'd chosen to live here.

Squaring her shoulders, she finally moved forward.

On her way past, she snatched her umbrella from the corner of the foyer. Oddly, it hadn't been touched. Or destroyed, like everything else she found.

If someone was still here, she had a weapon of sorts.

Ransom would only laugh at her.

No, Ransom would yell. She had no business being here, risking herself, he would say. And he'd be right in that, at least.

Yet the farther she stepped from the open front door, the more courage she gathered around her. Courage, or plain foolishness? Perhaps it was the latter. But Ransom wouldn't understand that she had to, *had to,* maintain some semblance of a normal life.

This wasn't really happening, she tried to tell herself.

If she blinked, the past hours—and this moment—would disappear. They would become something she had imagined, perhaps in Ransom's case even dreamed of, like some smitten teenager over a rock-star idol. His kisses would vaporize. His touch.

This terrible attack upon the everyday trappings of her life would vanish, too.

Just clothes, she thought. Only that.

Simple theft.

Still, she felt personally assaulted.

But had anything been taken?

Unsure, with muffled footsteps and a soft swish of satin, Cameron crept into the living room, her umbrella at the ready. One blow to a man's shoulders, across the back of his neck, even his skull, and before he recovered his balance, she would have time to flee.

So she told herself.

The reassurance didn't help. Her one armchair seemed a total loss. Stuffing spewed from a dozen long, deep slashes in the upholstery. Its legs were broken. Now she had nowhere to sit.

As if that were the point of this. The ludicrous thought almost made her smile, but she felt too terrified.

Her folding chair, where Ransom had sat that first night, had been thrown against the far wall. Sheetrock shards littered the carpet and a large hole desecrated the wall itself.

With a shudder, Cameron silently moved on, as stealthy as a burglar herself. Her steps dragged through the living room into the kitchen. There she discovered her meager supply of staples scattered over the tile. Flour coated the cabinet sides, the wall, the floor. Spice tins had been ground into the grouting with a heavy heel. Cameron rarely cooked for herself at home. By the time she finished her workday, she felt too tired to start dinner for one. Sometimes she brought a container with the excess of a client's meal from her last job, sometimes she picked up take-out Chinese food or a pizza. Sometimes she settled for a mug of hot chocolate. Not tonight, she knew. The box of dry cocoa mix mingled with the flour and the sugar on the floor.

She didn't dare cough from the dust that hazed the still air. With a faint rustle of satin, she continued down the hall to her bedroom. There, too, she thought, stomach churning. Every room had been methodically destroyed, and for once Cameron felt grateful that she hadn't furnished the apartment yet. How much more devastation there would be then.

Her umbrella held tight in a fist, she found everything in the bedroom ruined, yet nothing seemed to be missing.

The filmy curtains, the blinds she had installed for privacy after Kyle's visit—and Ransom's—had been ripped from their mounts. They lay on the carpet stained with lipstick, foundation and eyeliner from her bathroom. Only her prized antique chandelier—a first purchase—above the bed remained untouched. Not a single item from her drawers appeared to be whole. Cameron swallowed hard.

Even if she wanted to think so, this did not have the mark of simple burglary.

A calculated violence had been unleashed in this room. In every room.

Turning, she gaped at her bed. Or rather, her mattress on the floor.

It, too, bore the remnants of the smashed lipsticks, color streaking across the new comforter she'd bought. Its white background bore a pink tinge now, the soft blue floral print wore the grime from someone's shoe. Cameron peered closer to make out the shape of a sole. And then she saw it.

The image of violence seemed strongest then. Brutal, and deadly.

She knelt to pick up the battered doll, as if she were cradling an injured child in her arms, feeling that she, too, had been defiled. The doll from her childhood, the doll Kyle had brought back to her, flopped in her embrace.

Tears prickled, brimmed, then spilled over onto its damaged cloth body. Cameron wept.

The doll had been slashed open from chin to legs, like a woman raped and mutilated by a serial killer. Cameron pressed her cheek to it, as if to comfort—the doll, or herself? She couldn't separate them now.

She held the wide-eyed toy, its partially stiff spine feeling even harder, as if in defiance of the attack, and felt its beanbag stuffing scatter in tiny bits over the backs of her hands to bounce off the carpet. With each loss, it sagged more until all she could feel was that still-lumpy spine like a last vestige of courage. Her own, too. The beads of stuffing, like the lipstick stains on the comforter, became blood to her shattered mind.

*Who did this?*

This wasn't the work of a druggie searching for easy items to fence, or... *Oh God.* No. This was the work of a person with a specific purpose. Cameron feared she knew what that was.

She should call for help. Now.

But when she rose to look for the phone, she heard a sudden rush of movement from the closet behind her.

Before she could turn, a heavy object crashed down on her skull.

A man shoved past her. Into the hall. Toward the broken front door.

Already losing consciousness, Cameron crumpled to the floor in a pool of Emerald's bronze gown and coat.

"PLEASE. Don't yell at me."

Holding a tattered cloth doll, and perched cross-legged on the mattress in her bedroom, she wouldn't look at him. J.C. hunkered down in front of her, his heart lurching at the sight of her swollen eyes, her too-pale face. She still looked beautiful to him, but his pulse raced for a different reason. Cameron cradled the toy to her breast like a mother with a sick child and everything inside him hurt for her. Feared for her.

"I won't yell," he promised. Then, trying to appear in control, he searched through her dark, silky hair for signs of trauma.

A big goose egg was forming at the base of her skull. When he touched it, she winced.

J.C. probed more gently. "He hit you. More than once?"

"I...don't think so."

His mouth tightened. He let his hands fall away from her scalp, then folded his arms over his chest. *Hang on,* he told himself, *for Cameron.* But fury—and panic—welled inside him like the thick beat of his blood. *Don't lose it now, Ransom.* Glancing around, he discovered the weapon that had been used, a heavy marble vase.

He held it up and Cameron whitened another shade. She rubbed her temples.

"That was my mother's. She gave it to me just before she died." She tried to smile. "The first time in my life I was able to take something with me when I left Witness Protection and look what happens."

"Once was enough," J.C. muttered. "You're lucky it didn't kill you."

Obviously, her head hurt. Thank God he'd been close by. When she'd called him on his cell phone, her voice sounding thin and strained, J.C. had been standing in a nearby convenience store. Intending to spend the night outside her apartment building again or in the lobby with Fred, J.C. had been buying an extra-large container of black coffee. Innumerable stakeouts in his work had trained him to do without much sleep. Besides, staying awake helped him avoid nightmares. His first impulse had been to kill whoever had done this. His hands shook with the effort not to reach out to her now, to comfort rather than examine her injury, but he didn't have much practice. And after she'd ended their kiss in the limo tonight, he knew better than to try.

Her eyes focused on the doll. She stroked its comic face. "I shouldn't have come in here. Once I opened the door…"

"And saw that broken lock…" He couldn't agree more. "The threat to your personal safety was one thing. The emotional damage from seeing all this—" he indicated the whole room, certain he'd never viewed such destruction before "—could be even worse."

She said nothing.

J.C. rose. "Let's pick through that pile of clothes, find something other than Emerald's gown that you can wear. You need medical attention."

Cameron looked up at him, her eyes dazed. "I'll be fine. I'm a little dizzy but that will pass. Just give me a minute. I'm not really hurt."

"That's for a doctor to decide." J.C. didn't need a quarrel. He needed to find the nearest ER, but he also had to calm himself first. He'd be no good to her if he lost control.

He let the silence build for a moment. He didn't expect her next words.

"I think you may be right." The admission seemed difficult. "Someone was looking for the missing money in Dad's case. You may even be right about Destina being behind the break-in. And that he feels certain I have it." She paused. "Why else would someone ransack my apartment? Without taking anything?"

J.C.'s pulse hammered. Hearing his earlier suspicions validated didn't soothe him. If Cameron had been home when the intruder arrived, he hated to think what could have happened to her. The level of violence he saw here made him shake inside. This was like overkill, fortunately without the victim. J.C. began to sweat. He felt halfway to a full-blown panic attack as the haunting memories washed over him. Somebody—and of course he thought he knew who—was very angry with Cameron.

"So you're ready to believe there's some connection? Between you and your father and Venuto Destina?"

"A presumed connection—to me. I hope you're not going to gloat."

He faked a smile. "Would I do that?"

"Probably." She tried to focus on him. "I still don't know where that money is."

He held her gaze. "Cameron, believe me. I'm not gloating. I wish Destina had never been released from prison. I wish James hadn't died in that Denver alley. I wish your apartment wasn't a disaster right now. But since all that is fact, and you're not fighting it now, we have to deal with it."

"I suppose I can't deny the possibility any longer. Not after this."

"And the call to Emerald Greer's apartment," he reminded her.

He saw her mouth tremble. And cursed himself.

He'd gone too far. She'd had enough for one day, and suddenly J.C. didn't care if she tried to shove him away. Gently, he removed the ruined doll from her grasp then reached for her anyway, drew her up into his arms and held her tight. After another moment, he cleared his throat. Some things had to be done while the scene was fresh.

"We need to call the police."

"No," she said, glancing up with stricken eyes.

The law, he knew, would make the damage seem even more real to her. There would be reports to file, uniformed cops in her already violated space. J.C. knew how important this first home, her privacy, were for Cameron.

"I'll contact Gabe Whitney—my friend in the NYPD."

"Ransom, please—"

"He's a good guy. He won't fuss." J.C. looked around. "Did you touch anything?"

"Just the front door when I came in. And the doll," she admitted.

J.C. bit back a groan. With luck, she hadn't smeared any prints.

He held her close. "Gabe can handle this. As soon as he gets here, we're heading for the hospital. I don't like the look of that bump on your head." He leaned down to study her eyes. "Your pupils seem a little whacky. Let's get you a full exam and some X-rays, even a scan."

Cameron didn't resist his deeper embrace. J.C. wrapped his arms around her tight and let her rest against his chest. He felt the silk of her hair on his skin, smelled the light fragrance that seemed to define her. For nearly a year, he'd known something would go down, that James's death wasn't the end, and he had suspected Cameron at its center since Destina's release from prison. He knew the reality that she was Destina's target was slowly sinking in for Cameron. Not a pleasant thought.

"Tomorrow I'll get new locks installed," he said.

"Ransom, you don't need to—"

"Believe me. I need to. Let me do this, okay?"

He needed to keep himself busy. Or lose it completely.

Cameron slumped against him. She needed time to adjust to the notion that someone wanted that money—even wanted her dead.

SHE WOULDN'T THINK about that now.

Cameron hadn't found time in the emergency room at New York Hospital. There'd been too many questions to answer, too many tests to take. Later, she'd thought. *Later*. Now, with her X-rays on file and her scan completed, she was home again—at her own insistence. She surveyed the horror in her apartment but not in her mind. She could deal with the physical tonight. That was all.

"It won't take long to clean this up," she told Ransom.

He stood, grim-faced, a few feet from her, staring down at the mess and running a hand over the back of his neck. She didn't want to consider why she'd called him rather than Kyle, or the police. It had been a knee-jerk reaction. Since then, Gabe Whitney had come and gone to write his report. Tomorrow she would give him her statement, but not before she eliminated all traces of her intruder's handiwork. Ransom disagreed.

"You need to rest. The doc said—"

"I'm too wired from all the attention. My head only hurts a little now. I'm not as dizzy, and I can't go to bed before this apartment is straightened."

"Not as dizzy?" he echoed. "Forget cleaning. You have a concussion."

"A minor concussion."

Ransom scowled. "Didn't you hear what the doctor said? You're supposed to take it easy for the next few days. And before you tell me to get lost again, I'll remind you that he released you into my care. Otherwise, you'd be in the hospital overnight for observation."

"I don't need to be observed."

"On a regular basis—you sure do," Ransom insisted. "You're stuck with me." He prowled the room, kicking aside debris. "I didn't want to come back here tonight— and we're not staying."

"Just for half an hour," she said.

Ransom rolled his eyes. "And you think *I'm* mental?"

"I have a concussion."

Laughing, he gave up. "Well, at least when you pass out I'll be here to catch you."

Together, united for once in a common task, Cameron and Ransom tried to clean. Even the essential chores took longer than she'd planned, and by the time they restored partial order to the apartment, Cameron was still aching. Her head, too. And her spirit. She wouldn't tell him, but at the same time she felt drained, as if she'd been hit by a very large truck. Her legs had imaginary lead weights on them, and when she stopped moving for just a moment, she yawned.

"You finally ready?" Ransom asked. "My back's killing me. Let's go."

She suspected he was simply giving her an excuse to leave.

"But where to?" she said.

Her apartment was still not habitable and she wouldn't feel safe here for some time. The thought saddened her. She'd worked hard to give herself a home. And now, when she looked around at the still-damaged rooms, like another "halfway" house during Witness Protection, all she wanted was never to see it again.

Ransom threw an arm around her shoulders.

"We can spend the night at Emerald's. You have a key."

She hadn't considered that idea, but it worked. She doubted Emerald would care. Her only concern had been getting out of town. In fact, she'd given Cameron the key so she could continue working after the Zeus reception, not to lose pay. She was to feed Grace—and if he wanted, Ron, too.

Cameron started for the door. Then stopped. After retrieving a nightshirt and another change of clothes, she scooped up the torn doll from her bedroom and tucked it into her pocket. Small beans chittered onto the entryway floor. She would try to repair the doll later. Dazed, she rode the elevator to the street with Ransom. In the lobby, the Christmas tree glowed as if nothing had happened tonight, the snow outside had stopped and Fred was still on duty.

Surprised, Cameron noted from the wall clock near the elevators that it was 4:00 a.m.

Neither she nor Ransom felt hungry, yet she needed to eat. Cameron would have fixed eggs and toast at Emerald's, but she didn't think she could lift a hand. Take-out pizza seemed to be the solution, and on the way to Emerald's Fifth Avenue apartment, they stopped to buy two pies. Large, with everything.

At Emerald's, only blessed silence greeted them.

Gone were the hospital's harsh sounds, the clattering of bedpans and machines, the softer swish of gurneys across the glossy floors. There was no destruction here. Cameron breathed a sigh.

"This wasn't a bad idea. I'm halfway tired now."

"The adrenaline's wearing off. Mine, too."

Now they were left with only the total quiet in the vast apartment, and each other.

When she finished eating, Cameron knew she wouldn't rest quite yet. She curled into one of Emerald's armchairs in the white den and stared at a book.

Her head really did hurt. Not even the aspirins Ransom had forced her to take with her pizza did the trick. Finally, she felt him gently remove the novel from her hands. His fingers brushed hers and Cameron felt a buzz of awareness. Or was that her concussion? Putting a hand to the lump at the back of her head, she gazed up at him with half-unfocused eyes.

"Did I fall asleep?" The notion amazed her.

"Almost." He checked her pupils. "It's been a long day. You should go to bed."

The last word hovered on the air between them. She remembered his kisses in the limousine, and another jolt of desire flashed through her. She wouldn't let that happen again. But when he knelt in front of her, holding her gaze, she couldn't look away. And felt fresh tears sting her eyes.

"Come here." He pulled her down onto the carpet, into his arms.

"I seem to be spending a lot of time this way tonight." She blinked back the tears.

"You're not as tough as you want me to think. Let go, Cameron. Not many people have to handle what you did today. You could use a good cry."

"Again? And have you think I'm a weak female?"

"I don't think you're weak. The years in WP saw to that."

At the reminder, she glanced away, feeling an immediate wave of dizziness. Her voice caught. "What did my father do, Ransom? He was an accountant, not a hardened criminal like Destina. *If* he took money from Destina—who took the money from someone else in the first place, I'm sure—then where is it?"

"Not at your apartment." They'd gone over every inch during the cleanup.

"No, and it never was there." Desperate, she grasped at a straw. "If the intruder tonight failed to find the money he was looking for, then maybe he'll stop. He won't try to get near me again."

But even she didn't believe that now.

Ransom only held her tighter. His silence said the same.

"If I knew where it was," she murmured, "I'd give it to him. Tainted money."

He agreed. "Money, most likely, from prostitution and drugs."

She shivered again. "I can't believe, even if you do, that my father was involved. He balanced Destina's books. That's all."

"He may have believed in creative bookkeeping."

Cameron drew back too fast. Pain shot through her head but her eyes flashed.

"Think what you will about my father—"

"I think he double-crossed Destina. I think he snuck money from this account or that of Venuto's, then laundered it somewhere. I think he stashed it away for a rainy day—and in the end it got him killed. If you prefer to think he was white as snow when he worked for Destina in the first place, you're deluding yourself. But go ahead."

"He didn't know Destina was a crook!"

Ransom shook his head. "Come on, Cameron. You're an intelligent woman. Part of becoming an independent adult includes letting go of childhood illusions."

"Are you calling me a naive child?"

"No. I'm saying you have an issue to resolve. We all like to think our parents are flawless but the fact is, they're human. They make mistakes. They work for the wrong people sometimes, and temptation takes over. They—"

He broke off. His intense tone made her pause instead of lashing out before she said, "You're not talking about James now, are you?"

A muscle ticked in Ransom's jaw. It was the only sign that she was right, and Cameron didn't back down. He must mean his own father. So that was it.

"What did *your* father do, Ransom? What mistake did he make?"

Clearly, he didn't want to answer. He tried a smile that didn't work.

"If I told you, I'd have to hurt you."

Cameron didn't budge. She knew one thing about Ransom: he would never hurt her. Never. She couldn't let it go.

"Something illegal?"

"Yeah."

"And that humiliated you."

"Yep," he said, then admitted with a sigh, "he betrayed me. He betrayed my mother—and it killed her, just as

James was partly responsible for the breakdown of your mother's health. Her death.''

"How did he betray you?"

"Quit pushing," he said. He released her and got to his feet. At the white-manteled fireplace where a small stack of logs lay ready, Ransom struck a long match to light the fire. He stood watching the flames. Avoiding the issue.

Cameron could have left him there but she didn't.

He intrigued her.

Their ongoing awareness of each other, the chemistry they'd shared in the limousine tonight, was one thing to deal with. Her father's murder was another. Ransom himself made a third. Cameron wouldn't leave him to his mystery.

Moving slowly so as not to jar her brain, she joined him in front of the crackling fire.

"Obviously your feelings for your father influenced how you feel about mine. Tell me what *he* did, Ransom."

He ran a hand over the back of his neck. "He spent half his life in jail—where he belonged. That's all I'm saying."

"Why?"

When he only shook his head, Cameron sighed.

"And so—considering your own high moral code—you became a cop."

Ransom's jaw set. "Guess I did. Any charge for the psychotherapy session, Doc?"

She ignored his sarcasm. "It's easy for you to believe my father was a thief."

"Guess I do." Then, surprising her, Ransom slowly put his arms around her. "Listen. I'm sorry for my part in your father's death. I've been wanting to apologize."

Cameron frowned. "What part?"

He looked away. "No one in the program has ever been lost under the marshals' protection. I should have known what was coming down. We'd heard rumblings in the department about Destina. Rumor had it that he'd hired some new goons to do his bidding. One of them was a known hit man.'' Ransom stiffened. ''I didn't do my job well enough.''

Shocked, Cameron knew the truth as she said the words. ''Don't blame yourself. I know I've been, well, hard on the U.S. Marshals—particularly you. Kyle and I used to play a game in which we were the good guys for a change, you were the bad. You and all your buddies.''

Ransom must know she was trying to make him feel better.

''Who won?''

''We killed you all then rode off into the sunset.''

He winced. ''Happily ever after. A ghoulish game.''

She sobered. ''You don't believe in happiness, do you?''

''I've never seen it.'' But he tightened his embrace. ''God, Cameron. Today when I walked into your apartment, all I could think of was Destina. His hired killers. I saw what they did to James. Felt his blood on my hands. If that had been you…''

She felt his guilt as if it were her own. Was guilt the reason for that haunted look in his deep blue eyes? His burnout?

''I should have been more careful,'' she said. ''I'm sorry I scared you.''

He was trembling now. His skin felt cold, even clammy, under her hands, and when Cameron drew back to look at his face, he was sweating. Cold sweat, too, she supposed. For the past moments, he'd become more tense, not less, with every word about her father and Cameron's prodding about his.

''It wasn't your fault my father died in that alley, Ransom. I know that now.''

She pulled him close again, smoothing a hand over his

sun-streaked hair. It felt like satin, warm and heavy, when his skin felt so cold.

He shuddered.

Then he began to shake.

"Ransom, what...?"

"Panic attack." He was gasping for breath. "Since James's murder." He gulped in air. She could feel his heart racing. "Big-time, post-traumatic stress episodes, they tell me. Just...h-hold on. To...to me."

His request didn't come easily. But Cameron readily complied.

Ransom was human, too. He made mistakes. He had become so nerve-laden after her father's death that he was now inactive in his job. Medical leave. Now she knew why. Knew the rest of the reason for his haunted blue eyes.

She planted a light kiss in his hair.

"And I wondered if you were crazy."

He shivered, eyes shut. "I almost am. Sometimes."

"Is this my fault?" She laid a trail of kisses along his forehead, his temple, across his closed eyelids to his cheek. "Because of my apartment today?"

"Destina." His heart thundered beneath her hand at his chest. "You." Then she kissed the corner of his mouth, and he turned his head, his lips groping for hers.

She'd vowed this wouldn't happen yet she couldn't stop it. What had begun in the limousine seemed fated to continue here. Ransom's kisses alternated with hers until Cameron couldn't tell where they began or ended, or who had initiated them. She didn't care. When Ransom's hand lifted, shaking, to cup her breast, and he groaned, she forgot the past, the hiding, the pain of her injury tonight.

The hot sensations flooded her, drove her to her knees.

Ransom followed, his mouth on hers, his hands still on her breasts.

She held him, kissed him, until at last he stopped quaking. His skin grew warmer, his breathing leveled, his pulse slowed to a stronger, steadier beat.

He swallowed. "It's over."

His panic attack had gone, but the presumed threat to Cameron remained. She couldn't absorb that yet, even as his torn words whispered into her mouth. "I won't let him kill you. If he tries, he'll have to kill me first."

The notion sent another cold sweep down Cameron's spine. Abruptly, she pulled away. Her head hurt, but her eyes held his, and she hoped he didn't see panic in her now.

But that was what she felt.

As Ransom had claimed, her father's death wasn't the end but only another beginning.

*The missing money.*

Someone wanted that money.

Someone would hurt her to get it.

Would Ransom be able to safeguard her? Should she let him?

After his explanation she couldn't blame him for James's death, but with her history, she didn't know much about relationships. And despite their bond tonight, Ransom remained a symbol of her unhappy upbringing. She would be foolish to fall for him.

She would be even more foolish to trust him.

## Chapter Six

"Oh! Miss McKenzie—"

The next morning she heard Grace's surprised tone before she had fully wakened in Emerald Greer's bed. Grace stood in the open doorway, and the strong aroma of coffee from the kitchen half roused Cameron. "I didn't know you were here," Grace said, sounding fretful. "I was looking for Emerald."

Cameron sat up, yawning. Then clamped a hand over her throbbing head and fell back onto the sheets. Her concussion had set the room to spinning.

"I stayed the night. I didn't think Emerald would mind. I had a little mishap."

"You cut yourself again?" Grace's gaze shot to her bandaged fingers.

"No, nothing like that. I'll tell you later." Fuzzily, she thought of Ransom, who had slept on the den sofa, coming in to check her pupils at regular intervals for the rest of the night. Where was he now?

Between Ransom's nursing care and the lump on her head, she hadn't slept well. Cameron finally stumbled from bed. She needed caffeine to clear her head—of last night, and of her own confusion about Ransom, his protection and his kisses.

"I can't find Emerald," Grace cried, wringing her hands.

"She went to her fiancé's home. I assumed she'd told you."

"Yes, but—" Grace paused. "Emerald never showed up at Mr. Kayne's estate."

Cameron's pulse skipped. "Are you sure?"

"He just called. He's very worried. Her cell phone doesn't answer, either. I tried half a dozen times. Then I thought, maybe she hadn't gone after all, so I came in here."

Cameron frowned. "How did she plan to travel?" Once Cameron had taken the limousine, Emerald had needed other transportation.

"I reserved a rental car for her," Grace said. "I've checked with the agency."

Remembering that Grace had left early the day before, Cameron briefly explained the identity switch she'd made with Emerald that night, and Grace's brown gaze darkened. "I knew there would be trouble sooner or later. After those vicious calls—"

"She mentioned them to you?"

"I was here for the first few. Then she started sending me home at night."

Ah, so that hadn't been a whim on Emerald's part, or blatant cruelty toward Grace, but Emerald's need to be alone. To wait for her mysterious caller. Was he the fan who'd stalked Emerald, or Ransom's theoretical hit man for Cameron?

Instantly, she rejected the latter notion.

There was no need, she and Ransom had agreed, to inform Grace or Ron yet about Destina. Cameron half regretted confiding in Emerald about her past.

"She always leaves her cell phone on," Grace added.

Her voice stayed tight with apparent worry, or so it seemed. Then Cameron turned, slowly, took another look at Grace and changed her mind. Grace's frown had morphed into a faint smile.

"What?" Cameron said, thinking she'd missed some dark joke.

"Look on the bright side. Maybe she won't come back. We can all relax."

Cameron frowned. "If you're that unhappy with your job, why not find another?"

"At the salary she pays me? Emerald made me an offer I couldn't refuse."

From the evasive shift of Grace's gaze, that didn't seem to be the whole story. But Grace wouldn't say more and Cameron decided not to pry—for now. Cameron had her own secrets.

"Let's think this through. What else do we know?"

"She never picked up the rental car."

Cameron's breath caught. What had happened? An abduction?

Her pulse quickened.

Trying not to feel alarmed by Emerald's disappearance— it was too early to call it that—she gave Grace an encouraging smile. "Maybe she took a bus, or the train. Maybe it broke down."

"A bus? *Emerald?* But then she'd call."

One minute Grace seemed almost happy that Emerald was out of her hair, the next she seemed certain that foul play could have befallen her difficult employer.

She felt odd being in Emerald's apartment, in her bed, now that something seemed wrong. If someone, say, Edgar Mills had not only called Emerald but planned to abduct her, then why not waylay the limousine instead, with Cameron inside, dressed as Emerald? That meant he, or some other person, had seen through the disguise.

"And I thought our identity switch did the trick."

Leading Grace to the kitchen, Cameron poured them

both coffee and sat at the table. She didn't like the old prickling sensation in her neck that meant trouble, but she saw no sense in raising panic if she could avoid it. She tried to calm Grace's fears. And her own.

"Tell me, Grace. How did you meet Emerald?"

Their pairing seemed unlikely, but if she kept talking, Cameron might learn something that would help. She might forget Ransom's kisses, her apartment being ransacked and the way her head hurt.

Grace hesitated. Then she glanced up from her coffee, and seemed to make a decision. The same as Cameron's, it seemed.

"In Central Park one Saturday. She was jogging. It wasn't long before her surgery, though, and her bad knee gave out. She pulled up near the bench where I was sitting, reading a book in the sun." She paused. "Emerald rested, I told her about the story I'd been engrossed in. I'm addicted to murder mysteries." She said it as if the admission was something to feel ashamed about.

Cameron had a different opinion. "I love them, too."

"Do you?" Her eager tone helped break the ice. For the first time, Cameron sensed real emotion from Grace, other than her resentment toward Emerald. Now Grace's face lightened. "I'll give you a list of my favorites. If you'll do the same…"

"I'd be happy to." Cameron gestured. "Go on."

"After we talked, Emerald started to rise from the bench. Her knee buckled—and I helped to keep her from falling." Grace's mouth twisted. The brighter expression dimmed as quickly as it had shone. "I guess she decided then that I could be useful to her. Considering my background, I suppose I should be grateful. When we met, I'd been out of…work for some time."

"Your background?" So Grace really wasn't the brown-all-over spinster that Cameron had assumed.

Grace flushed. "I know I don't look it. But, well...I'm an ex-convict."

Cameron nearly spewed the rest of her coffee across the table. She tried not to sputter but choked. "I don't mean to probe—"

"That's all right. I rarely mention where I've been. The women's facility upstate isn't exactly an address from the right side of the tracks. I never say a word about the experience when I'm working here." As if Emerald might be listening, Grace glanced behind her. "Emerald cautioned me early on that her acquaintances and colleagues would not take well to dealing with a felon."

"I'm sure there's a good explanation. You're a well-spoken, obviously intelligent woman—" Cameron broke off. "Um, may I ask why you served time?"

"Murder."

The chill that raced down Cameron's spine could have cooled the vast apartment for an entire summer. *Murder.* And now, Emerald was...

"Missing," Grace said for her, and Cameron assumed that, without meaning to, she'd spoken aloud. "If anything has happened to her—beyond her usual selfish whim of the moment—I'll be the first suspect."

Cameron tried to relax in her chair. That explained Grace's mixed emotions. She must feel relieved that Emerald's overbearing presence was gone, at least temporarily, but on the other hand Grace knew she would have questions to answer. She didn't elaborate on her murder conviction, but Cameron hadn't missed the bitter note in Grace's voice again. Or that little half smile earlier.

"It doesn't seem a secret that you dislike her, Grace."

"Who doesn't?"

Cameron recalled Emerald's snide words to Grace. *I keep you around for amusement.* Having lived in Witness Protection, Cameron knew that ongoing pressure could warp people, and Emerald worried about her career. "I think she's a very lonely woman. Maybe that makes her unkind at times. To cover her unhappiness, she strikes out at other people."

"She may be lonely but she's a viper. Believe me."

"Grace…"

"She 'took me in,' as she puts it—and made my life a hell. I'm at her beck and call 24/7." She hesitated, a frown creasing her pale features. "That's exactly why I think something has happened to her. Otherwise, she would have contacted me this morning. Somehow. We may not like each other, but we do work together. And Emerald's schedule begins well before 8:00 a.m. every day."

It was nearly ten o'clock now, Cameron noted from the clock above the refrigerator. She'd overslept once she finally fell asleep.

"But last night anyone would have thought *I* was Emerald Greer. She would have looked like any ordinary person leaving the hotel, walking along the street, hailing a cab to the car rental agency…" *You're in danger. You're next.* Cameron set aside her coffee. "Wait a minute. If she took a cab to the agency—"

Grace shook her head. "If she took a taxi last night, it was a gypsy cab, unregistered with the Manhattan hack association. There's nothing on their log."

"Oh, Grace." Her pulse thumped. Cameron, too, was becoming convinced of foul play. There was another danger now, if not related to Venuto Destina, and if she hadn't agreed to Emerald's deception, switched clothes with her…

His name flashed into her mind. *Ransom.*

He must be nearby. He'd probably gone out for breakfast, so he wouldn't embarrass her by being in the apartment when Grace arrived.

Not liking the fact that she needed him again, Cameron jumped up and strode to the intercom on the kitchen wall.

When the security guard in the lobby answered, she described Ransom then sighed at the response. "Well, when you do see him, please send him up. Thanks." She turned to Grace. "A friend of mine," she explained. "He may be able to help us get to the bottom of this."

WHILE SHE WAITED FOR Ransom to return, Cameron took a quick shower, holding on to the marble-tiled wall to steady herself and keep her head from spinning. She had just dressed in jeans and a white silk shirt, when a loud crash sounded from the kitchen. One minor accident—no, two, after last night—seemed enough. Her healing finger stung, the lump on her head felt ultrasensitive, but in the next instant Cameron heard raised voices. One female, one male.

Grace and…Ransom? But the tone didn't sound like him.

After running a comb through her wet hair, Cameron bolted down the hall, fearing violence. The loud voices, the furious words, seemed to escalate with every step she took.

Cameron paused at the kitchen doorway then instinctively ducked back into the hallway, while keeping them in her line of vision.

Grace stood in the middle of the tile floor, glaring at Emerald's personal trainer, with shards of cups and saucers at their feet. She must have been unloading the dishwasher Cameron had filled yesterday. Grace pointed a thin index finger at Ron.

"Emerald owes you nothing more! I wrote your check three days ago."

"In advance? Things are improving for Miss Greer, then. Too bad I never got it."

Grace jabbed him in the chest, surprising Cameron again with her change of attitude, and Cameron remembered the day before, when Ron had demanded his pay. *I took him from a gutter,* Emerald had told her. Cameron didn't like his dark expression now, either. She took a step to help Grace, then when her vision blurred with the sudden movement, decided to stay where she was.

It amazed Cameron that Grace held her ground so well. But then, working for Emerald must have toughened her, prison, too, even though she didn't show it often.

"For your information, Emerald seems to have disappeared—and if the police ask me, I'll tell them they should talk to you."

"Why tell them?" A faint smile twitched his lips.

Grace filled him in on the sketchy details of Emerald's possible disappearance. "So if you think you won't be on the suspect list—"

"Speak for yourself, Gracie." Ron grabbed her arm. "Don't come after me, you scrawny little bird. I'm warning you. Keep your mouth shut. I may...hate the woman but I never touched her!"

Grace looked pointedly at his white-fingered grasp on her sleeve.

"I find that hard to believe. She always says you're a sadist. I can't imagine your abuse would stop with a few sets on the weight machines or a couple of miles on the treadmill."

"Imagine whatever you want. But the police won't overlook a woman who murdered her own husband!"

Shock ran through Cameron again. She took a step back. Nothing in Emerald's household seemed to be what it appeared. And if Grace had turned out to be a killer, then what could Ron be hiding?

"If you ask me, she's not lost," he said. "I'll tell you where she is right now. She's in the sack with some guy she met last night, another loser, in some backwater motel where the press won't see her. Don't worry about her. Miss Greer may have lousy taste in men, but she sure takes care of herself. If you think she's going to inform you of her every movement—every fling—especially now that she's engaged to Ted Kayne, you'd better think again. She's not your friend, Grace.''

''She's nobody's friend.''

''She's a bitch,'' Ron agreed.

Cameron tried to shut off the thought. *Tell me, bitch...what I want to hear.* But after last night's attack, she was having a hard time forgetting that call.

Grace raised an eyebrow, as if to acknowledge that she and Ron were in accord on one thing at least. With Ron's gaze trained on her, she bent down to pick up the shattered china. Cameron kept her eye on them both.

''Okay, so I've had trouble with the law myself,'' Ron admitted as if to give Grace a bone. ''The military.'' He went down on one knee to help her with the broken plates. He seemed more loquacious now that he and Grace had agreed on Emerald. ''I got a dishonorable discharge from the army for insubordination, spent a night or two with the MPs after bar fights, had too many jobs after I left the service that led nowhere—the last one I was accused of stealing money from the till at a fancy health club.'' He paused. ''Guess I should feel grateful that Miss Greer gave me another chance.'' He glanced at Grace. ''You get my point? We're just a couple of her strays. Don't ask me why she does it. Maybe we're some kind of tax write-off.''

''Unlikely but creative,'' Grace murmured, letting him help her to her feet. ''Still, if either of us is to be believed, that doesn't bring us any closer to finding Emerald.''

''You don't like my motel theory? Then she has enough enemies. Maybe one of them got sick of her throwing her weight around—and took care of business.''

''You mean killed her?'' Grace sounded horrified.

''Like a dream come true. Why not. Who would miss her?''

"Ted Kayne," Grace murmured.

At his name, Ron looked away. "Don't be too sure. In my opinion, Greer is a trophy—like all those companies he buys out. Another notch on his belt. He hasn't turned up here, has he? A few phone calls don't shout Valentine's Day to me. Hell, every time I'm here, he either cuts her off on the phone or has his secretary tell her to call him later. True love? I doubt it, Gracie."

Grace wrung her hands. "That's cruel, Ron."

"But an interesting notion. You don't agree?"

Her head pounding, Cameron had to acknowledge the possibility. If it came to that, she didn't doubt the police would question Ron and Grace. Maybe they were telling the truth. Maybe they were lying, and one—or both—of them knew exactly where Emerald had gone. Reminding herself that this was sheer speculation, Cameron held out the hope that Emerald would contact them soon.

Ron, it seemed, had other ideas. "Maybe Kayne has an insurance policy on her. If we're lucky," he said, "Miss Greer's bones won't turn up until doomsday."

When the doorbell rang, he started. His gaze lifted from Grace to Cameron who came out of hiding and made her presence known in the kitchen doorway. He drilled Cameron with a look that made her wonder if all along he'd known she'd been eavesdropping.

*I TOLD YOU NOT to get involved.*

Before the door fully opened, the thought leaped into J.C.'s mind. He pushed his way into the apartment. He'd ridden the elevator to Emerald's floor with his heart in his throat. Cameron looked the same, her face drawn with tension, and he tried to rein in his temper. Cameron wouldn't call him unless something bad had happened.

His first thought was last night's break-in.

"You okay here?" He glanced around the entryway then

into the living room where a plump but fine-boned woman stood beside a man he recognized as Ron Emory. Each held a few pieces of what appeared to be broken pottery.

Cameron's voice shook. "I'm fine. Emerald may not be."

She introduced Grace then stepped back in the entry hall.

J.C. studied Grace Jennings. She had a pinched look, as if her shoes fit too tightly and a nervous habit of wringing her hands. In his time J.C. had seen the same look on dozens of suspects.

The heavily muscled Ron, whom J.C. had met the night before as Emerald's chauffeur, eyed him with a wary expression. His dark gaze could bore holes through a skull and instantly J.C. knew not to underestimate him. With a nod of acknowledgment, he filed that away for later to focus on Cameron.

"I had a bad feeling last night. It never went away."

"Me, too," she murmured, and he guessed that instead of the "burglary" at her apartment, she could mean the kisses they had shared. Cameron made her announcement without looking at him. "Emerald never made it to Ted Kayne's."

J.C. groaned inwardly. He eyed her jeans and the white silk shirt that draped her breasts so sinuously his mouth watered. It had taken every ounce of his self-control not to go to her last night. His back hurt from lying on Emerald's sofa until dawn. Sleepless. And still aroused.

"Emerald's a grown woman," he said. "She could have decided to stop at a motel overnight."

"Yeah," Ron muttered.

Grace tried to set them straight.

"Mr. Kayne's home isn't far away—it's in Orange County."

J.C. wandered into the living room and took a seat. He pasted his most professional expression on his face. "Ron, what happened after I spoke to you last night then took the limousine?''

"With Emerald? Never saw her.''

J.C. frowned. The man was supposed to watch out for Emerald. Yet there had been time between J.C.'s sighting of Emerald and relieving Ron of his duties. She'd moved at a good clip. The Waldorf-Astoria was busy that night. It would be easy for Emerald to get swallowed up by the crowd.

He turned to Grace. "Tell me what you do know. For sure.''

When she finished, Cameron added, "I think her fan is back again. Not just on the phone this time.'' *And certainly not for me,* she might have said. She was pacing the room, driving him nuts. The next time she passed, J.C. tugged her down beside him. Her eyes met his. "The one your friend Gabe tried to arrest,'' she said.

"And you think Edgar Mills abducted Emerald.'' J.C. had his doubts. He hoped that she and Grace were over-reacting. "It's early,'' he pointed out. "Not even noon yet. You can't file a missing person's report on an adult until she's been gone for twenty-four hours. By then, she'll probably turn up. It's been what, twelve hours? Besides, he's not the type to ask for a ransom.''

Cameron's tone turned wry. "Meaning yourself?''

J.C. smiled thinly. He'd heard that joke before, and all through training. It was a bad one. Cameron must need the distraction. He wondered how her head felt, and now, after getting brained with a marble vase last night, she'd ignored his advice and gotten mixed up in Emerald's problem after all. A potentially bigger problem.

"I take it you haven't contacted the police.''

"Not yet.''

"So you rang downstairs looking for me. I'm flattered.

You want me to call Gabe at the NYPD.'' It wasn't a question.

''He has the case file on Edgar Mills. He knows Emerald. We may eventually have to call the police anyway—'' *Again,* J.C. added, but she didn't mention her apartment last night. ''It might as well be someone we know. Someone you know,'' she corrected.

''Which means I have my uses.'' Even a burnt-out Deputy U.S. Marshal, he thought, who right now felt himself hovering on the edge of panic again. *It could have been Cameron.* Grace looked from one to the other, and J.C. said, ''We have a history here.''

''*You* have a history. I'm making a fresh start.'' He noticed Cameron avoided Grace's eyes, which were full of curiosity.

''Clean slate?'' His tone was dry. Was she sending him a message about last night?

''Yes, and if you're thinking about my being followed and the same man phoning me here at Emerald's apartment—'' She broke off. ''Grace, will you bring us some coffee, please? Ron, would you help her pick up the rest of the broken china?'' She waited until they were alone. Then she turned on J.C., her hazel eyes snapping. ''You're wrong. *She's* the one who's missing.''

''Wearing your clothes.'' J.C. didn't blink.

She couldn't argue with that reminder. Or the fact that her own apartment had been vandalized. She'd try, though. Cameron must still be fighting her connection to Destina and the missing money.

''You don't believe in coincidence?'' she said.

''Nope.'' He held her gaze. ''Don't forget your appointment with Gabe this afternoon—about your apartment...'' He paused. ''In any case, I have no jurisdiction here. My job for Justice was—is—to protect government witnesses.'' There, he'd cloaked himself in his government-agent mask.

But it didn't help kill his rising anxiety because of Cameron.

"Kidnapping belongs to the FBI," he said, "and local officials—*if* Emerald was abducted." He didn't want to believe that. Because if it was true and Emerald was in danger, it was because she'd looked like Cameron last night, not herself. Even if Cameron chose to ignore this new connection.

J.C. had his hand on the phone when it rang.

Cameron motioned him to answer. J.C. couldn't ignore the caller.

"Who's this?" an angry male voice demanded, and J.C. identified himself. "Theodore Kayne here," the other man went on. "Emerald's fiancé. I didn't realize the authorities had been called."

"I'm here as a friend of Miss Greer's chef. I take it you haven't heard from her."

"I was hoping she'd answer. That she was home by now."

"We've had no contact with her either. Or the police yet."

"I want my fiancée found—and found quickly!"

J.C.'s mouth tightened. "Look, Kayne. Nothing can be done just yet. Officially."

"I'm sure it can. And will be."

The mild threat in his tone made the hackles on J.C.'s neck rise. He frowned into the receiver. *Don't throw your weight around, hotshot. Money doesn't buy everything.* If it could, J.C.'s panic episodes would have ended right after they began. He'd have spent his pension to put Venuto Destina on death row, if a judge and jury agreed. With his last penny, his own father's perfidy would be erased—not for his sake but his mother's.

He knew better.

"I understand your concern," he told Kayne in a cool

voice. ''But the law is the law. I can't change it. Neither can you.''

''Emerald Greer is a celebrity! An important person. Possibly the most talented female tennis player the game has ever seen. The rules,'' Kayne insisted, ''can be bent.''

''Not from my viewpoint.''

Kayne swore at the apparently unexpected obstacle. ''Who else is there now?''

Without answering, J.C. handed the phone to Cameron. If he didn't, he would say something he'd regret.


CAMERON LISTENED to Ted Kayne. She could feel her face whiten another shade.

When Ransom took her hand, she let him. She felt cold.

She might not want to face the issue, but this had to be said.

''There's something I think you should know, Mr. Kayne.'' She told him about the identity switch with Emerald after the Zeus reception but didn't mention her own apartment. ''I spent the night here,'' she finished. ''I'm sorry. Our playacting complicates the issue, I know.''

Ted Kayne's explosive response didn't help her nerves. Or her throbbing head.

''Why in hell would she do something like that?''

But Cameron could hear the terror in his voice.

While Ransom might have shouted back, she knew to lower her tone, to comfort. She would own up to her own part in this.

''Mr. Ransom's opinion is that someone may have taken Emerald—if she has really disappeared—by mistake. This person…may have wanted me instead.''

''You don't share his opinion.''

''I'm trying not to. In any event, Emerald is still out of touch.''

''I don't like the situation,'' Kayne murmured, quieter

now. His voice shook when he spoke again. "I'm going to need your help, Miss…"

"McKenzie."

"I'd drive down myself but until we're certain Emerald has disappeared and that it means foul play, I feel we should keep this under wraps."

"You mean, not call the police?"

"Or the media. Mr. Ransom—" he said the name with sarcasm "—seems capable enough, even if his manner is abrasive. I'd like him to stay, in case of contact with whoever may have taken Emerald. Keep Miss Jennings and Mr. Emory there, too. Anyone who calls or comes by the apartment will expect the household routine to be normal." He paused. "Because you wore Emerald's gown last night, I want you there, too. Until she's found, the press needn't know about our fears to the contrary."

"I'm not sure I understand."

She heard a sound on the line. Ted Kayne, tapping his fingers on his desk?

"I want the deception to continue. You will remain at the apartment. If Emerald has public appearances today that you could handle from the distance, please do so. I don't want any slips. Grace can run interference with reporters. She's used to dealing with them. Ron should show up each day as if to work out with Emerald. Let us hope that's only for today."

"I see."

"If compensation is a problem—" he had obviously picked up on her icy response "—I'll see to it personally."

Anger raced along her nerve ends. No wonder Ransom had used that tone of voice with Kayne. She'd lived most of her life under the government's thumb. She would not do the same for Emerald's future husband. Neither had Ransom.

"I don't need your money, Mr. Kayne. Emerald hired

me to cook for her and her staff and that's what I'll do. If there's anything else…"

"Let me speak to Grace."

Cameron started to hand off the phone. Then stopped. She had one more thing to say. "I realize you're a very important man. If Emerald is really missing, that may be of some help. But her staff—and I—and Mr. Ransom do not answer to you. If you want our help, treat us with respect."

When Grace took the phone, Cameron glanced at Ransom. He was grinning.

She gave him an abrupt nod, as if to say *so there*.

A few moments later, she finished telling him what Ted Kayne wanted.

"You're in this up to your neck now," Ransom said. "And no matter what you want, or what you believe, I'm not letting you alone." He held out a hand. "Until this is over, I'm your new best friend. Your Siamese twin."

# *Chapter Seven*

Stay at Emerald's apartment because that suited Ted Kayne?

Still determined to decide her own fate, Cameron would have balked at the notion. She would have gone home that afternoon to her apartment and finished cleaning up the mess. She would have told Ransom to keep away. Instead, she did stay.

Emerald's larger home had all the basics that were still lacking in Cameron's space—furniture, for instance. In the linen closet tall stacks of fluffy towels were hers for the choosing. The pantry held an array of staples plus gourmet items—balsamic vinegar, the finest olive oil, every herb and spice in Cameron's repertoire, genuine Belgian chocolate and handmade dried pastas from Rome. And to be honest, for the time being she felt safer there.

She would never admit that to Ransom, but since some vicious "hit man" had invaded her apartment and given her a concussion, she did, indeed, feel rattled—not just her brain. Besides, she didn't want Ransom trailing her home again, like a constant reminder that she had something to fear.

She could, however, avoid him for her own peace of mind. She couldn't deny the fact that the man disturbed her, mind and body. Ransom could rouse all her senses with just a look from that heated blue gaze. A word or two from his deep voice sent desire racing over her skin. He made her want things she had no business wanting. His powerful body, his sensual mouth...his touch. His taste.

But that wasn't all.

She couldn't stop remembering his comfort, either.

Cameron pressed her lips tight. She might fear for Emerald's safety and her own, but she also feared Ransom. And herself. It was better to keep him at a distance.

Bent upon keeping up a facade in the meantime that everything was normal, Cameron decided to cook up a storm. Peering into the refrigerator, she found enough left-over beef for a hearty ragout, and this certainly seemed the day for comfort food with a French twist. There was sufficient cabernet left in a bottle too for a rich gravy base. At least they would eat well while they waited for Emerald to surface. Even amid such borrowed luxury, Cameron prayed that would happen soon.

A while later she looked up from putting the finishing touches on dinner to find Grace climbing up to perch on a stool at the counter. Trying to forget Grace's earlier argument with Ron, Cameron smiled.

"You doing all right, Grace?"

"Surviving." She smiled. "You? How's your head?"

"Feels twice normal size." She touched the sensitive lump at the base of her skull and winced. "I'm still spacey now and then, but better, thanks."

"What about those fingers?"

Cameron held out her hand. "I took off the bandages. You spoil me."

Grace had been pampering her ever since she learned of the break-in at Cameron's apartment, which she and Ransom referred to as an ordinary burglary. Grace had objected to her even making dinner. But Grace had enough to do.

"The telephones seemed to ring all day," she reported.

"But it's never been Emerald."

"No," she murmured. "Just fifty calls about her wedding arrangements, another dozen with suggested public appearances for Emerald to make, the Zeus people checking about last night's reception, and a charity dinner/dance—she's the honorary chairperson this year." Grace yawned behind her hand. "Oh, and a number of photo shoots. World-Renowned Tennis Star to Wed—How Does a Modern Woman Juggle Marriage and Career?" she said. "Or, Marriage Now. Babies When? Take your pick."

Cameron smiled, glad the somber mood had lightened for a moment.

"The press never lets up."

"I think Ted Kayne is right. It's better to keep a low profile about this. If the media get hold of Emerald's disappearance, all hell will break loose."

"Let's hope they don't. And that she comes home soon." Cameron added, "If you need help with the phones, I'll be glad to take a turn. I'll pick up on the first ring, not to make my headache worse."

Grace toyed with the place settings Cameron had left on the counter.

"Thanks for staying. Not only does dinner smell wonderful—" she smiled "—but I wasn't looking forward to manning those phones all night alone. If you feel up to it."

So Grace was staying, too. That made her, Cameron...and Ransom.

"Will Ron be with us?"

"He might come in handy. The bodyguard thing, you know. I'm sure Emerald would turn over in her grave—" Grace broke off. "Oh God, I didn't mean...but you must think I did after our conversation earlier."

Grace had a point. But why say so? Cameron wouldn't take the bait and admit she'd overheard them. If Grace or

Ron were involved in Emerald's disappearance, that would come out soon enough.

"We're all under pressure. We say things that may not be true."

On the other hand, Ron's views on Emerald had seemed too strong, even over the top. Were his theories about her whereabouts—or possible abductors—the truth, or were they meant to divert suspicion from Ron? From the gym at the far end of the hall, Cameron heard the faint whir of the treadmill. Ron was exercising—to keep himself occupied? She stirred the ragout again in the heavy cooking pot then checked the fresh rolls baking in the oven. "Almost done," she said. "If you'll grab the salad from the fridge, we can eat."

"I'll call Mr. Ransom."

Cameron didn't exactly welcome his presence. Her memory of last night's encounter remained all too vivid—and dinner proved a silent affair. The phones had finally stopped ringing. With four people at the huge dining-room table where Emerald had eaten alone two nights ago, no one spoke. Everyone seemed to be listening for another call, or the opening of the front door. Cameron focused on the click of silverware on china, and, from Ron, a soft groan of appreciation for her cooking.

"This is great, Miss McKenzie."

"Cameron. That's my job. Thank you."

Ransom glanced up from his plate but didn't comment. His dark blue gaze held hers for a moment then slid away. Perhaps he, too, had decided that further tension wouldn't be a good thing, yet his opinion about Emerald, Cameron and Destina remained clear. As soon as he finished, he added his thanks then vanished.

"Mr. Ransom is using my computer," Grace said, explaining the faint snap of keys from her nearby office. "I think he's trying to get into the police database from here.

Maybe he'll learn something about Emerald's stalker that could help.''

Glad that he was occupied, and not lecturing her, Cameron cleaned up the kitchen then took a book into Emerald's den to read. Again, she couldn't concentrate but doubted her dull headache was the cause. Before nine o'clock, she heard Grace go into the spare room where she sometimes stayed when Emerald needed her, she'd said, and closed the door for the night. Ron would use the gym, in which Emerald kept a sturdy cot. With the endorphins flowing after his exercise, he'd probably sleep like a child. Ransom...

Aware that she wasn't alone, Cameron looked up.

Ransom leaned a shoulder against the door frame, watching her. She felt her pulse skip. Never mind their differences. If he wasn't the best-looking man she'd ever seen, she didn't know who was. Tall, lean, hard-muscled, with that shock of sun-streaked hair and those deep blue eyes, Ransom made her mouth water. When he folded his arms across his chest, his biceps bulged, and she couldn't take her gaze off his hands, strong and capable of giving a woman pleasure.

"You've read that page six times," he said. "Must be fascinating.''

"It's hard to focus."

"Need glasses?"

Cameron made a face. Her own bad joke deserved another. "You know what I mean. The silence— I think I preferred the phones ringing, even if Grace didn't.''

Ransom pushed away from the frame. He wandered into the room and flopped down on a deep-cushioned chair. And stared at her.

"Thanks for getting a few more clothes from my place," she finally said. He'd gone out in the midafternoon to get her new locks installed, coming back with her things and his in shopping bags. Did he expect this to be a long siege?

"Your plants are fine. I watered them before I left."

Cameron smiled her thanks, then rested her head against the chair back. "God, this is nerve-racking."

"Like a stakeout. Edgy. Boring, then terrifying."

She didn't like the sound of that either. "You expect something to happen? Other than Emerald walking in the door tonight?"

"We're close to that twenty-four hours now. Ted Kayne's wrong. When the time comes, we have to get the police involved."

Her heart skipped. "Then you think Emerald *has* been abducted."

"The longer I wait, the more I have to think possibly yes."

"But Kayne doesn't want the media to move in."

"He may not be running the show much longer." He frowned. "And this won't surprise or please you, but I'm still not convinced Emerald was the target."

Cameron straightened, her pulse tripping fast. Her tone cooled.

"And if she wasn't…then *I* am?"

He stretched out his legs, laced his hands behind his head and continued to study her. "Go ballistic if you want. But I've had all afternoon to think about this. I've decided that Kayne has given us an opportunity. If this deception continues as he 'requested' so nicely, with you staying out of sight here we can test any threat to you from Destina."

"You mean that effectively I will have disappeared, too."

*There is no threat,* she tried to tell herself. The intruder hadn't found the money. So why would he come back? As for Emerald…

Ransom nodded. "If Destina—or rather, his man—

snatched Emerald by mistake, they've discovered that by now. Be prepared, Cameron. Once he lets her go, assuming he might, he'll escalate his hunt for you again—and that missing money.''

Alarm swept through her. "If his people followed me before, then Destina knows where I am—even here. You think he'll let her go?''

He shrugged. "Depends on how well Emerald cooperates. If she plays the tennis star, the wronged celebrity, in other words the prima donna—''

"Her specialty,'' Cameron murmured with another glitch of her pulse.

"Then Destina's henchman may not care whether she gets home or not. If she can identify him, she's in even deeper trouble. Frankly, I hope she's been blindfolded, even drugged. I'm hoping she keeps her mouth shut.''

"And if the kidnapper wasn't Destina?''

Cameron held her breath. Then she and Emerald weren't connected.

"If someone only wanted to shake her up, maybe it's Mills, her stalker, who recognized her even wearing your clothes, then we may find Emerald—unharmed. Then you're home free, as far as she's concerned.'' He paused. "And I'll admit I made a mistake. As a bonus, you get to draw and quarter me for scaring the hell out of you.''

She smiled faintly. "Let the punishment fit the crime.''

When she rose, feigning a yawn to show she was ready for bed, he stood, too. Ransom wasn't finished. He always liked to have the last word.

"Cameron.''

"What?'' Her voice was weary. Suddenly she wanted to be tucked into Emerald's bed, beneath her Egyptian-cotton sheets, with the lights out and the draperies drawn. Away from Ransom.

Away from whatever was brewing between them. Away from her own growing fear. And his.

"I don't think I'm mistaken."

CAMERON COULD ONLY HOPE Ransom was wrong. The next day she felt as if she were back in Witness Protection—an even more confining existence than the one she'd led years ago. She felt trapped. Because of her injury, she couldn't work, which only increased her anxiety the better she felt, and Ransom rarely let her out of his overbearing sight.

He had taken her yesterday to the police precinct to make her statement about the break-in. His friend Gabe Whitney—a big, broad-shouldered cop to the core—didn't ease her mind. His morning visit today and his questions, his first report on Emerald's apparent disappearance, only made her head swim, then ache. She could blame that on her concussion, yet the lump on her skull didn't hurt as much now, and when she rose too quickly from a chair, her vision didn't waver on the edge of darkness. No, she had to face the truth in this at least. She felt frantic about Emerald and her silence.

When the doorbell rang that afternoon, she leaped to answer. By then, she'd had enough of Ransom's constant surveillance, enough as well of Ron and Grace's continual bickering which seemed to float through the stifling air. Cameron envisioned the mood in the apartment as a large black bird smothering them all in its deadly embrace.

Speculation had become increasingly somber among the four temporary residents of Emerald's apartment. Grateful for any distraction, Cameron was about to open the door when Ransom covered her hand with his. As she had the first night, she felt an electric jolt from his touch but tried not to visibly react.

"Security first," he said, taking a look through the peephole. He made a harsh sound then the locks snicked open.

Kyle stood in the hall. When had she told him Emerald's address? Again, she felt torn between joy at seeing her brother and her own uneasiness at how he'd found her for the second time in days.

Before Ransom moved to stop him, Kyle was inside.

His eyes flashed. "Where have you been, Cam? I called your apartment last night and all day today. I was worried sick. Then I talked to the old guy, that doorman at your building, and he told me you'd been robbed."

Feeling caught, Cameron glanced at Ransom. She would have to explain to Kyle. When she'd finished, she said, "I'm sorry. I should have left a message with your hotel."

Ransom's warning look told her to be cautious in what she said. Kyle had learned about her break-in, but he needed to know nothing more. Emerald's disappearance was not to be mentioned yet. Gabe had agreed to nose around first, then discuss the issue with Ted Kayne before the press—and the public—got wind of the story.

Cameron led the way into the den, where she felt most comfortable. More casual than the rest of the apartment, it was a place to relax. As if any of them could. Giving herself time to concoct some excuse for her own "disappearance," as far as Kyle was concerned, she took a seat on a sofa. To her surprise, Ransom sat close beside her.

"My guardian," she murmured. "You needn't protect me from my own brother."

Kyle didn't seem to hear. He examined the room then poured himself a drink at Emerald's bar cart. "Do you mind?" He held up the bottle.

"Help yourself," Ransom said. Sounding unhappy.

Kyle's visit obviously didn't please him. The mood around them darkened another shade. She saw that her break-in had upset Kyle. She couldn't blame him.

"You're right," Cameron said. "I should have let you know about the burglary, and that I'd be here for a while.

My apartment is still a mess.'' Kyle frowned and she went on, ''I realize you were worried. You had every right to be. But I'm fine.''

''With a concussion?'' Kyle drained his drink. ''Cameron—''

''A few days of rest and I'll be fully recovered.''

His frown darkened. ''And Ransom is here, too... because of Destina? I thought you didn't need his protection.''

For a moment, no one spoke. Cameron looked again at Ransom. He looked back. Then to Cameron's further astonishment, he slung an arm around her shoulders. He dragged her to his side and smiled down at her. The smile didn't reach his eyes, but Kyle wasn't looking at them. He stared into his empty glass and Ransom offered another excuse that made her twitch. ''I don't imagine this will thrill you,'' he told Kyle, ''but Cameron and I have been, well, seeing each other.''

Kyle's gaze jerked up. ''Cam, you have to be kidding. The last person on earth I'd picture you with is a U.S. Marshal.''

''On leave,'' she said, picking up her cue. She couldn't think how else to explain Ransom's presence either. ''Yes. I know. But only the other night you said yourself that Ransom—um, J.C.—had some interest in me. I wasn't ready to tell you then.''

''The feeling is definitely mutual.'' Ransom squeezed her shoulder. ''Right, sweetheart?''

Ransom had used the endearment, though he couldn't mean it. She had no choice then. ''Absolutely.'' She dropped her head against his solid chest and snuggled close. ''You're really the first to know except my employer,'' she informed Kyle, hoping her tone sounded properly enraptured. She could feel the hard thud of Ransom's heart under her cheek. Her own pulse skittered.

Kyle didn't look convinced.

"And Greer doesn't mind Ransom hanging around?"

Ransom's voice rumbled in her ear. "Emerald's engaged herself. Love must be in the air."

*Kyle will never believe us,* Cameron thought.

Just as Ransom apparently didn't buy Kyle's sudden visit.

"How did you track Cameron down?" he asked.

Kyle shrugged. "I remembered her mentioning Greer's name and approximately where she works. After that, it was a matter of asking the right people. You'd be surprised how informative one's neighbors can be."

Cameron didn't know her neighbors. In New York, that was nothing strange, but she raised her head. From the look on Ransom's face, he didn't believe Kyle either.

"Greer's neighbors," Kyle corrected himself.

"You didn't trail Cameron here and back to her apartment the other night?"

"Of course not. Why would I? I happened to arrive at the same time you did—you and Cameron. Now I see why. I should thank you for walking my sister home along those dark streets, but I'm not sure I approve of your 'relationship.'" He paused. "I stepped out of the shadows near her building just as you reached the entrance."

"Hey, coincidences happen," Ransom murmured, shooting her a look that she knew said otherwise.

Kyle bristled. "Are you calling me a liar?"

Cameron reached out a hand. Her supposed romance with Ransom could distract Kyle from the presumed danger she was in. "Let's not quarrel. Kyle, I know it will take time for you to accept J.C. and me, but please try. For my sake."

"You know your welfare is essential to me."

She forced the smile. "And I appreciate that. Even when

it's not convenient for me. Now, shall we have coffee before you go?''

He studied his empty drink. "I don't need coffee." He set the glass down on an end table then crossed the room. Ignoring Ransom, he drew Cameron to her feet, into his embrace. "I'd like you to come with me, Cam. We'll have dinner." He glanced around, as if he expected Emerald to walk in. "You claim you're feeling better. Soothe my nerves," he said. "We've hardly spent any time together."

Cameron refused to feel guilty. All she wanted now was for Kyle to leave, and the charade about Emerald, about herself and Ransom to end. Kyle bothered her, too.

"When you called and I wasn't home, my machine must have taken a message."

"Your machine didn't reassure me. You never called back."

She hadn't checked her calls but Ransom had—before her brother phoned? She rose to kiss Kyle's cheek. "Consider yourself reassured. I *am* an adult, responsible for myself now."

"I'm not sure you're doing a good job."

She might have felt insulted, but Cameron chalked up Kyle's comment to his worry about her. After all, they had shared long years in WP when the daily safety of each family member was critical. How could she blame him now for slipping back into their old pattern? She felt stuck there herself.

"She's not going anywhere," Ransom murmured.

"If my sister needs protection, I'm more than able to provide it."

Ransom gave her a sexy smile. "I already have that job."

"Then, what? I'm supposed to go merrily on my way, satisfied that she's in good hands?" He shook his head. "Her apartment was burglarized! Destina came that *close*,"

e said, indicating a small gap between two fingers. "Cam-
ron was hurt. Some protector you make. No wonder they
ok your badge."

She felt Ransom try not to flinch. His medical leave was
sore point but he didn't argue. She edged away from
yle, closer to Ransom.

"I'm safe here. With J.C. I'm better but still dizzy from
e concussion."

Kyle looked scornful but he backed down. "Well, as
ng as you're spending so much time here, let me have
our cell and work numbers. I don't want to lose track
gain. When I tried to call here, I discovered that Greer's
umber is unlisted."

Cameron stiffened. She couldn't refuse without making
yle suspicious. With an arm around Cameron, Ransom
ulled her near.

"Emerald doesn't want her unlisted number floating
round, even among family members of her employees.
ive us a few days more. When Cameron is home again,
nd feeling well, she'll give you a call." He overlooked
er own cell number.

Kyle didn't look happy but he accepted the notion.

Then, before he walked into the elevator, he hesitated.

"I'll take care of her," Ransom assured him. And low-
ring his head, he kissed Cameron squarely on the mouth.
he kiss lingered and Cameron felt her bones melt.

"That's what I'm afraid of," Kyle said.

AMERON'S LIPS still tingled from Ransom's kiss when, af-
r dinner that night, she headed for the den. She was
owning, troubled. Emerald was still missing. Remember-
g Kyle's obvious fretfulness on her behalf that afternoon,
he didn't know what to make of him either. Sixteen years
part was a long time. As she neared the den she heard

angry voices. Ron and Grace again. Their quarrels had become commonplace.

"You're nuts! What would I be hiding?" Ron growled

"If I knew, it wouldn't be hidden. You know more than you let on, Ron. If you ask me, you know where Emerald is right now—and I don't mean some motel."

"That's a neat trick. Put the blame on me when you've hated her since the day you first came to work here."

"I don't really hate her. Even if I did, that doesn't mean I meant her any harm."

"No?" His words bounced off the walls. "It doesn't mean you didn't, either. Oh, I'm sure everyone ignores you Gracie. Plump little partridge, how could you do anyone harm? But that's just the point. You could hire someone Someone big. Someone lethal."

"Your name would be my first pick—just like the police."

"What's going on in here?" Cameron said.

Ron loomed over them. "We were having a discussion."

"Your 'discussion' is disturbing the whole apartment. If either of you has any real information on where to find Emerald, you need to tell the police. Or tell Ransom."

"Right here." Behind her, Ransom laid a hand on her shoulder. He'd been working in Grace's office again. "Ron, time for an evening workout. Think I'll join you."

Ron looked him over. "Sure. You can spot me with the weights."

"And vice versa."

Defusing the situation, the two men headed for the gym. Leading Grace to the kitchen, Cameron agreed with Ransom. Ron needed to work off his aggression before Grace, or someone else, got hurt. But was Grace right, as Cameron suspected? Did Ron know something?

"Emerald should never have hired him," Grace said.

Cameron poured two glasses of chilled water then sat at
he kitchen counter with Grace beside her.

"I heard about Ron's troubles with military law." Cam-
ron waited, hoping the other woman would supply details.

Grace made circles on the countertop with her wet glass.
"And mine," she said. "I guess we're a pair."

"You really think Ron had something to do with Em-
rald's disappearance?"

"I wouldn't put it past him."

"He has his own suspicions about you."

Grace looked up. "And you think he could be right?"
Her pale eyes clouded. "Miss McKenzie—Cameron—I
nade a huge mistake years ago. I let my husband's abuse
lter my own beliefs that a human being's life is sacred,
hat love can heal." She shuddered. "He took his fists to
he one too many times—and I snapped. I'm not proud of
vhat I did. But I survived."

"And your husband died," Cameron murmured. So
nat's what had happened. Self-defense?

"I put a knife through his heart." She hesitated. "You
hink I could do the same to Emerald because I dislike
er?"

Her tone had made Cameron uneasy. "I'm not accusing
ou. I do want to find Emerald, though. Alive."

"What's your stake in this?"

Cameron hesitated. "I feel somewhat responsible for her
lisappearance." Then she pressed her lips tight. She'd un-
urdened herself to Emerald, but Grace didn't need to learn
et about her past. "Even if someone attacked her on the
treet, it could be because she looked like me that night."

"Well, we all have our crosses to bear."

Grace slid off the stool without having taken a swallow
f her water. Not looking back, she left the kitchen. And
eft Cameron with her statement.

She was still pondering the issue of Grace, Ron, herself—and Emerald's possible fate—when the mantel clock chimed midnight.

With a sigh, Cameron put the glasses in the dishwasher, then went to bed.

Of course she couldn't sleep.

She hadn't slept much at all in the past few nights.

*Where was Emerald?*

And what about Ted Kayne? Cameron wondered. Despite his almost hourly calls demanding information that no one had about his fiancée, Kayne had yet to show up. He had meetings, he told them, regarding an acquisition. He could better coordinate efforts to find Emerald from his offices than from her apartment. Et cetera, Cameron thought. Yet his concern didn't ring true.

*No true love there,* Ron had said.

Then there was Kyle. Cameron realized why his visit earlier hadn't seemed right. She *had* given him her cell and work numbers—the night he came back into her life.

Why did he pretend not to have them? Because he'd wanted to see her in person?

Her head ached, a dull pounding, and Cameron flipped over in bed again.

How had she left Witness Protection, tried to accept her father's death in that Denver alley, only to get caught up in another desperate situation? A knock at the door jolted her heart. Kyle was still on her mind when Ransom slipped into the dark room.

KNOWING SHE WOULDN'T LIKE the reason for his visit, J.C. didn't wait for an invitation. Not even his workout with Ron had eased his mind. He hadn't come to chat.

Or to note Cameron's loose hair, disarrayed from sleep—or the lack of it—and her loose nightshirt, which nevertheless caressed her rounded shoulder bones and clung to her breasts. J.C. forced his gaze away.

"I just took another quick look at your apartment. Your brother left no messages on your answering machine."

Her eyes widening, Cameron sat up, sweeping hair from her eyes. She probably realized J.C. still had her new key from yesterday. "Maybe he didn't mean that literally. He could have called—then hung up."

J.C. eased down on the edge of the bed.

"Then why expect you to call back? Cameron, you didn't see him for years. He abandoned your family. He never even knew when your mother had died. Until he showed up at your apartment a few nights ago he hadn't heard about James. Why are you so willing to believe him?"

He didn't say *trust*, but wondered if that was what she felt now. And if so, how she had come by it that quickly.

"He's my brother."

"I never had a brother," J.C. admitted, "but like you, remember, I did have a father." The pain ran through him again, like a knife blade between his ribs. "I know what I'm talking about. Don't let Kyle back into your life so easily. He could end up hurting you, too."

She didn't answer. Didn't know what to say, perhaps. The frustrating day on top of the break-in at her apartment, then Emerald's disappearance and Kyle's latest visit must have exhausted her. She probably wished she could sleep, but she knew as well as he did that she wouldn't. Yet his statement had apparently intrigued her. And she must have remembered their last conversation on the topic.

"Ransom, what did your father do? Tell me."

He ran a hand over the back of his neck. He shouldn't have mentioned his father. The last time, either.

"You need to tell me," she murmured. "It affects everything you do."

Hell, she had a point. Why keep avoiding the issue? But he didn't look at her when he answered. "Embezzled money. A lot of money. He worked for a bank. He started as a messenger, made head teller in a couple of years, married my mother, they had me.'' His mouth tightened. ''He got promoted to loan officer, then VP.'' His voice bore no inflection, but J.C. couldn't quite hide his emotions. ''Their new lifestyle required a certain appearance, so I guess in order to supply that he figured he could use a little extra every week. Pretty soon it was a great deal extra—and of course someone found out. A high-level officer of the bank. The same guy who'd hired him.''

Cameron didn't have to ask. ''He turned your father in.''

J.C. nodded, his body taut with tension. ''I live with what he did every day of my life. I try to understand why he raised me to be scrupulously honest, to believe in certain values, to honor my commitments, my obligations—then threw that in my face. I try to understand why he broke my mother's heart. And her spirit.'' He shook his head. ''I still don't understand why he did what he did.''

Cameron's tone was quiet. ''Then I guess we have something in common.''

''James?'' He lifted an eyebrow.

She slipped her arms around his waist. ''My father had his faults. He should have seen Destina for what he was and quit his job before Destina was indicted on racketeering charges. That doesn't mean someone had the right to kill him.''

''He's dead anyway. My father, too.'' He flinched at the memory. ''So is my mother.''

''And that's it for you?'' She drew back and touched his arm, as if feeling sorry for him. ''Don't you think the world is a more positive place than that?''

''Goes with the territory. I've seen a lot in my work. It sours you.''

''Yet there's a better man in there somewhere.'' She

tapped a finger against his wrist, then his heart. "A man who could believe in a happier outcome. In *someone*."

In the dark he studied her face. *You,* he thought, then reached out, trailing a light hand down her cheek, feeling the hum of awareness in his fingertips. "You're so soft, Cameron, not just your skin, but smooth inside…even after what you've seen."

"Is that bad?"

"No," he said. "It's probably good. But if you were in my shoes—in my job—that attitude could get you killed." He paused, holding her gaze in the dark. "It could get you killed now, Cameron." He leaned closer, his voice, his breath, whispering across her skin. "I'd sure hate to see that happen."

"I thought…" Her breath caught, probably at the look in his eyes. Need. It was all he could feel now. "I thought I was your current mission," she murmured. "*Not* in a romantic sense."

"You are my mission." But did she, too, remember that night in the limousine, then later when he fell apart? He couldn't get the taste of her out of his mind. The feel of her body pressed to his. Now, J.C. moved, easing himself onto the wide bed until he was half-lying beside her. He cupped her chin. "I'm not sure I can separate James's death, or the danger you're in from Destina, from how I feel about you. Personally." Then, without further thought, he had her in his arms. His head lowered to hers, and his lips sought hers in the dark and he stopped worrying about Emerald, about Kyle, about Ron and Grace, about James's killer.

Or even his own father.

For the first time in a long while J.C. thought about life. And hope.

And Cameron.

When his mouth took full possession of hers, and his

hand slipped under her nightshirt to glide up her side then gently take her breast in his palm, he groaned. J.C. had raised her shift and was peeling off his T-shirt now. His kisses grew hotter, deeper, until all he could feel was her mouth under his, the smoothness of her scented skin, and he could barely breathe for wanting her. He tried to caution himself. He was half out of his mind. He was wrong for her. He was everything she hated...

Didn't matter. His hand touched her breast and he knew. She was everything he needed. *Now.*

Then, before it had fully begun, to his shock and frustration, everything ended. With J.C. braced above her, Cameron pushed hard at his chest, as if she had sensed the depth of his feelings.

"*Stop.* We can't do this."

He tried to focus, to comprehend what she was saying. But before J.C. could even shift his weight, Cameron wriggled free then bounded from the bed, from the room.

# Chapter Eight

Shaken by her reaction to Ransom's attempted lovemaking the night before, and still troubled not only by Emerald's disappearance but the supposed burglary at her own apartment, Cameron sat cross-legged on Emerald's bed the next day, holding her broken doll.

That reminder of her past, like Ransom's kisses, only brought sorrow now. And more fear.

It had taken her a long time to admit her attraction to Ransom, even longer to acknowledge her growing feelings for him.

She didn't want him to grieve about his father. Or hers.

She didn't want him to sweat in panic.

She didn't want him to…care about her.

Her own emotions scared her.

They had no future, Cameron felt certain, only a past that bound them together. That, she told herself, was why she'd summoned some last vestige of strength to push him away last night. Before she couldn't pull back. Before it was too late.

In the distance now a telephone rang once. Grace had answered, and Cameron heard her low-pitched voice along the hallway. The call didn't take long. A moment later, Grace appeared at Emerald's door.

She looked pale. ''That was Mr. Kayne again. One of

his people thinks he spotted Emerald in a small town upstate.''

Ted Kayne, Cameron thought with disdain. His longdistance telephone bill was mounting by the hour, but he had yet to make an appearance. Instead, business seemed uppermost in his mind.

Grace named the town.

''Isn't that where Emerald came from?'' Cameron asked.

''Yes. But she hasn't been home in years, not since she started playing tennis.''

''Not since she left to train, she told me.'' Cameron paused. ''She would have been, what? Nine, I think she said. By now she would have lost most of her ties to the area. Then why would she go back there now?''

Grace shivered. ''If she didn't go willingly...if her 'fan' took her, that might explain his interest in her.''

''You mean, he might be from her hometown?''

She nodded. ''What if he went to school with her?'' Grace brightened. ''Let me see what I can find. Emerald brought a few items with her. We might get lucky and turn up a school photo—with names.''

''Good idea. There could be Valentines, notes from other students, friends.''

Leaning against the door, Grace said, ''What did your friends write?''

Was she trying to get close to Cameron? The feeling was new, and Cameron didn't quite know how to deal with it.

''I never had friends,'' she admitted. ''Not close ones.'' It was too dangerous.

Another wave of sorrow lapped at the edges of her mind. Yet last night, talking with Ransom about his father's crime, she had felt almost normal. Despite the painful topic, she had shared his guilt, his grief, and for a while they had seemed to be friends. In the light of day, she realized that couldn't be.

The doll in her arms told her how different their lives were.

Soon, on his own, Ransom would probably overcome his panic attacks.

He'd return to active duty as a U.S. Marshal.

With Witness Protection at last behind her, Cameron would struggle to make a success of The Unlimited Chef.

She would slowly furnish her apartment.

Maybe someday Ransom would even forgive his father.

And she would stop looking over her shoulder.

Would Destina's arrest—this time—end her paranoia? Or was she destined to spend the rest of her life in hiding, if not physically, then emotionally? Hiding herself behind a polite mask that never let anyone get near? How could she tell Grace, or anyone else, about her past? It was ironic, but only Ransom could understand. Or Kyle.

But then, she realized, so had Emerald.

"You see what you can find," she told Grace. "I'll help as soon as I finish here."

Grace flashed her an inquiring look and Cameron held up the doll.

"She hasn't lost too much of her stuffing. I'll see if I can mend her."

Mend myself, she added silently. In her own way, she felt as damaged as her doll. She had as much of a burden to carry as Grace herself. She needed to find time to talk with Grace. With her for company, she could avoid Ransom—and his hot, dark blue eyes.

"You found the sewing kit?" Grace asked.

"Ron got it for me. I hope you don't mind." They must be Grace's thread and needles. She couldn't imagine Emerald making neat stitches down the front of this doll, or anywhere else. "I'll return it when I'm through." Cameron stopped her before Grace stepped out of the room. "The phones seem quiet today.'' No news, she had begun to think, was not good news. ''Except for Kayne's call—''

''Nothing. Mr. Ransom's on my computer. Running some plates for a car that belongs to Emerald's supposed fan. And in some federal database. I don't know what he's looking for.''

Cameron's heart rate kicked up. ''Tell me when he finds something.''

As much as possible, she would stay away from him until news came about Emerald. After last night, she did feel safer that way.

Opening the small sewing kit, Cameron selected the right shade of thread. She cut off a piece, poked it through the needle's hole and tied a knot at the end. She hadn't forgotten her mother's lessons. They had filled more than one empty day in WP, but Cameron didn't smile.

Her mother had had scant time for anything but work. Her pay, her overtime, kept the family in food and clothes. Still, every evening her mother sat in some lumpy armchair in the corner of some living room, in some town or other, to mend the old or to make new skirts, blouses for herself and Cameron, corduroy pants and flannel shirts for Cameron's father or Kyle.

Now Cameron had just thrust her finger inside the hole in the doll's chest to pinch it closed for the first stitch, when she felt something.

Hard.

Lumpy.

The beanbag stuffing that had trickled out in Cameron's apartment didn't explain this. Those beans were smaller, lighter, she remembered. She fished around and, with difficulty, then surprise, wrenched free a mesh pouch.

She pulled it out and her pulse hammered.

She couldn't believe her eyes.

Inside the pouch an array of stones glittered.

*Diamonds!*

Lots of them.

She felt her face pale and her fingers shake. She dropped the needle in the bedcovers. The "burglar" had missed these, buried deep inside the doll's body cavity, but when the beans scattered, the diamonds became easier to find, closer to the surface. No wonder the doll's spine had felt so stiff.

This—not money in cash—was what Destina's thugs must be looking for, what Ransom believed Destina wanted of her.

Cameron opened her mouth to call Ransom.

Then shut it again. Tight.

She couldn't tell Ransom.

Cameron flew off the bed to lock the door. She didn't want to be seen. Then, unable to stop her heart from pounding, she laid the pouch of diamonds on the dark comforter and watched them sparkle.

Her breath caught. *My God.*

There must be tens of thousands of dollars' worth here, perhaps millions. She was no expert on gems—had never owned any—but these looked genuine. The stones flashed even in the natural light of the room, reminding Cameron that she didn't belong here.

These were temporary quarters, she told herself, just fancier than the kind she remembered all too well from childhood.

As soon as Emerald returned, Cameron would go home. But at home now, she knew, a possible killer could be waiting.

She was as much in need of protection as she had been with her family at the age of three, or thirteen, or twenty-three.

Her blood ran cold.

Ransom thought her father had known where the missing funds were.

*Had her father really put the diamonds here?*

But she wouldn't believe he was responsible, and these were jewels not cash. Cameron frowned. Years ago, she remembered, her mother had told her that Venuto Destina was a sometime visitor to their home—before his indictment, his trial, before Cameron vanished with her parents into Witness Protection because of his threat. What if he had hidden the diamonds? Destina's vow of revenge, it seemed, had been only partly satisfied by James's death. Now...

If Ransom was right, *she* was the target.

And despite her resistance to the notion, he was now her protector.

Yet Emerald had just been sighted in a little upstate town.

Was there really no connection between her and Cameron except for a mistaken abduction? If so, why hadn't they heard from Emerald herself by now?

Still puzzled, Cameron gathered the diamonds from the comforter's surface and cupped the pouch in her hands. What to do with them?

Her first thought had been to call Ransom.

But she couldn't.

He might protect her, in part because he wanted Destina, but he also thought her father was a thief. This cache of diamonds would only convince him he was right again.

Cameron couldn't show him.

Not yet.

She started to refill the doll's body with the diamonds then stopped. In spite of the "burglar's" vicious slashing at the childhood toy, he hadn't found what he was looking for. His action with the doll seemed more angry, thwarted, out of control with frustration. And if it was Destina, he might know where the diamonds were hidden. She couldn't take the chance.

Hoping still, even praying that her father was innocent, she stowed the glittering gems in their mesh pouch between Emerald's mattress and box spring. That would do for now. She would sleep on them tonight—like the princess on the pea.

Trying to quiet her trembling hands, she located the needle she'd dropped. She pulled the doll's torn "flesh" together and began to stitch.

Unfortunately, to be sure the diamonds stayed safe, she would have to go home. Tomorrow. There, Cameron knew, she would find the safest hiding place of all.

A place where no one would find them—not even Ransom—until Cameron had learned the truth about Destina and her father for herself.

And, assuming he was innocent, for James.

BY THE NEXT MORNING Cameron lifted her first cup of coffee to her lips with still-shaking fingers.

"Nerves?" At the kitchen table Ransom glanced up from the newspaper, but Cameron felt he'd been watching her, all too aware of her inner battle to appear calm.

"My other clients are wondering why I'm unavailable. My business is at risk—more than my safety." She cried, "Ransom, why hasn't Emerald been found?"

He didn't answer directly. "The plate for her stalker's car is clean. No outstanding warrants against him. And, according to Gabe, that car has been sitting in the guy's driveway for the past week. Broken water pump."

"Does that mean he's not involved in Emerald's disappearance?"

Which would mean this was all about Cameron. Like the diamonds.

"Either/or," Ransom said, setting the paper aside. "He's

being interviewed, but I can't take part." He ran a hand through his hair. "Unfortunately, these things take time." He looked at her again. "You sure you're okay?"

"Fine. Just…frustrated. By this time each morning I'm halfway through my first client's menus for the week. I don't know how much longer I can hold them off without losing every one of them."

"Except Emerald."

Cameron remembered her wish to be exclusive. "She's not here."

"If it's any consolation, Ted Kayne's supposed to show up tomorrow."

"That's big of him. Better late than never."

Ransom smiled faintly. "I see you and Grace share the same opinion."

Cameron shoved back from the table. "I need something to do. Cook," she added. "If I don't work, I'll go crazy."

On her way past him, Ransom reached for her hand. He tugged her closer and looked up into her eyes. "Hang tight, Cameron. A little while longer, okay? I know it's hard. Harder than WP."

"At least you understand."

There it was again, that connection between them that Cameron couldn't deny. She eased back and left the room. This morning she couldn't afford to be friends with him, or anything more. She needed to ditch Ransom. Somehow. She had to get out of Emerald's apartment then make her way home. Alone.

To her dismay, Ransom hung around the kitchen while she cooked, then he lingered over Grace's computer. Because her office was across the hall from the kitchen and the door stayed open, he could see Cameron's every move. The clacking keys nearly drove her mad.

By three o'clock she was biting her lip.

Then, as if by magic, Ransom suddenly left the apartment.

Grace informed her, "He's gone to see his friend at the NYPD."

Cameron breathed a sigh of relief. Maybe her luck was changing.

Then her heart sank.

"He told Ron to keep an eye on you." Grace studied her. "There's something else here, beyond Emerald's disappearance. I get the feeling Mr. Ransom is not simply trying to help find her—but is also guarding you."

"After the break-in at my place, he tends to be a bit paranoid. Not that he wasn't before." So did Cameron but she didn't point that out. "Listen, Grace. I need to go out for an hour or so. Tell Ron—"

"I'll cover for you," she said, "if you level with me."

Ah. So Grace—again—was not the mousy personal assistant she appeared to be. Cameron reminded herself that the woman had served time for murder. She shouldn't underestimate Grace where Emerald was concerned, either. What if she and Ron had made a pact, and their quarrels were just for show? What if Ron had abducted Emerald?

Then Ransom's theory was wrong. And what had they done with the tennis star?

Frowning, Cameron decided to come clean. Maybe she wasn't being fair. Maybe they were innocent. Grace and Ron weren't the only ones with a past, and if she convinced Grace she was one of them, Cameron could escape. After explaining about Witness Protection, she finished, "So you can see why being confined makes me half-crazy. I need to take a walk. That's all."

This was partly true—she would walk home—but Grace looked suspicious.

"Ron can go with you."

"Really, that's not necessary." Cameron smiled. "Actually, I'm meeting my brother.'' Earlier, Cameron had managed a brief conversation with Kyle. She couldn't blame him for worrying. "If you can just keep Ron busy for a few minutes while I slip out…''

Grace looked at her with new awareness.

"I guess there are all kinds of prisons. Even Emerald knew that.''

Cameron's pulse thudded. Grace had used the past tense, and Cameron was still analyzing her comment when she crossed the last intersection before her apartment. She was still shaking, too.

With one last look behind her, she entered the lobby.

The doorman was on duty and, grateful for a familiar face that had nothing to do with Emerald or Destina, she gave Fred a cheery greeting.

"Cold but crisp out there today,'' he agreed. Then stopped her at the elevator. "Miss McKenzie, some man has been here for you. Several times.''

For an instant she thought Ransom had followed her.

She wouldn't put it past him.

Perhaps his "errand'' had been fiction, for her benefit.

Or Grace had sent Ransom after her.

But when Fred described him, she relaxed.

"That would be my brother.'' Then she frowned. "I thought he realized I was staying at my employer's apartment this week,'' she added for Fred's benefit.

He shrugged. "I told him I couldn't let him in, especially after the trouble you had. That's all I know.''

Why would Kyle want in to her apartment?

Trying to quiet her suspicions, she went upstairs then fished in her bag for her new key. She was becoming like Ransom—more wary of people than she had been.

She would ask Kyle his reasons later.

After she deposited the diamonds for safekeeping.

KYLE WAS WAITING for her in the entryway of the Italian restaurant on upper Third Avenue not far from Cameron's apartment. By the time she stepped inside, out of the growing cold at dusk, she felt nearly normal.

Her hands had stopped trembling, and she hugged Kyle tight.

"I'm sorry for the other day," she told him when they were seated at their table in the bar. "I know you don't like Ransom."

"At first I thought I would." He checked the menu. "He's pretty uptight, it seems to me. I wonder why."

Cameron ordered an artichoke-dip appetizer with her wine. She briefly told Kyle about Ransom's experience in the alley with their father. "Still, it's not his fault that Destina finally got to Dad. Someday he may believe that."

Kyle reached for her hand. He warmed it between his. Then lowered his tone.

"Cam, I'm nearly wild at this point. How am I supposed to trust you with Ransom? He shakes like an aspen in a high wind. And I'm expected to walk away and let him 'protect' you? It almost killed me to leave you with him."

"And you've been lurking around my apartment building ever since?"

Kyle's startled expression met her gaze. "The old guy told you, huh? Sorry. I can't help myself. I kept hoping you'd come home. Without your bodyguard." He smiled. "I'm relieved you came alone tonight. Don't be too hard on me, Cam. I only have one sister. I don't want to lose her now that we've found each other again."

"You found *me*," Cameron corrected him. She still wondered why.

It wasn't that she didn't want to trust Kyle. Heaven knew, she needed to trust someone. Still, his timing seemed odd, as Ransom had pointed out. She didn't know why Kyle suddenly felt the need for family again.

The vague memories of his leaving years ago flitted across her mind.

Sixteen years.

"You can't imagine how glad I am to be with you," he said, releasing her hand. The waitress put down their drinks and Kyle dug into his stuffed-mushroom appetizer.

Cameron returned his smile.

Maybe it was time, now, to trust him. She couldn't blame Kyle forever for leaving her. He'd been only seventeen then himself to her twelve years old. Still a kid. Whatever had driven him away, she might learn later. Maybe it had been just frustration at their confinement, like Cameron at Emerald's apartment.

Still, the shadowed half memory of angry words, of threats, lingered in her mind.

"I've missed so much." Kyle sipped his beer. "I wish there was time to catch up on everything but there's not." He lifted an eyebrow. "I'm off to Houston soon. One more interview here, then to Texas. I wanted to see you before I go."

Disappointment swept her. On the verge of trying her artichoke dip, she pushed it aside. "Oh, Kyle. I was hoping you'd stay...until this Destina thing is resolved." Until Emerald is found, she added silently.

He looked into his glass. "I wish I could. I can't tell you how terrified I felt when I learned your apartment had been ransacked. Have Ransom, or the cops, made any headway?"

"Not yet. It takes time," she repeated Ransom's words, not feeling reassured herself. "Are you sure you can't stay?"

"I'll come back. As soon as possible. In the meantime, I'll call. Every day."

Cameron intertwined their hands. "Kyle, I need you."

The words weren't easy to say. Her resentment still hovered just beneath the surface, and she felt it again. He was leaving. Abandoning her.

Kyle squeezed her fingers. "Before I go, I want to caution you, Cam. Whoever among Destina's men violated your apartment—and you in the process—will return. Ransom knows that. So do I." He hesitated. "If you know anything about the money they were looking for, now is the time to say so."

Cameron's pulse thudded. Could he feel it beneath his fingers?

She pulled away. "I told you before, I have no idea where the money is."

For a moment, she felt tempted. She might feel inclined to trust him—or she had until he told her he was leaving—but with the diamonds safely stashed, she wasn't about to let him know where they were. For now, no one would know except herself.

Kyle wouldn't take no for an answer.

"Surely Mom and Dad discussed that money. You stayed in WP a lot longer than I did. Maybe I was premature in leaving, but their quarrels had me nuts. Mom's constant pleas…"

"She knew about the money?"

"Of course she did. You know how close they were." *You were so close to your father, he would have told you everything.* "The night I left they were going at it again."

Cameron remembered.

Not the actual words, but Kyle and her father fighting. Her mother crying.

"You and Dad sounded as if you hated each other."

Kyle slugged down the rest of his beer. "Sure," he said. "I did hate him then. I hated what he was doing to her. To you. I couldn't stay to watch that anymore."

"So you went to Gram's."

"Hell, I was seventeen—not ready to be on my own yet

entirely. I left, the marshals slammed the door behind me, shut me off from my family for good, moved you and Mom and Dad to…somewhere.''

"Phoenix," she murmured. She could tell him now. James was dead.

"Well, at least you had sun."

"Kyle, bitterness won't bring Dad back—or heal the breach you had with him."

"I wish it could." He shook his head. "Cameron, there's no way Dad went to his grave without telling someone about that money. Mom was already gone by then. I figure he—or even she—must have told *you*."

"I'm not holding out!" Cameron pushed away her wine. "*I don't know.* Why is this so important to you? Why won't you believe me?"

"Destina doesn't believe you, either. Until you give up the money, he'll keep trying to kill you for it." He ate the last mushroom. "*That's* why I care. No amount of money—and it must be big—is worth more than my own sister's life!"

Cameron blinked. She wanted to trust. She did.

She even wanted to tell him. Yet something made her keep silent.

"Ransom may be a bit messed up right now, but I don't doubt he can protect me—if that proves necessary again."

"And unless his feeling for you gets in the way of his judgment." His hand turned to capture hers again. Tight. "It's me you should trust, Cam. If you won't tell the police, even Ransom, where the money is, then tell me."

"I can't, Kyle."

HE REFUSED TO ACCEPT her decision.

They parted with terse goodbyes, a hard peck on the cheek.

"Call me before you leave town," she said, but he didn't answer.

Their new rift saddened her, and Cameron's heart still hurt when she reached Emerald's apartment. She couldn't believe Kyle's persistence—or his attitude.

Of course, she was lying to him.

Lying to everyone now.

Before she fitted her key into the lock, Ransom hauled her inside.

"Where the hell have you been?"

She had expected this greeting. "Your tracking skills are slipping, Marshal."

Cameron tried to move past him but he blocked her way. Ransom gripped her upper arms. His dark eyes flashed. "I turn my back and you try your best to get yourself killed. What were you doing at your apartment this afternoon?"

How did he know she'd been there?

"Tidying up." Fred must have told him. The doorman was a regular fount of information. She could see what happened. Ransom had come home, found her missing, raced over to her apartment. Then he'd lost her trail.

"And afterward?" he said, his mouth grim.

She didn't want to admit this. "I met Kyle for a drink."

Ransom's grip eased but his eyes stayed hard. "Well, I hope you enjoyed your little foray into the real world. I sure didn't."

She couldn't blame him for being angry. She had been thoughtless.

"I'm sorry I worried you."

He led the way into the living room. No one else seemed to be around. Ron and Grace must be in the office, the gym. Ransom frowned. "What did Kyle want?"

The question made her neck prickle.

"What makes you think he wanted anything? He's my brother."

"And he's been tracking you all over this city."

"So have you. He's worried about me!" She flung out a hand. "Everyone I know is worried, and I should be flattered but I'm not. My apologies."

She sank onto a sofa. Ransom paced the carpet.

"Did I miss something?" she said after a long, silent moment.

His mood didn't seem to be sour only for her.

Ransom's step faltered but he didn't stop. "While you were out, I talked to the NYPD. The sighting in upstate turned cold. No confirmation, no other witnesses. Kayne's man saw her from such a distance—no binoculars—that he can't make a positive ID."

"That's disappointing."

"Hell, yes." Ransom turned to look at her. "But there is some promising news. Emerald's watch cap has been found right here in New York." He paused. "*Your* watch cap. Can you identify the hat?"

She frowned but her pulse skipped. "It's just a plain navy blue knitted cap."

"No logo? No image—like Tweety Bird, for instance?"

"None." Cameron thought a moment. "There might be a tag inside. I think I bought the cap at Bloomingdale's. It has a designer label, if I remember right."

Ransom stared.

"It was on sale," she said.

His mouth softened. "As soon as the NYPD calls us, you can take a look."

"I'd be happy to." With that polite understatement, she rose. And walked from the room. "Good night, Ransom. I'm going to turn in early. It's been a long day."

Clearly, his mood didn't invite cheerful conversation. Still, some news was better than none. Her cap had been found. Emerald must be nearby.

Cameron flipped on the light in Emerald's room.

Before her hand left the switch, Ransom flicked it off.

In darkness he moved into the room with her. Heat radiated from him.

"You took ten years off my life today. If I stay around you much longer, I'll be an old man. No," he said. "I'll be dead. My heart is still thundering like fury."

He pressed Cameron's hand to his chest. He was right, and another brief wave of guilt raced through her. Her own pulse kicked into overdrive, not just because Ransom's anger seemed justified. Cameron remembered the rest of her deception—the diamonds in her apartment, the troubled meeting with Kyle. The feel of Ransom's hard muscle under her fingers now jolted her, too, the hot, deep blue of his eyes.

"I am sorry," she repeated.

"Not good enough."

"Then I don't know how to...what you want from me."

His mouth tightened again. "I want you alive. I want you safe." He crowded her against the wall. "Dammit. I want *you*."

"If this is some psychological means of reaffirming life after I scared you—"

"Don't get cute again with me." He lowered his head and took her mouth. Hard.

Cameron's stifled protest died the instant his lips touched hers.

She shut her eyes at the flood of sensation. All she could feel, all she could think of then, like before, was Ransom. She wouldn't refuse. His solid body pressed to hers, he skimmed his mouth over her lips, then planted little kisses on her cheeks, her closed eyelids, her hairline. His lips trailed downward again to the edge of her jaw, then her collarbone. With his nose, he nudged aside the opening of her shirt to nibble a path from shoulder to shoulder.

As he went, his hands worked busily at her buttons, popping one then the next in a line to give him space until he reached her waist. He bracketed it with both hands, leaned into her, and ground his hips against her.

She moaned.

"I want you now," he murmured, dropping to his knees. "Here."

She helped him with the one button, then the zipper of her pants. She covered his hands with hers to aid him in skimming down the fabric, hips to thighs to knees to ankles, in a long, smooth glide. Seconds later, she was naked.

Ransom still had his clothes on.

Embarrassed by the difference, she began to remedy the situation.

He didn't stop her, either.

Mutual consent, she thought. They were both adults. In another moment they were locked together, skin to skin, body to body, and Cameron had stopped fretting about the diamonds, about Kyle. This was now, as Ransom had said. This was here.

From the far end of the hall, Cameron heard the low murmur of voices. Ron and Grace, sharing a meal or a drink. In the past few days their quarrels had abated for the most part, but Cameron wouldn't have cared just now if they tore the place apart.

"Is the door locked?" she asked.

Ransom went to secure it, then fumbled in his pants pocket for protection.

He came back to the bed where Cameron lay on her side, watching his every movement. He had walked across the room with lithe grace, with purpose. Naked and fully aroused, he made her heart beat faster. She could feel her thighs loosen, her body soften with desire. He sank onto the bed beside her, then covered himself.

"I love a man who comes prepared," Cameron whispered in his ear.

"I love a woman who comes...apart."

In seconds, their kisses escalated. Their breathing quickened.

They had no future, Cameron had thought—and thought again now.

It didn't matter.

When Ransom slipped inside her on a long, slow thrust, she felt the catch in her heart, then deeper, deeper still. She wouldn't let the future in tonight.

Tonight, she was just a woman. A normal woman.

"Say my name," he murmured, his body moving faster, harder.

"Ransom."

"My first name."

"J.C." She had forgotten what his initials stood for.

"Jordan Christopher," he said. "Call me Jordan."

Holding him tight, she nearly wept. Cameron cupped the back of his head, his silky sun-streaked hair. *"Jordan...!"* But this wasn't only physical, she knew, even in the midst of sex. Whatever their differences or the outcome of the Destina case, of Emerald's disappearance, or how she felt about Kyle, one thing remained.

Cameron had fallen in love with J. C. Ransom.

She couldn't escape that, either.


IN THE MORNING she awoke. Alone.

Still groggy, Cameron struggled up onto an elbow, then glanced at the empty place next to her. She could see the faint imprint of Ransom's head, and when she bent close, she could smell his scent. So much for the afterglow. So much for a repeat performance.

Cameron heard sounds from the hallway. She peeked at the alarm clock on Emerald's nightstand: 7:00 a.m. Grace was up already?

Cameron didn't smell coffee.

The conversation from the hall intensified.

Then the door flew open and Ransom stood there in his jeans, zipped but still unbuttoned. For an instant, Cameron felt the soft flow of need wash through her body again, but he wasn't smiling. They weren't alone.

At his shoulder Grace hovered, wringing her hands, looking white and shaken. Ron did, too. For once his bulk didn't intimidate Cameron. His wide shoulders slumped and shock had transformed his harsh face. Ransom's gaze remained dry, hard and resolute.

Clearly, something had happened.

She didn't have to ask.

"They've found Emerald."

*Something bad.*

# Chapter Nine

"Emerald is dead."

For a long moment, Cameron simply stared at Ransom.

"But how...she can't be—"

"It appears someone strangled her." He looked away, then rubbed a hand over the nape of his neck. "Then she was shot. Once," he said. "We won't know which was the cause of death for sure until the medical examiner has done the autopsy."

The room swam around her. Cameron put a hand to her own throat. "Where—"

He tried to gentle his voice. "She was found near LaGuardia Airport. There's a wildlife refuge there. Marshland. It's a good place to dump a body."

"My God." Cameron shook her head, still not wanting to believe. Even Ransom's harsh statement didn't get through. "I saw her less than three days ago..."

"We won't know the time of death either until the report comes back."

"But she—we—switched clothes. I thought I was helping...that she'd be safe."

Ransom gripped her shoulders. He waited until Cameron looked up.

"Denial's a first reaction. But you do understand what I'm saying?"

Cameron knew. Yet she couldn't quite take it in. In the

next instant she didn't stop to think. Or to remember the night before, when Emerald might already have been lying in a swamp—and Cameron had been in bed with Ransom. He was standing there now, solid and strong, and she felt herself begin to crumple. She moved into his embrace before Ransom had lifted his arms to envelop her. She leaned her forehead against his collarbone.

"I know what you're saying."

*Murdered.*

J.C. DIDN'T BELIEVE in mincing words. *Emerald is dead. Murdered.* Three days later those same words still echoed inside him but he hadn't changed his mind. He saw no reason to sugarcoat the truth. Standing near Emerald's grave, he swept his gaze past a mob of reporters, then over the assembled mourners. Oddly, many of them didn't seem to be filled with grief. Including Theodore Kayne.

As he'd expected, Cameron appeared to be taking the situation the hardest.

J.C. thought he knew why, and in addition he had to consider his own behavior. By taking Cameron to bed, he'd taken their involvement with each other to a new level. He wasn't sure Cameron welcomed that—or him.

J.C. half listened to the minister's drone. The eulogy, like the sunny winter morning, didn't fit the occasion. J.C. had expected a cold rain, or even snow. He expected a heartfelt tribute to the slain tennis star. Instead, he heard weak praise from a man who clearly hadn't known Emerald even as well as Cameron did. He would have put his arm around her shoulders, but during the service she had moved away from him. Because she didn't want him to see her grief? Or because of their night together in Emerald's bed?

Standing next to Grace, she held a single rose and J.C. watched her step forward. Laying it on the bronze casket suspended above the grave, she then pressed a hand to the shiny surface in farewell. A dozen cameras flashed, recording the event. J.C. winced.

She felt guilty for the deception with Emerald, he knew. Probably guilty for her part in making love with him, too.

After seeing that Cameron didn't falter when she stepped back beside Grace, J.C., squinting into the harsh sun, glanced again at Kayne.

He was surrounded by members of the media.

J.C. couldn't get near him. He didn't have much experience with high-powered tycoons—crime bosses were as close as he came—but Ted Kayne hadn't shed a tear. J.C. had seen ruthless Mafia types weep like children over a loved one's death. Square-jawed and silent, Kayne only shook the clergyman's hand. The service had ended yet Kayne didn't move toward his former fiancée's grave. He held no flower.

Was there another reason for his taut, almost abrupt manner? Beyond his obvious lack of affection for Emerald?

His body language spoke volumes. Kayne had spent the past few nights in a hotel suite at the Plaza. He hadn't set foot inside Emerald's apartment, even last night when Cameron and Grace had held a short wake. Kayne had never asked to see Emerald.

Of course, he could be a tight-ass who never showed emotion.

Or, he could be a killer.

J.C. turned his attention to Grace.

He would question her later. Since Emerald's body had been found, Grace had seemed inconsolable. An act? he wondered. Or genuine tears? It took little to cause them. Even the sound of birds twittering in the trees around the grave had brought more sorrow to her. Cameron had spent hours with Grace trying to console her.

Then there was Ron.

The bodyguard/personal trainer appeared equally distraught.

Despite that, J.C. had questions for him, too.

Neither Ron nor Grace had adequate alibis for the time

of Emerald's disappearance. The medical examiner estimated her time of death as mere hours after she'd vanished.

Both had criminal histories.

Last but not least, in J.C.'s mind, was Edgar Mills, Emerald's stalker.

With a final glance at Cameron to make sure she was still on her feet, J.C. wandered to the edge of the crowd.

*Crowd* wasn't the right word. Except for the press, no more than a dozen people had shown up for Emerald's interment, even fewer had come to the apartment the night before.

"Mr. Mills." J.C. laid a hand on his shoulder and the man jumped. "Sorry to disturb your grief, but may I have a few minutes of your time?"

People were moving away from the graveside now, returning to their cars, a few of them stopping to chat. An air of visible relief could be detected. Most people, J.C. had learned, felt uncomfortable at another reminder that they, too, were mortal.

J.C. had learned that himself while holding James McKenzie in a Denver alley.

Edgar Mills shrugged. He didn't meet J.C.'s eyes.

"A woman like her, she should have had enough friends to fill a stadium."

"Well, she'd been off the circuit for some time. People forget."

Edgar whirled on him. To J.C. he came as a surprise. He was not a large man, in fact slight and thin with narrow, rounded shoulders. Which didn't mean he couldn't also be a killer.

"Nobody should forget Emerald Greer!" His shoulders slumped. "I know I never will. She was everything to me."

"And to Ted Kayne." J.C. watched his reaction.

Edgar's dark, too-bright eyes flashed with anger. "Ted Kayne would have married her for a trophy. That's all she was to him! His spokesperson for Zeus Sportswear. I tried to tell her that."

"In a bunch of threatening phone calls," J.C. murmured. "Doesn't sound like a devoted fan to me, Edgar. Or a would-be lover."

"My love for her was absolute! It was also pure." Eyes brimming, he glared across the grassy expanse between them and Ted Kayne. Sunlight sparkled, reflecting off dark sedans and the funeral limousine. Yet Mills had stalked her years ago. A reformed lunatic? J.C. wondered. "I would never touch Emerald. Never harm a hair on her head. Her beautiful head," he almost whispered. Then he dissolved into tears.

J.C. heard a few sparrows nearby, chattering as if to comfort, and searched his pockets for a tissue. He didn't find one. Finally, he settled for touching Edgar's shoulder again.

"I'm sorry." His grief seemed to be the real thing. "I'd like to talk to you some more—maybe tomorrow."

Edgar sniffed. "You know where to find me. The police already have my car."

"You have a record on file for stalking Emerald. And no alibi for the time of her death, Edgar." J.C. walked with him halfway to the winding road that ran through the cemetery. "You need one. You need to explain those phone calls…"

"You said I made those calls, not me." Beside a large, heavily carved marble monument adorned with angels, Edgar blinked. J.C. had turned away, looking for Cameron, when Edgar blurted, "Marshal? I wrote Emerald a note or two. But I never sent them—I didn't want trouble with the police—and I never made any threatening calls."

LATER THAT DAY Cameron sat with Grace in Emerald's den, helping her with the telephone messages of sympathy that continued to pour in. Strange, she thought. People could make a quick phone call, send flowers or write a note, but couldn't trouble themselves to attend the funeral.

Maybe they feared scrutiny by the police.

Law enforcement was investigating Emerald's murder,

with Ted Kayne's demands most likely ringing in their ears, she assumed. Ransom's private search for Emerald had ended with the announcement of her death.

Cameron knew he felt responsible in part.

"You should get some sleep, Grace." She squeezed the woman's hand.

"I can't sleep. I keep thinking about her." Grace shivered. "She wasn't an easy person to work for, but she didn't deserve to die." She lifted her gaze to Cameron's. "I know Ron and I talked about her, but we didn't mean everything we said. That was frustration talking." She covered her face with one hand. "I can't believe she's gone."

Ransom came into the room. He must have heard what Grace said.

Cameron glanced at him. They hadn't spoken much after sleeping together the other night, and since Emerald's murder was discovered, she couldn't think what to say. Or even how she felt except for the now-undeniable fact that she seemed to be in love with him.

He was wearing his government-agent face now.

"Grace, I need your help. I'm waiting for the telephone log on Miss Greer's account. But what can you tell me about the calls she supposedly had from Edgar Mills?"

Ransom sat on the edge of the coffee table, bracing his powerful forearms on his thighs. Cameron tried not to see the taut muscle rippling beneath his suit pants. He'd looked very handsome today. Then she chided herself for noticing after all, for noticing him at a funeral.

After the other night, would she ever be able *not* to notice?

Or forget.

The realization that she couldn't made Cameron uneasy—and widened the gulf between them.

"All I know about the calls," Grace said, "was what I heard myself. Twice."

"After Emerald's engagement was announced."

"Yes," she murmured, staring down at her hands. Cameron held one of them in hers, but she sensed Grace wanted to wring both of her hands together.

Ransom didn't appear to notice. "Tell me again what the caller said."

"'You're making a mistake. Don't do it.' That's all he said," Grace reported.

Cameron's heart beat surged. They were not the same message she had heard.

"No threats? No promised violence?" Ransom probed.

"None."

"You think it could have been Edgar Mills?" Cameron asked.

"The log will tell us." Ransom softened his tone. "Grace, your resentment toward Miss Greer is well known. I've heard it, Cameron has heard it, certainly Ron—"

"Are you accusing me?" Grace leaped up from the sofa. "I killed my husband, yes. It was self-defense, even if the judge didn't agree, but he's dead—and I paid for that crime. I did not hurt Emerald! I told the police and I'm telling you. I had nothing to do with her death!"

Cameron reached out but Grace stepped away.

"It's true," she murmured. "I swear. Do you know why I murdered the man I once loved, Mr. Ransom?" She took a sharp breath. "Because he beat me, yes—but also he beat my daughter. She was just a child but he wouldn't stop. I had to keep him from hurting her anymore. I grabbed a kitchen knife and stabbed him." Shaking, she dropped her face into her hands. Tears flowed between her fingers.

Cameron wouldn't look at Ransom.

"I'm sorry, Grace," he said.

Grace shook her head. "They took my daughter away from me, put her into foster care. I served my time—and when I came out, she was gone. At thirteen she became a runaway."

"You don't know where she is now?" Cameron felt a wrench of pity for Grace.

Grace shuddered. "No. I've tried so hard to find her."

When Cameron glanced at him, Ransom looked sheepish. Then his U.S. Marshal expression dropped into place again. "I'm sorry for your losses. But I hope you understand that I need to do everything I possibly can to get Emerald Greer's killer."

"I hope you do, Mr. Ransom." Grace swept tears from her face. "Because it was Emerald who helped me try to locate my daughter."

The philanthropic side of Emerald Greer was not one Cameron had seen in the short time she knew her. She wondered if Ransom believed Grace.

To Cameron, Grace didn't seem like a killer. Even though once she had been forced into it, to save her child.

In the case of Cameron's father, James McKenzie had been murdered in cold blood. Deliberately.

Grace didn't appear to fit the bill, but Cameron knew Ransom had to question anyone who might be involved in Emerald's murder.

She also knew who he held responsible.

Venuto Destina.


HIS THOUGHTS STILL ON Grace Jennings, J.C. went down the hall.

Cameron was in the den. Grace had gone to bed. After the long, emotionally draining day, Emerald's apartment was again quiet, except for the slam of heavy metal that sounded from the in-home gym.

Ron was working out again.

Therapy, J.C. supposed. At the funeral Ron had obviously mourned.

Which surprised J.C.

After a quick rap at the open door to announce his presence, he found Ron lying on the bench, muscles straining to hoist the enormous stack of weights on the bar he held. With the effort, the words gritted between his teeth.

"I suppose you have questions for me, too."

"Not officially. That jurisdiction belongs to the NYPD

now, where the murder occurred—and the FBI due to Emerald's kidnapping.''

Ron had flinched at the word *murder*.

"But you're doing what you can.'' Sarcasm laced his grunted tone.

"Yeah. And your lack of an alibi for the night Emerald disappeared has been sticking in my craw for days. The police, too, from what I hear. Want to try again?''

The barbell reached its highest point above Ron's body. His arms quivered with the effort. "Sure. I worked that day. I went home, had a beer, a couple of burritos, then picked Emerald up for the Zeus reception. You took over there. When I tried to track Emerald, she had disappeared. I never saw her again. I went home to bed. By myself.''

That wasn't hard to believe. Ron didn't have the personality of a crowd pleaser. Or a ladies' man, despite his impressive build. The barbell clanged back into its holder, and Ron sat up, sweating. His eyes could bore a hole through the metal plates he'd just lifted. Or through J.C.'s skull. J.C. imagined that would please Ron right now.

He also sensed he was hearing only half the story.

"You didn't like Emerald,'' he said.

"Who did? Grace may snivel now that Emerald's gone, but that's a woman talking. I'm not changing my opinion of Miss Greer.'' His gaze avoided J.C. "Anyway, Grace is more frightened of the police trying to pin this on her than she is broken up over Emerald.''

"You're sure of that?''

"Hell, can't you see it? The tears, the hand wringing...''

"After her years in prison, I imagine Grace has no love for cops.''

Ron shrugged his massive shoulders. "I don't either. That doesn't mean either of us killed Emerald.''

His tone shifted, J.C. noted, every time he mentioned her name.

"Apparently, she had her good side. She helped people. She helped Grace—and you. You must have felt grateful.''

"Sure. She gave me a job when no one else would. So, yeah, I guess I did feel grateful." His voice took on a bitter edge. "When she wasn't jerking my chain about how she'd saved me. Or trying to cheat me out of my pay."

"You said she had debts. Large ones."

"Didn't much care when they got paid either—or if they got paid. She had this attitude…arrogant, as if she was entitled to whatever she could get."

"A Star complex."

Ron shrugged again. Then he wiped a hand towel around the back of his neck, over his chest and threw it on the bench. He stood.

"I gotta go. No sense all of us shacking up here together." Now that Emerald was gone, J.C. added silently. Ron hadn't finished the thought. "But let me give you some advice, Marshal. Leave Grace alone. She didn't kill Miss Greer. I know that much."

"What about you, Ron?"

"No way." He didn't say more. Ron brushed past him, making sure he shoved J.C. back a few inches, and strode to the door.

"Nice try, Emory. Know what I think? I think you were in love with Emerald Greer."

Ron eyed him with a hostile gaze. The fight seemed to drain from him, and his balled fists fell open at his sides. His voice dropped low. "She could be a real witch. Most of the time I didn't even like her."

"Did you dislike her enough to make phone calls about her engagement to Ted Kayne?"

"Hell." Ron flushed. "Maybe a few. Just to set her straight, you know?"

Which still didn't explain the vicious threat Cameron had heard. J.C.'s money was on Destina—through one of his goons—but this made sense, too. Ron Emory, desperate at the thought of losing the woman he craved, a woman probably beyond his reach except in her home gym for an hour each day, or when she needed a ride somewhere, would try to scare her off about Kayne. And hope she'd turn to Ron.

Was that where it had ended?

Ron held J.C.'s gaze a moment longer.

J.C. murmured, "You were afraid of losing her."

"I never had her," Ron admitted. "But I did love her— too much to kill her."

HAD IT BEEN Cameron's fault that Emerald died?

Still curled up in Emerald's den, Cameron couldn't get the notion out of her head once she let it surface. She'd felt guilty enough that the switch of identity with Emerald for one night might have caused her abduction. Now Emerald was dead. And one by one the suspects in her murder were being eliminated.

*Edgar Mills.* Ransom had said he seemed harmless, a worshipful fan who took his adoration a bit too far, but not, at this point, a violent man. The phone log included no calls from him, and Mills's pathetic grief over Emerald had been painful to view. He'd been too frightened after the stalking incident to call her, he'd claimed, or to send a note.

*Grace Jennings.* Cameron had seen for herself that the woman was overcome by Emerald's death. She didn't have a solid alibi—she'd been at home, alone, with a migraine that night—but her one brush with the law had taken any courage she possessed. Years out of prison now, Grace still seemed a shattered woman who might resent Emerald yet feel grateful to her—like Ron—for giving Grace a job, another chance.

*Ron Emory.* He puzzled Cameron. On one hand, she almost liked him. On the other, his size intimidated her only slightly less than his attitude. He and Grace had stuck by Cameron while Emerald was missing. Both had been a big help in handling regular business and new inquiries from a suspicious press. Both were productive and efficient. But did that exonerate Ron, who was big enough to handle Emerald Greer without effort?

"It's not Ron."

Ransom's voice brought her head up. Cameron stared at him. He'd come into the room without her realizing he was there.

Her thoughts scattered. For a long moment she couldn't speak. When he crossed the den with that lazy walk, sheer power rippled down his frame from his wide shoulders to his biceps and washboard abdomen. With effort Cameron tore her gaze away from the muscled strength of his thighs and, forcing her glance upward over his broad chest to his strong throat, then the hard line of his jaw, she briefly settled on his sensual mouth. Which was a mistake. By the time she met his dark blue eyes, she was trembling.

"How did you know I was thinking about Ron?"

"I could see your wheels spinning. He's gone home, by the way."

"There won't be any need for his services now," she said sadly.

"He told me he'll come around to help Grace—and you—for the next few days or a week. However long you need him."

"That was nice of him. What makes you think he's innocent?"

Ransom sat down beside her, and Cameron fought the urge to shift away. She didn't have to. Ransom moved closer. His solid shoulder brushed hers, giving Cameron the impression of heavy bone and sleek muscle. His hard thigh pressed against her softer one, making her all too aware of their differences. Male to female. The enticing physical contrast caused Cameron's pulse to thump in response. She could smell the faint tang of his aftershave, crisp and woody and overlaid with the scent of man, and felt her fingers twitch. She hadn't been this close to him since the night they'd spent making love, and Cameron felt awkward, as if he would guess her feelings for him.

Her inappropriate feelings.

The closer she got to Ransom, the more he also reminded

her that her father's death remained an open case. Their conflicts still loomed between them.

Cameron waited for his answer.

"Why do I say he's innocent? Gut feeling. Ron was in love with Emerald."

Shocked, she could only stare.

"True," he said. "Call it a hunch, but every time he said her name, it sounded like a lover's touch."

The phrase made Cameron look away. Only a few nights ago, she had lain in Ransom's arms, called him Jordan, admitted that she loved him—at least to herself. She didn't want him to see that now in her eyes.

"That's new," she murmured.

"And statistics would say that only makes him more of a suspect." He shrugged. "Maybe Ron was good at hiding his feelings—behind all that muscle. Then Emerald died and he couldn't hide them anymore."

She glanced up. "You can be a very perceptive man, Ransom."

His mouth thinned. "We're back to that, are we?"

"What?"

"You calling me Ransom." He touched her cheek and her skin warmed. "Next thing, you'll be telling me the other night was a mistake."

She couldn't say it. Even if it was true.

But when he moved toward her again, she backed away. Cameron's spine hit the corner of the sofa and she could go no farther. Ransom, however, could. He had her trapped between his arms, hands braced on the sofa, before she breathed again.

"Know what I think?" Ransom murmured, his blue gaze holding hers. "I think you're scared."

"Of course I'm scared." Deliberately, she misunderstood. Her heart was pounding. She couldn't breathe right. He was too near. "Someone killed Emerald. Someone wants to kill me—"

"Scared about us."

She tried to laugh. "*Us?* You can't be serious." She choked on the word.

To show that he was completely serious, Ransom dipped his head and kissed her. The shock of desire shot through her so fast, Cameron's head spun. She clung to his strong forearms like a lifeline, feeling hard muscle and heavy bone and even the tendon, taut as piano wire, in his solid wrist under her fingers.

She couldn't seem to get enough air. "Just because I lost my senses once doesn't mean I intend to lose them again."

"So you say. Who are you trying to kid?"

"So I know." But he had a point. Cameron shrank back against the sofa, desperate to save herself. "Or are you forgetting the way we met?" Okay, he wanted to talk. She would talk. About them—and why they were so wrong for each other. "Considering the circumstances now, I find it hard to believe you could forget. I know I haven't. I won't."

Ransom groaned, like a man in pain. "Is this the old Deputy U.S. Marshal bit? The bad guy who makes life a living hell for the innocent little girl? Drags her family from one place to another? Takes her away from her newfound friends? Her toys?"

The man who sent need rushing through her woman's body?

She could barely get the words out. "And thinks her father was a crook."

He leaned closer, his chest brushing her breasts. Cameron's skin tingled.

"You may have been a skinny kid with that same big gaze when I first saw you. You still have those hazel eyes that beg a man to make life okay again, the same eyes that turn me inside out." He kissed her, longer this time. Sweeter. "I had to wait for you to grow up. But honey, the strings have been playing in me for a long time. Be kind," he said with a half smile that caused havoc with her remaining senses. "Put me out of my misery."

She was losing the battle. When he would have kissed her again, Cameron turned her head away. Wanting to whimper and beg.

"That's beside the point."

"No," he said, nuzzling her ear, "that's exactly the point." His mouth trailed along her throat, and more liquid heat ran through her. "I want you. You want me."

Cameron straightened as much as she could with Ransom's body all but pinning her to the sofa. "Destina," she murmured in desperation, like a splash of cold water. "The money is still missing. My father is still dead. So is Emerald."

With a sigh Ransom eased back. He gazed at her for a long moment, his deep blue eyes still hot and hungry. But disappointed, too. Maybe even hurt by the rejection that had saved Cameron from another mistake. A second later, he was all business again. And she was able to breathe. A little.

Distance, she thought. It was better that way.

Safer. She hoped.

"You're wrong," he said. "I know you feel Emerald is dead because of you, but that's not true, Cameron."

"It is! If she hadn't been dressed as me, wearing my watch cap, I would have been abducted. Not her."

"And you've been going over every other suspect in your mind tonight. Trying to find someone— Emerald's fan or Grace or Ron, even Ted Kayne—"

She tried to smile. "I hadn't gotten to him."

"But you would have. And you'd have come up empty."

"Not quite," she admitted. She couldn't hide that from herself any longer.

"So what are you left with?"

Cameron took a long breath. He already knew what she'd been trying to keep from herself. When her apartment had been broken into, then Emerald disappeared, she'd known who was probably responsible. Until now, she couldn't accept it.

"Destina."

Ransom shut his eyes, as if he couldn't believe she'd finally acknowledged the truth. Then he opened them and came close again, lowering his head to kiss the hollow of her throat, his eyes still on hers. Cameron shuddered at the rush of sensation she felt but didn't stop him.

Emerald's funeral, Grace's sorrow…her own guilt…

She tried not to feel overwhelmed.

Ransom's voice turned husky. "I told you. If he comes after you—as *we* know he will—he has to come through me. That's not going to happen." He kissed a trail along her jaw to her mouth. "I'm here and I'll protect you. And when this is over, when Emerald's killer and your father's is behind bars…"

She covered his lips with her hand. Ransom raised his head to study her.

"Full retreat?"

"Yes."

He sighed. "Then I take it I'm sleeping here in the den tonight."

Cameron only nodded. She loved him, but contemplating a future with him had to wait. Cameron knew practically nothing about relationships. Ransom hadn't said he even wanted one beyond the physical. She didn't know if anything more was possible, couldn't know until Ransom closed the case. And her father's name had been cleared.

"Can't change your mind?" he said.

"No."

She felt Ransom's arms wrap her tight. He whispered in her ear.

"We'll get him. Then we'll talk. About us."

WE'LL GET HIM. *We.*

The next morning Cameron reminded herself that Ransom still thought her father was a thief and a liar. He wanted Destina—but he also wanted the missing money. Cameron knew exactly where it was, in diamonds not spades, and that only distanced her further from Ransom. She tried not to acknowledge the fact that she herself was impeding the investigation.

When the doorbell rang, she welcomed the break from her own thoughts.

She felt as if she were spinning in increasingly unhappy circles.

Glad that Ransom had gone out early to watch the police question Ted Kayne, she opened the door to see her brother standing in the hall again.

"Kyle. This is getting to be a habit. I thought you'd left town."

"I heard about Greer," he said. "I didn't want to run off. You're alone."

Then why hadn't he called? Or come to the funeral? He was peering behind her, and Cameron stepped back to let him in, remembering their clash the last time she'd seen him. Remembering that Kyle knew nothing about Emerald's disappearance.

"No," she said. "Grace Jennings is here—Emerald's assistant. We were going through her things. Come have a cup of coffee."

She led Kyle into the kitchen. His dark gaze searched the area.

"Ransom here, too?"

"Not at the moment. I forget, do you take cream or sugar?"

"Just black." He grasped the cup she handed him, then leaned against the counter rather than sitting down. "Cam, this is getting out of hand. With Greer dead, surely you can see that the wisest course would be to come back with me to Houston."

Cameron gaped at him. "I have a business to run here. I can't leave. Ransom—"

"Is way out of his depth. Now that the police are handling the investigation into Greer's death, he's not needed. I don't trust him anyway. My apartment in Houston is plenty big for both of us. You sure can't go back to your place.'' He swallowed more coffee. ''Nothing makes sense except that you let me take care of you. You're still in danger—and how did you get mixed up in Greer's death anyway?''

Cameron decided to tell him. Emerald was dead now, and her unwitting connection to Destina still nagged at Cameron. The switch of clothes, Emerald's disappearance, her murder... When she finished, she said, ''So I believe it's partly my fault that Emerald is dead. I'm staying here until her killer is behind bars.''

''Dad's killer,'' he corrected her.

Cameron acknowledged that with a brief nod. ''You're right. There is danger. There's nothing I can do for Emerald now, but there must be some way I can help Ransom—and the police.''

Kyle slammed his cup down on the counter, hard enough to break it. ''You're not being rational, Cam! What would Dad or Mom say if they knew I let you remain in a situation like this? Venuto Destina wants that money.'' He kicked the shattered pieces of the cup aside. ''He trashed your apartment, killed Emerald Greer after mistaking her for you— I have to admit Ransom was right about that. If Destina doesn't get the money, and soon, he won't stop at burglary. Next time he'll kill you!'' His eyes dark with temper, Kyle advanced toward her. Cameron took a step back, but he kept coming then grabbed her arm. ''Wasn't Greer's death enough? Answer me!''

Startled, she pulled away. ''Why are you so angry?''

She wasn't the only one who found his reaction alarming.

A gasp sounded from the doorway. Grace stood there, wringing her hands.

He ignored her. When Cameron tried to push past him, he caught her shoulders. Before she could free herself, he shook her, hard, until her teeth clamped together. And Cameron bit down on her tongue. She tasted blood.

As if he couldn't stop, Kyle lifted one arm. Frightened by his unexpected burst of fury, she cried out, afraid that in the next second he would strike her.

"Kyle, let me go!"

# Chapter Ten

Cameron's cry brought Ron running from the gym. In a single heartbeat, it seemed, he raced into the kitchen. Before Cameron took a breath, one big hand shot out to collar Kyle. With a hard shove, he sent Kyle slamming against the wall. Ron started after him again.

"Call the police, Grace."

Cameron laid a restraining hand on Ron's bulky forearm. "It's all right. I'm all right," she corrected herself.

Yet her pulse continued to hammer, and when she lifted her hand from Ron's arm, her fingers shook. Tucking them out of sight, Cameron folded her arms. Kyle's outburst amazed her. He had never touched her in anger before. Then another shadowed memory of the night he'd left home sixteen years ago flashed through her mind. Angry words had escalated into physical violence...

"You're okay?" Ron scowled at her. "You sure?"

She hesitated. "I'm sure."

It might be a long time before she actually forgave Kyle, but she didn't want Ron taking her brother apart.

"This guy has no right to manhandle you." Ron glanced at Grace, as if to corroborate her explanation of the night before. The reason for her husband's murder seemed to quiver on the air, and Grace's features remained white and shaken.

Kyle slumped against the wall. His harsh breathing broke the silence.

"You misunderstood. I love my sister. She's the only family I have."

Ron's jaw set. "I know what I saw."

"Then maybe you need an eye exam."

Ron edged close to Cameron, putting an arm around her shoulders. The weight of his embrace nearly buckled her knees and Cameron stiffened her spine.

Her brother had acted unwisely, perhaps in frustration. But who could better understand her past, their past, than Kyle? As he'd pointed out himself, they were each other's family—the only family they had left.

Hostile glares clashed across the space between Kyle and Ron. Finally, Cameron sighed.

"I think I'd better explain, Kyle. Until now, Ron and Grace weren't aware of our troubles with Destina."

A few minutes later she finished telling Emerald's personal trainer and her assistant about her past, not merely in Witness Protection, but the threat to her that remained and most likely linked Destina to Emerald's death. Her past, her "normal" life in New York were now an open book. She glanced up to see Ron and Grace studying her.

"I see why you told me you never had friends," Grace said. "Living in hiding, being on the run from Venuto Destina, must have been difficult."

"We had a dozen names," Kyle agreed. "A dozen places to live. None of them came close to feeling like home. I don't blame Cam for wanting to stay here. From Emory's reaction, and now yours," he said to Grace, "it's obvious she does have friends at last. I know she likes her apartment here, and that it's become home to her. But you have to agree with me. Cameron isn't safe."

Grace, then Ron, watched her for a silent moment before Grace stepped forward. "She'll be safe with us." And the three of them, Grace, Cameron and Ron, formed a circle of support. Cameron blinked. Twice.

"You've given me something new, something to hold on to. Even the few days while Emerald was missing, I felt a connection with you." Cameron hesitated. "I'm sorry about Emerald. If I had done things differently—"

"You didn't know. How could you?" Grace asked.

"Don't beat yourself up, Cameron. Emerald may have caused her own murder." Ron's expression looked sad yet affectionate. "She never did know when to keep quiet."

Ransom had speculated about that himself, and Cameron forced a small smile.

"She did have strong opinions." Then the smile faded as quickly as it had come. "But never mind her being outspoken. How frightened she must have felt then…"

Grace hugged her again. "We can't dwell on that, though. What's important now is finding Emerald's killer. Your father's killer," she said.

Kyle frowned. "I'd feel better if we left that to the cops."

"And Ransom," Ron put in.

Kyle shook his head. "I'm not leaving my sister's life in the hands of some guy with half a working brain."

Cameron frowned, too. "Ransom has panic disorder. A medical condition. It's a direct result of his being there when Dad died. He felt as helpless then as I do now after Emerald's murder."

The common bond—another bond between them—didn't ease Cameron's mind. On one hand, she had her brother now. The easiest thing would be to take Kyle's advice and go with him to Houston. Cameron's pulse leaped. But then, she'd still have the diamonds in her possession—and Kyle might find them. No, she was better off here. On her own.

Until Destina was behind bars, Cameron would keep her father's secret.

The diamonds would be the last nail in Destina's coffin. She owed her father that much.

After Kyle's manhandling, even if she wanted to trust him as family, Cameron realized her long-ingrained habit of mistrust wouldn't be broken that easily.

Feeling regret that she couldn't trust Kyle completely, or Ransom, Cameron eased away from Ron and Grace. At least she could show them that Kyle's outburst hadn't turned her from him. She leaned up to kiss her brother's cheek.

"Go back this time to Houston. I'll be fine. I promise."

"I wish that's all it took."

"Kyle, please. You have your own life to think about. Getting a new job, paying off your debt, finding a way to be happy yourself after all the years in Witness Protection."

Returning her kiss, Kyle gave a long sigh.

"If I didn't have an interview in Houston, you couldn't blast me out of here."

"But you do," Cameron said softly.

Kyle wouldn't meet her eyes. He must feel guilty for leaving her again.

"Yes. I do." He added, "Then I'll be back."

Cameron walked him toward the door. "I'll count on that."

By the time he returned, she promised herself, Destina would be history and she would find a way to trust Kyle. Because he *was* family and, beyond Grace and Ron, she couldn't deny his concern for her. Despite her attraction to Ransom, despite the one night they'd shared and the emotional bond that kept growing between them, despite the very love she felt for him, she needed to trust her own blood first. If she couldn't do that, she had nothing.

J.C. HAD KICKED HIMSELF all the way from the NYPD precinct station where he'd watched the police grill Ted Kayne through one-way glass then back to Emerald's apartment. He wasn't alone. J.C. wished he had found some way to discourage this surprise visit. Worried about its effect on Cameron, he deemed it a case of too little, too late.

In the elevator Kayne kept his pale blue gaze glued to the floor numbers flashing by.

"I suppose Grace Jennings and Ron Emory won't welcome me, but I need to pay my respects," Kayne insisted. "At the funeral, with so much media attention, I didn't find an opportunity."

"Right," was all J.C. said, tight-lipped.

When they stepped into the apartment, he fell behind. Let Kayne make his own excuses for what appeared to be an appalling lack of grief for his fiancée.

Cameron greeted them. She came from the kitchen, wiping her hands on a dish towel and carrying the distinctive scent of cinnamon. It turned him on. He couldn't get enough of those spices, the scents she always seemed to carry with her, in her clothes, in the soft silk of her dark hair, her even softer skin, her breasts, and in the tantalizing hollows of her hipbones. J.C.'s lower body warmed in reaction. He welcomed the sensation. He'd had enough of Ted Kayne's presence. Of murder. Like a reminder that the world held other, far more pleasant surprises, Cameron's spicy scent tempted him. They weren't so different in that. She was baking, J.C. supposed, to keep her hands, and her mind, from losing control. When she saw Ted Kayne, her mouth thinned in obvious disapproval.

Kayne offered his hand then seemed to think better of it. He leaned to kiss Cameron's cheek and J.C. felt his gut clench. *Hands off. She's mine.* "I can't tell you how sorry I am about Emerald."

Cameron pulled back. "I suppose grief strikes us all in different ways. With some, it takes longer." She glanced at Grace, in the hall behind her. "Others show their sorrow as soon as the news arrives."

Kayne's lips flattened. "Just because I don't throw myself into a coffin, sobbing, doesn't mean I feel no grief."

Grace wrung her hands. "All those business meetings must take your mind off Emerald's *murder*. Or perhaps that wasn't a surprise to you, Mr. Kayne?"

Ron Emory joined the group. "Grace is right. If you really cared about Emerald, you would have done more to find her. Maybe if you had helped, instead of hiding behind your shiny corporate image, she'd still be alive." He paused. "Or is it more convenient for you that she's not?"

Kayne widened his stance, as if ready for a fight.

"Meaning what? That *I* killed her?"

"Or had her killed. Same thing," Ron muttered.

Kayne raked a hand through his dark hair. "My staff did everything possible to find Emerald, even though…" He trailed off. "At least the police now seem satisfied that I had nothing to do with Emerald's murder, either personally or through some other means. At the time of Emerald's death, I was in a hotel suite—registered to me—meeting with my board of directors. Twelve men can attest to my presence."

Cameron eyed Kayne with reproach.

"What I can't understand is your total neglect of a woman who was pledged to marry you. You treated Emerald as if she didn't matter to you at all. Your fiancée was missing. Yet you still conducted business as usual." Cameron took a breath. "In my view, that's not love."

Kayne pushed past them into the living room.

"Love?" he said. "Emerald and I had a different type of relationship. An agreement, really, like a business deal."

Wanting to applaud Cameron, J.C. went into the room behind her. He could see the stiff set of her shoulders. He wasn't the only one who wanted to throw a fist at Kayne's well-tanned face, right into his gleaming white teeth. He put a hand on the nape of her neck to show her that he, at least, understood her.

Loved her.

The thought nearly knocked him to his knees. Sure, he'd been attracted to her from the start, years before she left Witness Protection. Before she even noticed him, except with resentment. Yes, their lovemaking had been every bit as exquisite as he'd imagined, but what he felt for her went far beyond a physical connection. She'd gotten under his skin. Made him believe goodness still existed in the world. Made him believe in *her*.

He half smiled. Well, what do you know?

He was a goner.

Returning his attention to the matter at hand, J.C. decided to defuse the friction that Kayne's presence was creating. "You've paid your 'respects,' Kayne. Time to go," he said.

"Not without my property."

"Your property?" Cameron repeated.

"The gifts I gave Emerald. Her diamond, of course, went with her to her grave. I couldn't begrudge her that. She did have a romantic streak," Kayne said. "In my view, such middle-class pretensions are unnecessary. How many people do you know who marry then spend the rest of their lives in perfect bliss?"

The notion suddenly appealed to J.C. He glanced at Cameron and saw her wistful expression, too. In Kayne's mind, he supposed, they were both saps.

J.C. didn't care. After watching, openmouthed, while Kayne snagged a few items from Emerald's desk—a platinum paperweight encrusted with a tennis racket made of rubies, a gold letter opener—he trailed Kayne into Emerald's bedroom.

Cameron couldn't keep quiet. "Mr. Kayne, is this necessary?"

He looked toward Grace and Ron. In the bedroom doorway, they stood, arms around each other, eyes stunned. Even Ron didn't move. "I paid for every one of these." Kayne slipped a crystal unicorn into his inside jacket pocket.

Like a checkbook, J.C. thought, and shook his head. He couldn't prevent Kayne from removing items he'd paid for, but J.C. had never seen a more tacky display of poor taste in judgment. Theodore Kayne was not only a wunderkind of the corporate world. Or a powerful man. He was a poor excuse for a human being.

Ron finally had enough. "You may have an alibi—" Abruptly, he released Grace to charge across the room "—but I know you murdered Emerald, and not to avoid marriage or take back a few trinkets! If the cops don't see that—"

Ted whirled, his hands full of jewelry. "Are the police to believe a man with a tainted past of his own instead? Or Grace, who served time for her husband's murder? I think not." He wandered to the closet and perused the gowns there, including the bronze satin Cameron had worn the night Emerald vanished.

Kayne ripped the gown from its hanger, then ground his heel into the thick, shiny fabric, just as the intruder at Cameron's apartment had done. Next came a black velvet, then a striking red floor-length sheath. Shocked like Grace and Ron, J.C. stood frozen.

He told himself again that Kayne's alibi was solid.

He couldn't be the killer.

In that moment, J.C. almost wished he were. So he'd have the pleasure of seeing him behind bars. But why this plunder of Emerald's clothes?

"Please! Don't," Cameron said, reaching for one of the gowns.

"She's dead! Have them, if you like. They're yours."

He turned on Grace. "Or perhaps Miss Jennings would care to dress herself in garish silk and satin. Emerald won't need them anymore."

Hands shaking, he tucked a last diamond bracelet into his pocket then stalked from the bedroom. J.C. stared after him. What was Kayne's real motive here? Ron tried to stop him, but Kayne kept going. In whatever fury he felt, his strength outdistanced even the burly weight lifter.

"A business deal," Kayne murmured, half to himself. "We were nothing but a contract with Zeus Sportswear to bind us."

Then he glanced at Ron.

And J.C. knew. He had just admitted his own love for Cameron, if not yet to her. In an instant he recognized another man with a vulnerable heart, like Ron. Ted Kayne.

"You could have had her, Emory. Sure as hell, she didn't want me."

Ron's face tightened. "What are you saying?"

Kayne laughed bitterly. "The last time we spoke—the night she disappeared—she wanted to break our engagement. That's the reason she was coming to see me. You poor bastard, Emerald was in love with *you.*"

TED KAYNE'S WORDS were still ringing in his ears later that day when J.C. made a telephone call to Venuto Destina's estate. He'd been trying to connect, without success, for some time—but especially since Emerald Greer's death.

The stakes were higher now.

He couldn't escape the feeling that Cameron was in greater danger than before. The first telephone call she'd intercepted at Emerald's apartment, the break-in at her own place, the murder…everything pointed to her as the target. And Destina as the triggerman. With Destina at last home from whatever private clinic he'd been in, according to the NYPD and the media, J.C. had his chance.

Cameron was next. Unless he stopped it.

Tapping his fingers against the marble tabletop in Emerald's den, he waited for Destina's son to come on the line. When Tony's deep voice boomed through the receiver, J.C. winced.

"Listen, Ransom. I'm saying this once. *Leave my father alone.*"

"If he's innocent, why not let him talk to me?"

"We don't have to talk to you. I spoke to your superior. You're not on duty, and from what I hear, you may retire—permanently—soon."

J.C.'s pulse lurched.

"Is that a threat?"

From Destina. Retire, or be killed.

"I don't care enough to threaten you, *Marshal.*"

And what about J.C.'s colleagues? Had they written him off, too?

J.C.'s jaw hardened. He wasn't going to quit before he could write Closed on the thick file that at least in his own mind, bore Cameron's family name.

"My father is not a well man," Tony Destina continued.

In J.C.'s world, that didn't let him off the hook.

"He was well enough to walk out of federal prison."

Tony exploded. "That was for the cameras—and you know it! He has his pride. He walked in, he walked out. Few people noticed the support he had to lean on."

"If pride is the issue, then why not let me ask him a few questions?"

"For whose benefit?"

The flat tone didn't stop J.C. "Mine," he said. "His, too, if he has nothing to hide."

"My father owes you nothing. You've hounded him long enough, you and the rest of your government stooges. Venuto Destina is a law-abiding citizen."

J.C. bit back a smile. "Maybe he ought to run for mayor

of the little town he bought there in Connecticut, then. Lock, stock and barrel. He's a natural leader, after all.''

"Look, you. One more phone call from me and you're—"

"A dead man? Like James McKenzie?'' He made a sound of reproach. ''Emerald Greer? I never thought killing women was your father's style. Or yours, Tony.''

He swore. ''I ought to hang up—''

''Don't. I'm not finished. I know you're head man of the organization now—at least in title—but you're still your father's son. If Destina wants to prove his innocence, he'll talk to me. Tomorrow. And you'll listen.''

"What makes you think—''

A sound in the background stopped Tony's coming tirade. Sure as his father's black soul, he'd been about to hang up as threatened. J.C. heard another voice now, deeper and throatier from years of smoking. Venuto Destina.

A second later Tony came back on the line.

He blew out a breath. "My father won't see you. Not tomorrow, not ever.''

J.C.'s heart picked up speed.

He might be on medical leave, but he knew Venuto Destina better than any other deputy in the U.S. Marshals. It wouldn't be good to see him again. But maybe this time J.C. could discover the clue that could tack Destina's hide to the door.

He would avenge James McKenzie—for Cameron's sake.

And allow Emerald Greer's soul to rest.

His own, too, J.C. thought.

He took a breath to steady his nerves. In his job—a job he meant to keep—he rarely took no for an answer.

"Twenty minutes, Tony. That's all I ask.''

"You wouldn't last that long before I threw your ass out on the street.''

"Okay. I'll do it in fifteen."

"Show up here, Ransom," Tony said with a growl, "and you'll be sorry. I'll see to it personally. Nothing illegal involved."

"So you say."

The threat—meaning his job, he supposed—didn't trouble J.C. in the least. He was used to trading insults with the Destinas. Even if Tony pitched him out as soon as he reached the family compound, J.C. had every intention of keeping their appointment. Or, the lack of one. He had questions to ask. And he wanted answers.

"I'M GOING WITH YOU," Cameron said softly from behind Ransom as he hung up the phone.

"Like hell. You're staying here," he said without turning around.

Her pulse thudding, Cameron didn't acknowledge the command. She watched him set the cordless receiver back in its cradle, saw the rigid set of his shoulders. Along the edge of his shirt collar, the nape of his neck turned a dull rose that told her, more than his words, that he was upset. And at the same time, excited. A strange exhilaration seemed to radiate from him. Cameron felt it, too.

"Destina won't see me," he told her.

"But you're going anyway."

"How did you—"

"I won't be left behind. This is about my father."

"It's about a federal case in which you have no official role."

"Neither do you," she pointed out.

He turned to stare at her. Unblinking. "Assuming Destina changes his mind once I get there, with luck and some persuasion I may be able to crack this case. Do you know how long I've waited to say that?"

"I've waited longer," Cameron said. "For twenty-five

years, I lived in fear and hiding. I'm done, Ransom. Don't try to leave me behind. I go with you or—''

''What?'' he cut in. ''You slash my tires?''

Cameron crossed the room. She jabbed a finger at his chest. All solid muscle, it scarcely moved under her touch, but Cameron felt the steady beat of his heart. ''I'll follow you. You'll never know I'm there.''

''In what? Emerald's borrowed limousine? A New York cab?''

''Ron will drive me.'' She paused. ''Or Grace. It seems they've become loyal to me since Emerald's disappearance. Now that she's…dead, I feel responsible for them.''

He grasped her hand. ''You're not going, Cameron.''

''You can't stop me.''

Ransom tried intimidation. ''These people are not average folks, I tell you. Let me deal with them. On my own.''

''Don't insult me. I can handle whatever happens.''

She'd survived so far, hadn't she? She wouldn't let Destina find her weak.

Ransom folded her hand to his chest, gently squeezing her fingers.

''Your brother is right. So am I.'' Before she could protest again, he went on, ''I can't begin to tell you how much I admire your spirit. Through all this—Emerald's death, especially—you've held up better than I could have hoped. You're a strong person. But you're still a woman—''

''Oh, please, Ransom. Don't play the gender card.''

''—a woman who has gone through too much. You don't need a trip to see Venuto Destina. That lump on your head's still there. I can sense right now that it hurts. If you won't listen to me, remember what the doctor said. Rest.'' He paused again. ''Let Grace and Ron pamper you for a few more days. At least for tomorrow, while I'm gone.''

''You won't be gone. I'll be there, too.''

Ransom sighed. ''This isn't about you changing clothes

with Emerald. If something happened to you, I'd never forgive myself.''

That was a risk, but one she had to take. Cameron didn't
want to be responsible for Ransom blaming himself again,
yet she had her own reasons for facing Destina. She had to
see him for herself. If Ransom went alone, she'd never have
that satisfaction.

"A warning, Ransom. If the next words from your lips
are, 'Stay home and bake some cookies,' I will personally
wash out your mouth.''

"With soap?" He had the audacity to grin at her. "I'd
really like something a bit more…friendly." He gazed at
her half-open mouth and impulsively drew her into his
arms. Before she could protest, he swept her up in a passionate kiss that left her weak with desire.

"Oh. I see." Cameron stepped back, freeing herself a
few moments later when she regained her bearings. For
those fleeting, unforgettable seconds, she'd been tempted
by the lowered tone of his voice, the taste and feel of his
lips claiming hers as their breaths mingled and hearts beat
in unison. "Now we use the seduction ploy. Ransom
waltzes Cameron into bed—again—and all's right with his
world. I never knew you were so manipulative.''

"Me?" He blinked at her, all fake innocence.

Cameron couldn't help laughing. Then she sobered. "I
can appreciate your valiant efforts. But believe me, I'm not
about to be distracted. I'm going with you to see Destina.''

He feigned disappointment. "Jeez, I thought I was better
than that.''

"Your masculine skills are not in question. Your meth-
ods are.''

Ransom gave up. "Cameron, dammit. What would Kyle
say if he knew you were planning to sneak out after me?
To put yourself in jeopardy?''

"He'd say I was walking into the lion's den," she murmured.

"You obviously don't trust me."

"I'm trying," she murmured.

"Less than half an hour, and I could have what we need to put Destina behind bars for the rest of his apparently unwell life. Well, that's a crock, because he's probably healthier than I am. But I'll find out for myself. Tomorrow. As soon as I know, you'll know."

"Exactly."

"I'll call you on my cell phone."

Cameron batted her eyelashes. "And I'll be waiting, breathlessly, to hear that deep male voice? Reassuring me that it's safe to come out from under the covers?"

A muscle ticked in Ransom's jaw.

Cameron squared her own shoulders. If he thought she would fold, he didn't know her at all.

Never mind their night of passion—when he'd learned everything about her body, at least. Forget the fact that just looking at him made her ache with need.

He still thought her father would be at the bottom of Destina's woodpile, figuratively speaking, and he still thought James McKenzie was as much a thief as the famed crime boss himself.

Ransom's expression turned grim. "I don't want you there, Cameron."

"Because you think I can't take the heat?"

He sighed. "I'm speaking from experience. It's not easy to learn that the person you trusted most in your life wasn't worthy of that trust. I don't want you hurt."

He meant his own father, of course, as well as hers. And for another moment Cameron wavered. She knew what that admission had cost Ransom. What it might cost her. But she had to find out.

"If what you believe is true, I'll be hurt anyway."

His tone hardened. "Do you have to hear it from Destina?"

"Yes!" She took a step toward him again. "Do you know why?"

He looked away. "Damn. You're gonna tell me."

Cameron didn't back down. "Because Venuto Destina destroyed my family! Despite your objections, and Kyle's, I need to see the man who caused the people I love so much grief. The man who broke my mother's spirit—who probably killed my father in the physical sense and who—"

Cameron stopped. She'd almost said too much.

Not yet, she thought. *Don't tell him.* Not yet.

"I won't wait for him to come after me," she finished.

She would hear the truth herself first from Venuto Destina—the man who may have hidden the diamonds in her doll so many years ago.

Or she would die trying.

## Chapter Eleven

Ashton, Connecticut, boasted a population of thirty-seven hundred people. In mid-December the sleepy little town had a three-inch coating of fresh snow. On the drive through town, Cameron had enjoyed the Christmas lights, the pine boughs and red ribbons that decorated the quaint gas lampposts, the towering blue spruce in front of city hall decked with ornaments and glowing for the season. The brick sidewalks, drifted with white snowfall, and the turn-of-the century buildings only enhanced the scene. Like a picture postcard of New England, Ashton looked peaceful and serene. It was hard to imagine the crime boss living in such a place. At the edge of town, she felt her stomach tighten. When Ransom navigated the last turn onto Venuto Destina's private road, Cameron turned to him. "What do you really think we'll find here?"

"If we get lucky, Destina will give away something we need."

"But if he gives away nothing?"

"Then we keep digging. I hope it won't come to that," he added.

Cameron couldn't agree more. With Emerald's death, she felt a growing anxiety herself to resolve the case. Before she could move forward in her own quest for a truly normal life, she needed to know who had planted the diamonds in her doll long ago even if it turned out to be her father. And if it was Destina who wanted her to surrender them now—or die.

Destina's gateposts were made of stone, his gates of black iron.

After Ransom identified himself on the intercom, they stayed stubbornly closed. Cameron took over then. She told Ransom to punch the button again and spoke across him into the intercom. "Tell Mr. Destina that Cameron Mc-Kenzie is here."

Less than a minute later, the gates soundlessly swung open, and Ransom's rented sedan rolled through onto the perfectly paved asphalt that led to Destina's immense home. Ransom flashed her a look of amazement, which Cameron answered with a smile. She hoped it didn't seem smug, but she had proved useful after all.

"He'll see me," she said.

Destina's stone and brick three-story structure looked impenetrable, like some ancient fortress, and Cameron couldn't help but catch her breath at the sight. A curl of dark smoke rose from a chimney—one of several—and she smelled burning wood in the cold, crisp air. She couldn't shake off the overlying impression of evil.

"I'd give anything not to be here," she said, wanting to run now that she'd gained admission.

"I can leave you in the parking area. You can wait for me there."

"Never."

Ransom shot her another look, then killed the engine and exited the car. "Let me do the talking. You keep quiet—and watch the action unfold."

Cameron saluted him. "Yessir. Sir."

He probably didn't believe her capable of silence.

With a faint smile, Ransom took her elbow to guide her up the front steps.

"Remember. I'm in charge."

Destina's son, Tony himself, answered the door. It surprised Cameron that no butler seemed to be in residence, and she told herself with a half smile to match Ransom's that it was hard to get good help these days.

In her career as a chef, Cameron *was* the help.

Not that she had any experience lately. Absent from her job because of her own concussion then Emerald's death, Cameron had already lost one client, but Grace Jennings had referred another. So far, she seemed to be holding her own. How much longer that would last, Cameron had no idea, but she needed to resolve this then get back to work.

Her normal life, she reminded herself, was waiting.

Destina's son stepped back in the entry. "After our conversation yesterday, I can't say I was expecting you, but persistence pays off." He glanced at Cameron.

He didn't appear pleased. A handsome man with dark hair and eyes and a lean, athletic build, Tony guided them toward his father's room, or so Cameron assumed.

"The feds have already questioned him," he reminded Ransom, "about James McKenzie—a traitor if there ever was one."

"My father was not a traitor," Cameron said, her voice taut.

Ransom flicked a glance at her that motioned her to silence.

"They questioned him about Emerald Greer, too," Destina continued. "Neither murder had anything to do with my father. So what are you doing here, Ransom?"

"Asking my own questions." He gestured at a closed door off the second-floor hallway. Tony had paused in front of it. "Your father is in there?"

"You still don't believe me. But he's in poor shape." Tony knocked softly on the wooden panel, then pushed the door open. "See for yourself."

Cameron peered over Ransom's shoulder. In the dark-ened room, she could see little but shadows. Then her eyes adjusted and she made out the figure of a man on the huge, walnut-carved bed opposite her, his wizened shape barely discernible beneath the covers. A small man, she realized. No, a shriveled man.

This was not the Venuto Destina she had envisioned, despised and feared, or even vaguely remembered from her childhood. Uncle Ven, she had called him then. The nick-name came back to her now. So did his kindness, and the toys he'd brought each time he came to visit her family.

Like the doll he'd given her.

Cameron entered the room behind Ransom—and shiv-ered at the chill in the air.

Destina's hoarse voice broke the silence. "Ransom. My son said you were here—uninvited, of course."

"Venuto." With a nod, Ransom walked closer, then stopped with Cameron at his heels. "Tony tells me you're ill."

"On my deathbed."

His raspy tone could barely be heard. His appearance shocked her. It seemed incredible that this spare little man had changed her life, and that of her family, years ago. She put her hand on Ransom's shoulder. He felt warm and solid beneath her touch, like comfort, and she wanted to cling to him. Her heart thundered inside, and her palms went damp.

"I didn't believe him," Ransom said.

Yet she could see the truth, too. Venuto Destina lay im-mobile in the wide bed, his muscles shrunken, his voice a mere whisper, his eyes sunken in his skull. He looked very ill indeed.

"My son does not lie."

Ransom stepped closer to the bed, but Cameron hung back, unwilling to get near the shell of a man she had feared for most of her life. "And you, Venuto?" Ransom asked.

"The truth is easier to control."

Ransom sank down on the edge of the mattress, crowding Destina.

Dark eyes flashing, Tony immediately moved to stop him.

But his father lifted a hand. "Let him stay."

Not glancing at Cameron, Ransom met Destina's gaze. It seemed he had forgotten her. In the near darkness that permeated the room, his deep blue eyes drilled into Venuto.

"Tell me what I want to know."

"About McKenzie?" Destina's voice croaked in the stillness. The pungent scents of medications wafted through the air. "Nothing," he said.

"About Emerald Greer."

Destina laughed, then choked. For long moments he couldn't seem to catch his breath. Or speak.

Tony Destina stepped forward again, his tone angry. "My father needs rest. If he knew anything, he would have told the feds."

"I am the feds," Ransom said.

Cameron prayed that would be enough to protect them.

YOU ARE THE GOVERNMENT, Cameron had told him the first night he came to her apartment. Now, J.C. sat on Venuto Destina's bed and silently thanked her for not refuting that fact. He needed her cooperation. One false move on his part—or hers—and Destina's son would throw them out into the driveway. If they were lucky.

J.C. reminded himself that they were in this room only because of her. Tony was right. He had no official reason to question Destina. His own curiosity, his concern for Cameron's safety, wouldn't be enough to satisfy his supervisor, since he was on medical leave. J.C. hadn't told Gabe his plans. No one knew they'd come here. It was not beyond the realm of possibility that both he and Cameron might never be seen again. Like Emerald. He might be inclined to panic, but he didn't have a death wish.

With that caution to himself, J.C. cleared his throat.

"Emerald Greer disappeared off a Manhattan street. I figure you know something about that, Venuto."

"A tennis player is of no interest to me."

"Unless she appeared to be someone else."

The old man raised himself in bed. Tony jumped to do his bidding, plumping pillows behind his back then offering a glass of water when Venuto coughed again.

"I heard nothing of this," he managed to say.

"Maybe you didn't have to hear. Maybe you already knew. Or got an unpleasant surprise when one of your goons hauled the wrong woman into a car."

"I don't know what you're talking about."

J.C. sighed. "Okay, play games if you want. The newspapers never reported this but I'll make it easy for you. Emerald Greer was dressed in Cameron's clothes that night."

Surprise—or its imitation—flickered across Venuto's heavily lined face.

Tony laid a hand on his hunched shoulder. "My father has been in a private clinic since the day he left prison—where he had suffered a series of minor strokes. He needed specialized treatment on the outside, therapy."

"Hey, that's compassionate release. Saves the government money on all those medical bills." He didn't lie. Sending a prisoner home to die could be a cost-cutting maneuver as much as it showed true compassion.

J.C.'s gaze wandered over Venuto's slight frame in the bed. His legs hadn't moved. He had dragged himself higher on the pillows with obvious effort. His speech seemed slow, even halting, and not quite clear. It was possible.

Certainly he'd been out of touch over the past weeks. And Tony's statement matched all the rumors.

"He may never walk again," Tony said in a hard voice that seemed to mask pain over his father's illness. "He may never be able to dress or feed himself. He requires round-the-clock nursing. He's a stroke victim, Ransom. And at the clinic, we learned he has lung cancer. Is the man you see here capable of murder?"

"Come on, Tony. The Destina family has any number of hired guns. If Venuto didn't order them to kill McKenzie and Greer, you did."

His dark eyes flashed. "Call me a killer, and you put yourself at risk, Ransom."

"A possible killer," he corrected himself. He'd skated too close to the edge. "And you just proved my point."

Tony indicated his obviously expensive suit. "You think I need blood on my hands? I don't. You think I want my wife and kids to live in constant fear of reprisals, like I did? Like my mother and my brothers?" He made a slashing motion that had Cameron taking a step back to avoid him. J.C. held his ground. "The answer is no. If you think that," Tony said, "you're crazier than I've heard you are. I'm a legitimate businessman. So is my father."

*Now,* J.C. added. The unspoken word seemed to vibrate in the dark, moist air.

He shrugged. "If you call prostitution and drugs legitimate. *Murder.*"

"Who's out of commission here, Ransom? You've been in the dark too long. My family has nothing to do with illegal activities."

"History doesn't lie."

"What is it they say? 'History repeats itself,'" Tony said, "*if* a man doesn't learn from it." He turned to Cameron. "I know why you're here, too. You think we had something to do with your father's murder. I even admire your guts for wanting to confront my father. But he's innocent. You think we killed Emerald Greer—apparently in your place? You couldn't be more wrong.''

''Mr. Destina…'' Cameron began.

J.C. reached out to grasp her hand. He gave it a warning squeeze.

*Let me,* it said.

For now, she seemed to agree. Cameron pressed her lips tight, as if to prevent herself from speaking.

Tony held her gaze. ''I have a degree from Yale. I have an MBA from Wharton. I have made it my life's mission to remove my family—my father—from any type of activity that would draw the attention of law enforcement.'' He paused. ''In any of its many forms. Including the U.S. Marshals.''

J.C.'s tone was dry. ''There's still a lot of money missing in the McKenzie case.''

''Yes, and James himself knew where it is. He's the one you should have looked at, not me or my father.'' He spoke to Cameron again. ''I can assure you, Miss McKenzie. You were not—nor are you now—our target.''

J.C. tensed. He couldn't be wrong. Yet Tony insisted he was.

''That money is small change to me. To my father. We have no interest in it.''

Venuto shifted in bed. His breath rasped in the silence.

''Come 'ere.'' He motioned to Cameron with one gnarled hand.

J.C. tightened his grip on her fingers but Cameron tugged free.

''Let her go…Ransom. Would I harm a woman…who was like a daughter to me?''

A DAUGHTER? With her heart in her throat, Cameron moved closer to the bed. He had become a pathetic old man, but the only thing she wanted of Venuto Destina was to see him behind bars.

"We will speak alone," he told Ransom.

"Forget it. I'm staying."

"This is…between me and…Cam. No one else. You go, too, Tony."

His son resisted. "I'm not leaving you with either of them."

"You protect me…too much. Please. I have things to say."

Cameron turned. "I'll be okay, Ransom."

Destina seemed inclined to take her into his confidence. Maybe she would learn something on her own that could help the case. Something about the money—the diamonds now—or her father's death, if not Emerald's. Venuto Destina had called her Cam, like Kyle. The shortened version of her name—her original name—had been intentional, she was sure. Destina wanted her trust.

He wouldn't get it, she thought. And reminded herself that this old man, who indeed appeared to be on his deathbed, had ruined her family, tried to ruin her life. But to gain information, she would hear him out.

When they were alone, he reached for her hand. She let him draw her down to sit on the edge of his bed as Ransom had done. His fingers felt cold, bony, but she didn't pull away. Ransom's confrontation hadn't worked.

Perhaps her own method would.

She prayed Destina would confess to her about the money.

"I am a sick man. I have little time left." He coughed again. "I am…at the point of settling my accounts."

Her heart lurched. Did he mean that money? Would he admit he'd put the fortune in her doll? She took a breath. "I think that's a wise decision, Mr. Destina."

"Venuto. We are old friends, are we not?" He managed

a smile, although one side of his mouth drooped. "Do you remember before the trouble started? When your father worked for me? When I came to see you on Sundays?"

"And brought gifts," she added.

"Ah. You do remember. There was a…red wagon. A hobby horse with real hair for its mane, straight from Italy and the town where I was born."

"There was a doll."

His face brightened. "Your favorite, I recall. A simple thing, made of cloth…with little beans inside. She had a silly grin."

"I still have her. Kyle brought her to me."

"Kyle?"

"My brother." Destina wouldn't know his WP first name. "She's still my favorite," Cameron said. *And she has a stash of diamonds inside, not beans.*

"Your father and I were great friends then, too."

A stab of grief, as fresh as yesterday, nearly made her weep. This sad, old man, her father…they *had* been friends, she remembered in vague snatches of some tableau from the past. She could see a healthy Venuto laughing, her mother's smile lighting up the room. Venuto's son…

"Tony used to come with you. I'd forgotten."

"He was very fond of you. For a ten-year-old boy."

She brightened. "We played marbles on the sidewalk in front of our house."

"You see? We share a history. Your Ransom is wrong."

"Or you are trying to divert me."

He laughed a little. "Ah, I see you are still so clever. But you, too, are wrong." He grasped her hand tighter. "Cameron… I am not your enemy. The money belongs to our past, to a…terrible time. When I was arrested, I lost my friends."

She couldn't imagine friends mattered to him, except as

a means to some end. "And you vowed revenge because my father testified against you."

His eyes filled. "Yes. A sad time. I was angry... trapped."

Her voice thickened. "You were also guilty, Mr. Destina."

He nodded. "Of some things, yes. I have...regrets." He studied her a moment. "I see you don't believe me. You are as suspicious as your Ransom."

*Your Ransom.* He'd said it twice.

"How do you know——"

"My eyes are old. Yet they still see." He gave her a lopsided smile. "He is a difficult man. Strong-willed. But he has...honor. Even when he tries to blame me for James's death...or that tennis player's."

Destina, it seemed, respected Ransom. He even held some affection for her. Was it all an act, or a genuine attempt to make restitution for his sins?

"I've looked forward to this meeting for a long time," she told him. "Now I don't know what to think."

"To hate me. Or to forgive," he murmured.

"Yes."

"I would choose forgiveness." He struggled against the pillows and, despite herself, Cameron hurried to help make him comfortable again. For another instant she saw him as he'd been years ago, younger, a vibrant man whose boisterous laugh could make her giggle. "Do you know why?" he said.

"It's not easier."

"No, but...I prefer this to bitterness. Or revenge." He gazed at her with watery eyes. "There was a time, yes, when I would have killed James for what he did to me. I spent my children's growing-up years in prison, away from them—and from the wife I loved."

"Because *you* made mistakes! Not because my father testified."

He inclined his head in agreement. "That was my way, then. A violent life. But do you not see, Cameron? I no longer need revenge."

"How do I know that?"

Did he think she'd make it easy for him? She had losses, too.

"I mean what I said." For a moment he stayed silent, obviously exhausted by conversation. "I mean this now—I no longer blame James. I forgive your father."

She was shaking. "He doesn't need your forgiveness!"

"We all need forgiveness." He looked at her, unblinking. "I feel sorry for him, in fact. No," he said when she tried to rise and free her hand from his. "Don't leave before I tell you why." He shook his head. "I am sorry because during the years in prison when I aged and grew old, so did he. And I realized that, in those same years, his life in Witness Protection was an equal punishment…a prison of his own."

Dear God, he was right. Cameron pressed her lips tight.

"You understand," he said.

"Yes. Maybe I do…a little now."

"Then we must end this. I will send you back to your Ransom. Go home, Cameron. Leave an old man to his dreams of happier days."

She had learned nothing that would close the case, find her father's killer or allow her to release the missing diamonds to Ransom. Yet she had not wasted time.

"Mr. D— Venuto." She covered both of his hands with hers but he stopped her.

"Tell my son that I give you my blessing. And your brother—" For another second, he held her gaze, appearing confused, as if trying to remember Kyle. Then his lined face cleared. "Ah, yes. How is he?"

"Struggling," Cameron admitted.

"An affliction of the young." She felt Venuto Destina's still-sharp gaze on her back all the way to the door. "Give my greetings to…Benjamin."

"THOSE TWO should win an Academy Award."

J.C. pushed hard on the accelerator, and his rented car shot down the long driveway from Destina's stone house to the road. Goodbye, he thought. Good riddance. He couldn't leave fast enough.

"Just an act?" Cameron didn't seem as sure. "I thought so, too, at first."

"Now you've changed your mind." What had Destina said to her in private?

"Not exactly. Venuto is still responsible for all the lost years my family had." She paused. "But he and his son may be telling the truth."

So it was Venuto now. J.C. scoffed at her obvious naïveté. "Tony may have degrees from fancy Ivy League schools. He may even be a good businessman." J.C. swung the car onto the entrance ramp of I-95 to New York. "Scratch his shiny veneer, and I'd bet my pension you'd find dirt underneath."

Cameron stayed silent for a few seconds. "Venuto told me that forgiving is better than being bitter, Ransom. You and Kyle might think about it."

"Now he's a self-help guru? You listened to that?"

She touched his shoulder, as if she understood his misgivings when, clearly, she didn't. She'd been had.

"You can't simply discount him," she said.

"Boy, he really sucked you in."

"Ransom, maybe he's changed. People can, you know."

"Sure he has. And leopards don't have spots."

"So it's your opinion that Destina and Tony were putting us on."

"It was quite a show," J.C. agreed. He didn't take his eyes from the road to look at her, but he could sense Cameron's disapproval. She shifted in her seat, then ran a hand through her hair. Dark and silky, he remembered, not wanting to remind himself—his body—by risking a glance at her. "How can I convince you that the Destina family has been in business for generations without changing a thing? That house belonged to the old guy's grandfather. If they're out of drugs, or prostitution, I'm more screwed up than I thought. Hell, I shouldn't have to convince *you.*"

"But what if Destina *didn't* kill my father?"

"Sure," J.C. muttered. He cut around a tractor-trailer then whipped back into the right lane. Today hadn't gone as he'd hoped. Not only did he fail to get information from the Destinas, but now he'd alienated Cameron who seemed to believe Destina was her new fairy godfather, not the scumbag who'd murdered her father.

Incredible. So was her next question.

"What if Destina had nothing to do with Emerald's death either?"

"You're not gonna quit, are you?"

"No." She turned to face him. "I won't quit—just like you—until I find my father's killer. I won't quit until the man who murdered Emerald is behind bars. You can't be rigid about this, though, Ransom." She took a breath. "Consider this. What if the killer wasn't one person but two? And the murders aren't connected at all?"

"Then we're back to square one."

He shrugged, kept his gaze on the road ahead and glanced at the green sedan that loomed in his rearview mirror. It had been with them all the way.

"We're being followed. You still think Destina's lily white?"

"Followed?" Cameron whirled to look out the back window.

"Mr. Green stays with us, slowing when I slow, picking up speed when I do, passing the same traffic and staying in the same lane. But maybe he's just an escort—to see we get home safely."

She didn't miss the sarcasm in his tone. J.C. didn't miss the fear in her eyes. Cameron had a thing about being followed, and he couldn't blame her. He'd just discovered he didn't much like it himself.

"Ransom, let's pull off. There's a rest stop not far from here. I just saw the sign."

"Pull off, for what? To let the Green Man take his best shot at us?"

Her face paled and he cursed himself. "Maybe he's not really tailing us."

"Sorry, but I don't feel like trading bullets to find out. If he wants a trip to New York, let him spend his gas."

"You don't think we're in danger?" She was staring out the back window again.

"Yeah, I think we're in deep water. Am I going to give him the satisfaction of knowing we're on to him? No."

"But if Venuto isn't guilty, then why follow us?"

"And if he is…?"

"I see what you mean." Sounding disappointed, she sank back into her seat. "I just have this hunch," she said a moment later, "that he and Tony had nothing to hide. Did you see the surprise on Destina's face when you mentioned my change of clothes with Emerald?"

"I told you, the guy's a good actor. Better than you know."

She smiled. "Venuto said you're strong-willed. I think you simply want to be right rather than wrong. If Destina isn't the killer and his son didn't order my father's death or Emerald's—I mean, mine—then who is responsible?"

"That does leave a question."

Cameron picked at a hangnail while J.C. negotiated the

increasingly heavy traffic nearing the city and tried not to look at her. The notion that he actually loved her was still new in his mind, and he didn't know where in hell their relationship could lead. But maybe that didn't matter at the moment. He'd rather sneak a glance at her after all, because he couldn't help himself, and watch the silken fall of dark hair around her face, the soft pout of her mouth as she contemplated her encounter with Destina. Or was she pondering her feelings for J.C.? What were they? he wondered. Then he caught himself and checked the rearview mirror again. Right now he had one thing to deal with: getting her home.

"So if it's not Venuto," she picked up the conversation, "then what if it's Ron?"

J.C. shook his head. "Or Grace? No, we've been over that. They may be getting on better than I expected they ever would. But their bond only goes back to Emerald's disappearance. If either of them—or both—were the guilty parties, they'd make sure we never saw them in the same room. They wouldn't want to rouse our suspicions."

"Emerald's fan?" Cameron said, ticking off her next suspect.

But they'd eliminated Edgar Mills, too. "The guy's a loser, but beyond his fascination with Emerald, he's no more capable of murder than, say, Ted Kayne."

"I'd think Kayne was very capable—of almost anything."

"You may be right. He's still not our killer."

"Because he has an alibi from twelve men who probably wouldn't dare cross him? His board of directors make a neat excuse."

"And yeah, for saying what he wanted them to, he might line their pockets with a lot extra in their Christmas-bonus checks." J.C. shook his head. "Still not our man."

"Why?"

He took the chance, and shot her another look. Lord, with her fingers she had tousled that silky dark hair, and her hazel eyes had gone wide and luminous, almost the way they looked when he kissed her, when they... He stopped himself.

"Because, sweetheart. Ron, Grace, Edgar Mills, Ted Kayne...none of them had a motive where your father is concerned. Opportunity with Emerald, yes. But the double motive, no. Emerald didn't count. Keep your eye on the ball, McKenzie."

Her already-pale face whitened when reality set in. J.C. could see her try, then reject, any other answer. An answer he'd thought she accepted days ago. But then, Destina could be a persuasive man. In her touchy-feely moments with him, she'd almost forgotten herself.

"I'm still the target."

"Destina's disclaimer aside, yes. 'His' money is still missing. Don't believe it's small change to them. And Destina still thinks you have it, through James."

"So...what do we do now?"

In one regard he liked her use of the word *we,* even if he wouldn't take her up on it where the case was concerned. J.C. glanced in his rearview mirror again. The green sedan was still trailing them, but if their man was Destina, which J.C. had believed all along, he wouldn't make his move here. The middle lane of the highway kept them safe. For now.

But night was falling.

The night was another matter.

He frowned. "I need to look at the transcript from the marshals' interview with Destina. We're missing something here. Or I am."

He decided to lose their tail. Frustrated, he whizzed into the left lane, passing a line of slower-moving cars and a couple of battered delivery vans headed for Manhattan. After a few more maneuvers in the growing rush-hour chaos, the green sedan fell back, then out of sight. At least one thing had worked today.

"What do you want me to do?" Cameron's wobbly tone told him she felt more frightened again than she had before. His fault. J.C. covered her hands with one of his own. She had both hands twisted together, like Grace.

"I didn't mean to worry you."

"But I can help."

Sure, she could—and get herself killed. J.C. felt the strong sense of rightness in his gut. Destina was their man. He just needed to find the proof.

"You can help me," he said, "by staying alive."

## Chapter Twelve

"I need to go home, Ransom. My home."

Cameron hadn't spoken for the rest of the drive from Ashton, but when Ransom turned toward Fifth Avenue and Emerald's apartment, she'd made a fast decision. Sleeping in Emerald's bed no longer seemed appropriate, and as Ron had said, with the tennis star gone, Cameron had no place there.

She needed to get back to work. Tomorrow.

She needed to sleep in her own bed. Tonight.

"Then I'll help you finish cleaning up," Ransom said.

Cameron started at his words. She had nearly forgotten, too, along with her fears of Venuto, that her apartment still showed signs of invasion, and the only thing she'd taken pains to restore was the hiding place for the missing diamonds. If Ransom stayed, he might guess where they were.

She wouldn't put it past him.

He might be wrong about Destina—or not—but like Venuto, he had a sharp eye and a quick mind.

Part of her didn't want him there for fear he would discover the truth. But another part ached to spend one more night making love with J.C., feeling his body become a part of hers. Feeling herself take flight at the instant of release. An even larger part, which frightened her, wanted him to wrap her tight afterward in his strong embrace, yearned to have him chase away the ghosts, to make her feel safe and warm.

"No," she said. "I'll be fine. Really."

He smiled. "Cameron, I'm not leaving you alone."

"But I don't have an extra b—"

"Don't argue. I'm sharing your bed tonight."

With a weary sigh, Cameron subsided against her seat. She could protest. She could try to convince him that she had no need of his protection. But she knew that wasn't true. Whether or not she wanted to believe it, because of the money, her life was still in danger. And deep down, the notion of having him in her bed thrilled her beyond words.

She glanced behind her again but didn't see the green sedan.

"We lost him on I-95," Ransom murmured.

He left his car on the street outside her apartment building, and after greeting the night doorman, they rode the elevator to her floor. Cameron had lapsed into silence again. If she spoke, she wouldn't be able to control the tremor in her voice. Scared? she thought. Oh, yes. Scared of her own feelings for Ransom even more than she was afraid of Destina...or some unknown killer.

Cameron couldn't shake her intuitive sense that whoever was after her, and the missing money—diamonds—was not connected to Venuto Destina. No matter what Ransom thought.

Should she tell him now?

Then she wouldn't be a target or have to fear for her life. She wouldn't worry that he'd stumble across the diamonds on his own.

Except—then Cameron would lose her one chance to clear her father's name.

She wouldn't risk that, even for love.

By the time Ransom slipped her key into the lock, she was shaking.

Not fear now, she told herself, but nerves.

Or was that anticipation?

As soon as the door closed behind them, Ransom checked the rest of the apartment. Then, apparently satisfied that they were alone, he returned. In a blink his deep blue eyes went from wary to dark and seductive. He crowded Cameron against the living-room wall with that look of intense purpose she had come to love.

"I know I rattled you before. I know you're ready for this to be over, and Destina to pay for his crime—"

Heart suddenly thumping, Cameron danced out from under his arm.

"I'm even more ready for dinner. Let's see what I can find."

"Uh-oh." Ransom trailed her into the kitchen where Cameron discovered broken pottery still piled on the counter and dented pans stacked in the open-doored cupboard. "She's cooking again," he muttered.

Cameron tried a grin that didn't quite work. "It's my profession."

"Well, mine's catching bad guys. And I know what the domestic hustle means. Keeping your hands, your mind occupied is good. I oughta know. I'll get going on the living room while you get started on something wonderful to eat."

He'd guessed she was frightened but didn't know why. What if he found the diamonds? "I'd hate to disappoint you," she said.

Ransom turned with a grin of his own. His warm gaze slid over her.

"You never disappoint me."

Flushing, she spun back to the counter—and heard him laugh, low and full of promise. She had sent him to Emerald's den to sleep just days ago. Tonight, there would be no escape from the passion he could rouse in her with a simple touch. And after that...

"Ahem." Trying not to think about Ransom, Cameron busied herself. With a secret smile, she admitted she didn't want to escape. Quickly, she scrubbed pots and scoured the counter. She sorted plates and cups and put the worst of them in the trash.

Moments later, an impromptu casserole was baking in the oven. The scent of onion and garlic and mingled spices wafted through the air. Every light in the place was on now, and if she ignored the mess still on the living-room floor, she could believe that this was home again. And safe.

"Not bad," Ransom said, coming back into the kitchen. "The cleanup won't take much longer." He slipped his arms around her at the stove. He nuzzled her neck, and she knew she was far from safe. "Smells great," he said. "I could get used to eating right."

She missed a breath. Did he mean permanence for them? A life together?

"I bet you live on burgers and fries."

He kissed the sensitive spot beneath her ear and Cameron shivered in response.

"Feel good?" he murmured.

"Mmm." Terrific. But could this last? When he learned what she'd hidden...

"You'll feel better. Later. I promise." He eased away to peer into the oven at the bubbling casserole. "I need to build strength first. You're right, I've all but bought a franchise in the fast-food business."

"You know how much fat's in that stuff?"

"Yeah, yeah. You cocky chefs are all alike. Superior."

"Your body will thank me."

Ransom laughed, right next to her ear. "Honey, that's an invitation if I ever heard one. Between us, we might forget the rest of this rotten day."

Cameron turned and met his eyes. Ransom dipped to take her mouth in a long, sweet kiss that hinted of endless hours in bed and whispers in the dark.

"Rotten week," she murmured.

Ransom drew back. His gaze serious, he tilted his head.

"If you hadn't gone with me today, Destina wouldn't have let us in."

"So he told me."

"What else did he say?" Ransom asked, as if he could no longer resist.

Cameron had avoided relating their conversation. It was private, part of her past, and now, about to be resolved. But partly, she wanted to hoard those moments for herself until she could take them out to make sense of them, of her life and her family's lives at last. That didn't include Ransom.

"Venuto reminded me of things forgotten," she finally said.

"No mention of the missing money?"

"I'm sorry I didn't get the information we need." Guilt pierced her. "He would never tell me even if he had it."

"He said James knew where it is."

Cameron turned to check the casserole. "Think what you want, but I'll never believe my father was a thief. I'll prove it to you."

"How?" he said. She could feel him watching her.

Their tender moment had been shattered, and Cameron wished he hadn't mentioned Destina or the money. The diamonds hovered at the edge of her mind.

She whacked the spoon against the side of the pan in dismissal.

"Food's done. Dinner's ready."

"How, Cameron?"

"I don't know! But I will."

When she had time to think, she would figure it out.

There must be someone, someone who knew her father and Destina.

After dinner she and Ransom tidied the rest of the apartment. He helped her hang fresh towels, scour the bathroom, then put clean sheets on the bed—or rather, her mattress on the floor.

"It's not the Ritz-Carlton," she said.

"But you're glad to be home." He must have noticed her smile.

"Yes. I am."

Together, they flung a new comforter into the air then settled it on the bed. Cameron plumped pillows. Then she couldn't think of anything else to do. When Ransom started toward her with that look of dark purpose in his deep blue eyes, she folded both arms over her chest. She was deceiving him with the diamonds—creating her own risk, possibly endangering him, too. "Maybe…this isn't a good idea."

"It's the best idea we've had in days."

"Ransom, you said when this is over, we'd talk. But it's not over."

His voice dropped low. "And we're not talking."

Before she could step away, he had her in his arms. Ransom looped them around her waist, at the same instant his mouth swept down to hers. They kissed, and he unfolded her arms to place them around his body. With her chest revealed, he started to work on her buttons.

"Wait. I think we should—"

"You knew this would happen tonight. So did I. Let it happen."

"But Ransom…"

"Jordan," he said into her mouth.

Then her shirt was open, his hands were covering her breasts, her nipples stood up hard and tingling for his touch, and Cameron moaned. When Ransom's mouth captured the stiff peak, she clutched his head to her, tight, hearing her sharp intake of breath, then his, loud in the utterly quiet room. Overhead, her antique chandelier swayed gently.

''We should...turn off the light.''

He shook his head, golden hair sleek and smooth against her skin.

''I want to see you.''

Tonight, she had him. She wouldn't be alone. They had each other.

Cameron worked feverishly then at his clothes. In seconds, still kissing, he was free in her hands, as ready in his magnificent arousal as Cameron's body was soft and liquid for his entry.

Together, they fell onto the mattress.

Together, they grappled for each other, hands on hands, mouths on mouths, and when his tongue slipped between her lips, he slid inside her. Quickly, by unspoken consent, they rose higher and higher, his thrusts becoming harder, faster, deeper, until at once, with a single cry, they hit the climax.

Cameron tumbled over the edge of a high precipice and went free-falling. Ransom fell right behind. She felt the rush deep within her, felt him tremble in her arms. When he dropped his head to her shoulder, and his lips found the tender, rounded bone, the soft, warm skin, he groaned again.

''I'm sorry. I didn't mean to frighten you today.''

Cameron stroked his hair. Felt the damp heat of his body.

''That was a fabulous apology.''

He laughed a little against her skin. She didn't care about Destina or the diamonds, and she guessed Ransom didn't care about closing the case. It was always that way between them.

''We'll be okay, Cameron. Soon.''

''I'm okay now,'' she whispered. ''Jordan, I love you.''

HE HADN'T SAID the same to her.

The next morning, Cameron tried not to let that bother her.

Humming a little tune, she dressed for work.

Ransom, she reminded herself, had wakened her with kisses. In a high mood, he'd insisted upon fixing their breakfast, and Cameron smiled at the memory of hot coffee and more kisses, never mind the eggs and toast he'd also made.

Before they finished, Ransom had taken her to bed again.

Maybe, Cameron thought, actions did speak louder than words.

Ransom had asked her to wait for him in the apartment. He'd left, whistling, hands in his pockets, and all but floated down the hall to the elevator like a man in love. Too bad he could be so closemouthed. He would spend a few hours at Gabe's office, he told her, accessing the transcripts of the marshals' interview with Destina. Then he'd come back to see her to work.

Unfortunately, she couldn't wait.

Her psychiatrist client had phoned right after Ransom left.

"Come here today or I'll find a new chef."

And he was right. Out of necessity, she had neglected her clients. She couldn't afford to do so any longer. Cameron fastened her gold studs in her ears, and told herself it was broad daylight. She feared the darkness, not the sun. Irrational, perhaps, but she felt fine now. Even her head didn't hurt. After last night in Ransom's arms, she wasn't afraid. Before she stepped into her shoes, she was already reviewing her own talk with Destina, exploring the past, looking for a new suspect.

After so many years, she was indeed back to square one.

But then who had telephoned Emerald's apartment that night?

Who had trashed Cameron's home, presumably to find the diamonds?

Who else but Destina would want them?

And who had followed her and Ransom from Venuto's compound yesterday?

In Ransom's mind, that person must still be Destina. Cameron wasn't sure. What greater, unknown threat might loom over her now?

It hadn't been easy for her to dismiss the man who had threatened her family since she was three years old, the man she assumed had killed her father.

She checked the diamonds to be sure they were safe, then grabbed her tote bag from the hall table.

Cameron shuddered, but she refused to live in fear. She slipped the dead bolt on her door then opened it onto the empty hallway. She would take a cab to West End Avenue, spend the morning cooking for the psychiatrist who was still her client. She had abandoned her own routine long enough.

By the time Ransom returned, she'd be home again.

Waiting for him.

He would never know she'd been gone.


IN SPITE OF her determination to pick up her life again, fear followed her home at noon. Cameron had put in a long morning, and already tired, she knew she had the inclination to jump at shadows. Still, she couldn't shake the feeling that someone stayed behind her, just out of sight, on the almost empty street.

In the softly falling snow, in daylight, he should be easy to spot.

Her first thought, of course, was Ransom. Yet all she could summon were memories of the night before, of Ransom wrapped around her like a comforting blanket, of his arms, his hands, his mouth on her.

The slow tingle of renewed awareness didn't take her by surprise this time.

She was becoming used to it. Welcomed it.

*We're not talking,* he had said then. But they would. Soon.

At the last corner, on Seventy-fifth and Third, Cameron glanced over her shoulder. She saw no one. Not that any assailant who meant her harm would allow himself to be seen.

Scoffing at her usual paranoia, she crossed the street, her stomach growling with hunger because she hadn't eaten, and headed for her building. Fred stood inside, his dress-coat collar turned up against the cold after helping another tenant with packages or opening the door. He greeted Cameron with a jaunty grin.

"Working today? You need to set holiday hours, Miss McKenzie."

"I believe you're right." She shivered not from the below-freezing temperature outside, but from the near fright she'd felt. The lobby, decked out with wreaths and twinkling lights on the tree, warmed her spirit. "I'll speak to my boss about that."

Fred laughed. He knew she ran her own business.

"She's a slave driver, that one."

Cameron laughed, too. "I can't even find time to do my Christmas shopping." Then she stepped into the waiting elevator. Somehow she had managed to avoid asking Fred if anyone was looking for her. She needed to break her bad habits, or she'd end up in a loony bin.

When the elevator stopped at her floor, she entered the hall, her door key in hand. She felt ready for lunch.

As soon as she walked into her apartment, Cameron froze. She felt another presence. In the entry hall, her heart took up a noisy pounding, and she tightened her fingers around her key. For an instant Cameron couldn't move.

Another break-in? *Oh God. Who's here?* Her intruder could be the driver of the green sedan that had trailed her and Ransom yesterday. Then, just as quickly, she relaxed. Her new locks were intact.

"Ransom?" she called out. "I'm here. I hope you're cooking—because I'm too wiped out to even boil an egg."

"You work too hard."

With the familiar voice—not Ransom's—the light snapped on and Cameron blinked against the brighter glare, then faced her brother.

"I have to pay my bills," she said.

Kyle stood at the entrance to the living room. He was wearing a heavy overcoat—and a displeased expression.

"It's eighty degrees in Houston," Cameron pointed out. *What was he doing here?*

She peeled off her gloves. She took her time folding them, then laid them on the entry table. Buying time to collect herself, she removed her coat and hung it in the closet. The bad feeling she'd sensed before returned, but she couldn't say why.

She whirled on him. "How did you get in here, Kyle?"

He shrugged.

"I have certain skills you may not know about."

She had wanted to trust him. But her pulse was still thudding. Had he picked her lock? She didn't like his non-explanation, and despite his promise to call, she hadn't heard from him in days. Had he even gone to Houston?

"Did you get the job?"

"Job?" he echoed. Then, "Oh, the interview. No. They decided the match didn't fit." He followed her into the room. "But I guess it's true what they say. Every rejection brings me closer to a real acceptance. Meaning, a job offer."

"You didn't tell me when you were coming back."

"I didn't know. I flew standby. The airports are loaded

with early Christmas travelers. Took me the whole day to get on a flight.''

"I see. But you were worried about me.''

"You know I was.'' He gave her a quizzical look. "Something wrong?''

She shrugged. *Yes,* she thought. But what, exactly? "Just irritated. I don't like walking into my own house and finding someone here.''

"Unexpected,'' he said, "but I'm still family. You said I could—''

"I don't remember saying anything. Are you hungry?''

He laughed a little. "I helped myself to some of your leftover casserole. Damn, but you're a good cook. I've been here awhile. I suppose you'll scold me for that, too.''

Then why was he wearing his overcoat, as if he'd just arrived—or needed to be ready for a quick getaway? Cameron went into the kitchen. Sure enough, his plate adorned the bistro table she'd bought recently. A half-full glass of milk sat in a puddle on the counter. Cameron pushed the refrigerator door completely shut without looking inside. Suddenly, she didn't feel hungry herself. Or tired.

"I saw Destina.''

"That was foolhardy,'' Kyle said.

"Ransom went with me. Or rather, I went with him.''

"And how was the old bastard?''

"Very ill. Weak. Dying. I can't believe he's running that multicrime organization. Even more, after talking with them, I can't believe his son would be involved in murder—Emerald's or Dad's, for that matter.''

"You always were gullible,'' Kyle said, clearly on Ransom's side.

Turning, Cameron leaned against the refrigerator. She really felt irritated now.

"If you have another theory, I'd be happy to hear it. At this point I'm out of options.''

"Yes," Kyle said, "you are."

He came toward her and Cameron fought not to stiffen her shoulders.

"If you're going to insist I fly back to Houston with you, don't bother."

Kyle framed her face in his hands. "You know I'm right. I've been right since the day I found you. I may not approve of your relationship with Ransom, but on one thing he and I agree. Your safety is in jeopardy, and unless you let me—"

"I'm in love with him," she said.

"You're what?" Kyle's gaze darkened.

"I'm not even sure it's possible for the long term, but that's how I feel."

He scowled. "Cam, it's one thing to have a fling. I realize that during Greer's disappearance, after you were hurt, you lived in close quarters with him. But I'm telling you, don't rely on him. When you need him most, Ransom will crumble."

The back of her neck prickled.

"Is that why you're here? To pick up my pieces?"

She eased out from under his arm to pour herself a glass of water. Her mouth felt dry, and a strange image buzzed at the edges of her mind. She couldn't stop moving.

In the living room again, Cameron headed for her one armchair. The stuffing poked through a dozen holes in the upholstery and the springs sagged, but she sat down anyway. Her head felt muzzy. Memory danced in front of her eyes.

*When you need him most...*

Kyle had said that before. He'd said it to her mother the night he left.

Sixteen years, she thought, and in all that time she hadn't been able to remember.

The kaleidoscope of images shifted, then refocused in her brain.

Kyle and her father, quarreling. Fighting.

Their voices had wakened her. Fright couldn't hold her in her bed. She'd crept down the steps to see what was happening. They had come to physical blows that night as Cameron watched from the stairway of the small, dreary house. She saw her mother weeping, her father bleeding, as Kyle had bled when Ransom punched him not long ago on her behalf.

*You selfish monster, what have you done to her? You'll kill my mother yet.*

*Kyle,* their mother had pleaded, tears streaming down her cheeks. *He's your father. Show him some respect.*

*Respect?* A china vase shattered against the brick fireplace. It was painted white, Cameron remembered, but they never used it. The chimney needed cleaning, her mother explained, and they couldn't afford to pay the sweep. *He works you into the ground—and why? Because he's too self-centered to be a man.*

*I'm willing to help. You know he can't work. Even with new identity papers, he can't submit references. If he could find a job as an accountant, that might only lead Destina to us.*

Her father weaved across the room. *Are you calling me a coward, Kyle?*

*I'm calling you a robber! You stole money from Destina.* When their father protested, Kyle lunged at him again. *Liar! You're nothing but a damn liar.*

Kyle had spun around to their mother then, his knuckles raw and bruised. *I pity you. When you need him most…*

Shaken now, Cameron studied her clasped hands in her lap. She'd heard Kyle come into the room but couldn't look at him.

"I don't need you to take care of me," she said. "You ran out on me before."

"You remember that?"

"Mom did the best she could. So did he. I won't believe Dad was a liar—or a thief. It hurts me that you thought he was, probably until the day he died."

He cocked his head to study her.

"Kyle, they were family, too. And you left. Why?" she said. "Because of the money? Destina, not Dad, probably knew where it was all along."

"Then why did he kill him?"

"I don't know that he did," she murmured.

Kyle's gaze sharpened. "And Emerald Greer?"

She shook her head. "I don't know."

Kyle knelt in front of her. "If you have that money, and you don't get out of here, Destina will find you. It was stupid, Cam, going to his compound. You and Ransom might never have come out again—alive."

"Another thing you agree on." But her pulse began to pound again. When Kyle reached for her hands, she pulled back. "How did you know he lives in a compound?"

Kyle's gaze flickered. Then he recovered.

"Everyone knows. TV makes sure of that. When Destina was released from prison, I saw Tony outside the gates of their estate. I recognized him, and the place. You may not remember, but Destina had Christmas parties there." He paused. "In fact, that's when he gave you the cloth doll I found at Gram's. How is Tony?" he said with a bitter twist to his mouth. "He and I used to play marbles, stickball."

"He's fine." Cameron swallowed, dryly. She looked away. His question about Tony had made her heart beat faster. "What else did you think you'd find at Gram's, Kyle?"

All day she'd tried to figure out the case. Tried to put two and two together—Destina, Emerald, her father, the money—but always came up with three. Now she knew: In that first flash of memory, she had known. And by the evasive look in his eyes.

She had tried to trust him.

Needed to trust him.

Now he'd inadvertently handed her the correct answer.

Cameron surged to her feet. Kyle fell back then righted himself and stood, too. They faced each other in the all but empty living room of her apartment, the first real home Cameron had ever known.

And she remembered the rest.

In the last seconds of her father's life—in that Denver alley—he had called out to her. He'd said another name, too.

But Ransom had heard wrong. Until now, she hadn't realized.

Her father hadn't said "Ven" for Venuto Destina.

He'd said *Ben*...

Destina himself had provided the missing link. *Give your brother my greetings.*

It was Kyle's original name. His birth name, the only one Destina knew. The name her father had used.

"Oh, Kyle," she said.

And then he grabbed her.

# Chapter Thirteen

Farther downtown, at the computer he'd "rented" from Gabe, J.C. scrolled through the transcript of Destina's interview with the U.S. Marshals. On this second pass, he continued to frown at the screen.

*Nothing,* he thought.

He could no longer discount the possibility that Cameron could be right. The ailing Destina might have no connection whatsoever to her father's death or to Emerald Greer's.

Exiting the program, he leaned back in his borrowed desk chair.

Gabe had lent J.C. the office—then discreetly disappeared. "Do your thing," he'd said in parting. "I don't want to know about it." With the door shut, the computer on, at the NYPD-issue desk J.C. ran a hand through his hair. His superiors wouldn't be thrilled to learn he was here—if they ever knew—but J.C. felt he had no choice.

After gaining access to the U.S. Marshals data bank, he'd still made no progress. Maybe he should go back to Cameron's apartment, try to learn more of her private conversation with Destina, search for some clue in her mind.

Another scenario immediately presented itself, and J.C. shifted in his chair.

The memory of their lovemaking last night made him tighten all over, and he wished he was with her now, wished that their passionate interlude following the visit to Destina hadn't ended so soon. Yet J.C. hadn't wanted to linger this morning either, to feel tempted by her again, when he felt so near to closing the case.

He breathed a sigh.

Yeah, like that had worked. Despite the trip to Ashton and the hours here, he was no further than he'd been yesterday.

Who else? he wondered. Who but Destina had motive, opportunity, a weapon?

J.C. ticked off a few facts. James McKenzie had been shot to death. A single bullet straight through his jugular vein had felled him like a redwood tree. But Emerald?

He swung back to the computer, tapped in the necessary commands, and clicked on her case file with the NYPD. According to the medical examiner's report, which Gabe had let him see, Emerald was a victim of strangulation, as suspected. The bullet through her brain thereafter had been overkill. She'd already been dead when the shot was fired. Insurance, J.C. supposed. Or panic on the killer's part?

He knew all about panic.

Even now, it slithered down his neck to the base of his spine.

Straightening in the chair, J.C. forced himself to concentrate. If he lost that focus, he'd be finished, and the hard grip of anxiety would send his body spiraling out of control.

Until he cracked this case, he had to put everything else out of his mind, except for Cameron's safety. He wasn't about to lose his concentration where her life was involved.

So what did he have to go on?

The two autopsy reports didn't mesh, as far as method was concerned, although the gun used in both killings had been the same. Same gun, same killer. J.C. imagined that Emerald Greer, up close and personal, had become too much of a handful for her abductor. In fury, or even fear for his own life, he'd attacked, rendering her unconscious—like Cameron, he realized, when her apartment had been burglarized. A little more pressure, and Emerald had been dead. But by an amateur's hand, not a professional after all? Then the gun...

Hitting the Page Down key, J.C. scanned the rest of the document.

And learned nothing new.

In his view, everything still pointed to Destina. Even the small-caliber handgun was the sort preferred by hit men, and another wave of wariness rolled through him. His stomach churned and he could feel his heartbeat soar.

Why couldn't he shake the feeling that Cameron hadn't obeyed his order to stay behind the locked and bolted door of her apartment until he got back? Because he knew her too well now, he silently answered himself. J.C. picked up the phone and punched in her number. He wasn't surprised when Cameron didn't answer. She wasn't home. He left a pithy message to demonstrate his irritation, then phoned Grace. Cameron wasn't at Emerald's apartment either, and he began to really worry.

She was on the loose. Probably trying to pick up her career, then. For a minute he racked his brain, trying to remember the names of her clients. She hadn't told him, he finally decided. Some psychiatrist on West End was all she'd said, a judge...

That didn't help either.

Grace didn't have the names herself.

J.C. hung up, spun back to the computer, closed the NYPD file, then returned to Destina. Somewhere here there must be a clue.

J.C. couldn't deny that feeling either.

With Emerald dead, but the money still missing, whoever had asked questions on the street was still out there. Still looking. For Cameron.

Yesterday the green sedan could have been from Destina. Or not, J.C. had to admit. He stared at the screen until his eyes burned.

And then, suddenly, there it was.

''Dammit!'' he said aloud.

The name seemed to jump at him from the case file. It fit—so perfectly—with James McKenzie's last words that J.C. cursed himself for not seeing it before.

In the next instant he was on his feet.

He had missed the damn connection.

Just as he'd lost James, he could lose Cameron now.

The name pulsed in his blood, keeping time with J.C.'s heart.

*Benjamin. Benjamin. Benjamin.*

He had to find her before her brother did. He had to save her.

''OH, KYLE,'' Cameron said again, facing him in her apartment. Then, ''Ben.''

She held up a hand to ward him off, but Kyle wrestled it behind her back, clamping both of her wrists in a tight grip.

''Tell me where the money is!''

She couldn't help lashing out. ''You killed Dad for it! You killed Emerald!''

Neither murder had been Destina's doing, and the feeling of utter betrayal that raced through her almost brought her to her knees. In her determination to lead a normal life, to be free of the past, she had ignored the truth. No wonder Kyle had offered his support, which would give him access to her life...and the missing money he sought. Money was what he and James had argued about.

In hiding the diamonds, she had made a decoy of herself for her own brother.

She fought against his hold, remembering that before, in

Emerald's apartment, he had used physical force. She had overlooked that.

Her mouth tightened. "I should have known. After everything else—after abandoning our family—you said you had financial problems now."

He didn't try to pretend ignorance.

"Tons," Kyle murmured, his eyes on her like a predator about to sink talons into its prey. "I have expensive taste. I've tried to make up for all those miserable years in Witness Protection."

"So it was you who started asking questions after Destina's release from prison."

He half smiled, a bitter smile. "I'd already taken care of Dad—unintentionally. I didn't mean to kill him," he tried to reassure her, "but he just wouldn't talk. After that, until Destina was free, I had to keep silent. Of course, if I hadn't, his lackeys might be blamed, or Tony, as your friend Ransom thought. But I played it safe. Guess that's one thing I learned from WP. How to bide my time."

"You thought you knew where the money was in the first place—with Dad."

He laughed. "That's all I wanted. Too bad he decided to keep his secret from me."

"He kept it from me, too, Kyle." She fought not to glance toward the mantel.

Kyle shook his head. "Now, Cam, you know that's not true. When I left home, you were too young, and while Mom was still alive, she shared his secret. But he would have told you before he died."

"He didn't know he was going to die! He was murdered. It doesn't bother you that the money wasn't his? That the money was from drugs, prostitution—"

"Plus a dozen other rackets Destina dabbled in. I hope you weren't really fooled by his little one-act play yesterday. If you were, I'm disappointed in you."

"I was fooled by you, Kyle. You used my love, my need to trust you, the very fact that we're family." Of all the killers she had envisioned, she'd never thought of Kyle. She tugged against his grasp but his fingers only clamped down harder. A wave of dizziness followed the flash of pain. "You make me sick. I wish... I wish I'd never seen you again."

Did she imagine his flinch? In the next second, Kyle's gaze hardened.

"Well, our little family reunion seems to be over, then. Fine," he said. "Let's do some business." He twisted her wrists until she gasped. "You tell me where the money is, I take it with me—and I let you live."

There was no way he'd allow her to go free, Cameron knew. She could identify him. She shifted her gaze away from the mantel. It kept wanting to stray there, to the place where her father's ashes sat in the copper urn.

"I've told you, I don't know—"

"Please don't expect me to believe that. I've been patient long enough." He wrenched her arms again and she cried out in pain. "There's more where that came from, and don't think I won't use whatever means I have to. I *want* that money! Tell me where you've hidden it, Cam! Tell me now."

She tried to stall. Her life depended on buying time. "You're insane. If I had the money, I would have used it." She remembered Ransom's suspicions that first night. "Do you see expensive furnishings, clothes?"

His gaze ran down her form. "Everyone wears jeans. Even the rich."

"I'm not rich! I'm struggling the same as you are. Trying to make a real life for myself, Kyle—an honest life. You followed me home. You know where I work, how hard I work. How can you think that I—"

"Because you're just like him! Good old dad pinched

pennies. That didn't mean he was innocent. He cooked the books for Destina until the feds came down on him. Before they arrested Venuto, Dad liquidated an offshore account— Destina always laundered his money and our father knew exactly where it was.'' Kyle marched her across the living room, right past the fireplace and the mantel, into her bedroom. ''Now start remembering.''

Cameron tried to resist but he pushed her into the other room. If she held Kyle off long enough, kept him talking, Ransom might come back. He'd promised to meet her here. Stalling didn't prove that hard for Cameron. She needed to understand why her father, too, had apparently lied to her. Her tone softened with sorrow.

''Then Dad *was* a thief.'' Ransom had been right in that at least.

''Come on, you can't really believe that he was just a victim of Destina's crime family. Once Dad testified against him, he knew Destina would threaten revenge. And he was right.''

''So Dad tried to put something aside,'' she murmured. ''For us?''

That didn't exonerate him, but it seemed very much like James.

''Insurance,'' Kyle said. ''If Destina did come after him, as Ransom expected, Dad had a not-so-honest means of survival for his family at least.''

Kyle turned her in the middle of the bedroom.

''Now start thinking. I'm sure—'' he tightened his hold until she gasped again ''—that you'll come up with that money in no time. The alternative will be very painful.''

And permanent, Cameron silently added.

In that moment she knew she had one small advantage, if not one that would save her. Kyle knew about the money. But he didn't know that their father had converted the bulky cash into diamonds—and hidden them in Cameron's beanbag doll. If he did, Kyle would never have given it to her, never approached her at all, begging her forgiveness.

All along, she'd felt guilty that she couldn't trust him.

All along, her instincts had been right.

How ironic that Destina hadn't been after the missing money for which her father had died. He and Tony had told the truth.

"I can't help you if you don't let go!" She pulled again at the bonds of his strong hands wrapped around her wrists.

The sense of Kyle's betrayal, even her sorrow at James's thievery, suddenly seemed stronger than her inclination to hesitate or run. Her "family" would never be whole again, but if she wanted to survive, to face life without the constant need to flee from danger and to hide, she had to confront Kyle. If she didn't win, she would die.

A momentary flash of memory caught her. Ransom's face above hers, his body within her, his absolutely honest—honorable—expression, his haunted, dark blue eyes. Hurry, she thought. *Please hurry.* The thought that if she failed now, she might never see him again blurred her vision.

"Tears, Cameron? I'm immune to them. Why don't you simply direct me to the proper place? I assume that's here, in your apartment."

He'd unwittingly given her the chance to buy more time. "No, I... I rented a safe-deposit box. At the bank. It's not far from here."

He shook his head. "No. You didn't. We lived for too many years in WP. You know better than to leave anything important—and the money is very important—somewhere it can't be reached. Instantly. In cash."

He was mostly right. She hadn't come that far. Yet.

"I'd like the rest of your story first," she said, one ear cocked for any sound from the hall. The turning of her lock. Thank heaven she hadn't bolted the door when she came in. Hearing Kyle in the apartment, she had left herself the escape hatch. Now Ransom could simply walk in...if he got here in time.

"So you looked me up in New York," she began for him. "Did you really think I'd just hand over the money and wish you well?" Let him think she could be greedy, too.

"Huh. Not as dull-witted as you seemed. Yes," he said. "I thought exactly that. I hoped you would be that glad to see me. You'd trust me. And share."

Cameron trembled. "I can't imagine all you want is half the money."

"Now, if I admit to wanting it all, you'll never tell me. Will you?"

She took a guess. "Is that why you called Emerald's apartment, knowing I'd be there that night? Because you had already followed me? Did you hope to scare me—so I'd welcome you in my life again after sixteen years?" *Tell me what I want to hear...*

"You didn't exactly turn cartwheels when you saw me, but I had applied a bit of pressure, yes." He paused then went on as if pleased to be the center of attention. "I needed you to rely on me. I figured if you felt frightened enough by that voice on the phone first, you'd panic—and gladly hand over the money to get rid of it."

Her head began to throb. *Tell me...or I'm coming after you.*

"When you abducted Emerald, you must have realized your mistake. You meant to take me. Didn't you?"

Kyle shrugged. "I didn't count on finding her in your clothes, I admit. What a vile woman she was, too. Never shut her mouth. Not once after I dragged her into a car not half a block before Fifth Avenue. She was trying to hail a cab," he said, "in a snowstorm. Not so bright, Miss Greer. Everyone knows it's impossible to get a taxi in New York in bad weather. Which worked for me, very nicely. She made an easy target.''

Another wave of sadness hit Cameron.

''She believed she was safe—in my place. That no one would accost her.''

''Not your fault,'' Kyle murmured. ''She threatened to chew my ass all the way to hell and back. She'd turn me in to the police, she said.'' He smiled. ''Interesting, how worked up she could get, considering she never knew I was your brother, never knew what I was after.''

''Why did you kill her?''

''She got in my way. Her presence proved inconvenient, and so did her mouth. I didn't need threats of prison from some has-been tennis player. Frankly, she became tedious. When my head began to ache from the noise, I throttled her. I squeezed and squeezed. Again. And *again.*'' His eyes seemed lit from within, by madness. ''I'd brought the gun as backup—in case *you* proved difficult, instead. No matter how hard I squeezed, Greer fought me. I could hardly leave her by the road alive. I couldn't afford that mouth of hers. So I shot her to make sure.''

Abruptly he released Cameron's wrists, and she rubbed them to restore circulation. Kyle *was* insane. And she was running out of time.

''Don't think of going for the door,'' he said, mistaking her glance toward the outer room. Where was Ransom?

''I have nowhere to run. You'd catch me, Kyle.''

''True,'' he said. ''And you'd suffer.''

''Then what do we do now? Because I'm not giving you that money. It isn't here,'' she lied in desperation, ''and you know it. You searched this whole apartment.''

''Ah. Yes. And nearly ruined everything. When you came in, I was afraid you'd see my face. I was trapped in the bedroom. I hid in your closet, and when you turned your back...sorry, but I had to hit you. Better to leave you out cold than to short-circuit my own quest, shall we say.''

The bump on Cameron's head still hurt. ''You didn't find it.''

''No, and that does make me wonder. Perhaps you're more clever than I give you credit for. Because somewhere in these rooms a fortune is hidden. My fortune now.''

''We won't be alone much longer,'' she said, praying for Ransom to come.

''Long enough.'' He spun her around toward the closet. ''Empty it. Lucky for me, you haven't either furniture or goods. This shouldn't take long.''

Slightly dizzy, she slowed her movements. She pulled everything from the closet, piece by piece, pausing in between each one. All the while she felt Kyle's growing impatience, his increased tension. If Ransom didn't come soon...

Dear God, let him get here before she reached the living room. The mantel.

Stalling again, Cameron picked up the doll from her bed. She had restitched the long gash, replaced its beanbag stuffing, but now Kyle tore it from her. He ripped the doll open again, then flung it on the floor in disgust when he found nothing inside but the beans.

''Wouldn't it have been ironic,'' he said, ''if I'd missed that before.''

''And you'll miss it again.''

''I'm entitled to that money, damn you! I spent too much of my life in WP because of it—because of *him!*''

''And when you found him, when he wouldn't tell you where it was, you killed him. Your own father.''

''He owed me. I had the devil's time finding him, then he wouldn't reveal his secret.''

Cameron's pulse tripped. Had she unwittingly led Kyle to their father, somehow, as Ransom once accused?

Biting down on her lip, she began to strip the bed. She owed her father this chance to put his killer in prison.

A slight sound from the hallway caught her attention. Ransom. It had to be. She needed to tip him off to Kyle's presence. "I'll never give you that money, Kyle. Never!"

The front door opened. Ransom's footsteps clattered across the entryway floor. To her horror, Kyle had pulled out a gun.

"Ransom! Watch out!" she yelled.

Then Kyle backhanded her. And, again, the world went dark.

AT THE SHARP TONE of Cameron's voice, reality registered for J.C. She was not alone. A split second after that, he reached for his gun. Taking a stance, the semiautomatic cupped in both hands, he swept the living room. The soft thud of a body falling to the bedroom floor a second later zipped his heart into high gear.

His worst fears threatened to overwhelm him. His first thought was Kyle McKenzie. Having put two and two together from James's last words, he'd driven like a madman from the precinct to Cameron's apartment. Hoping one second, then fearing the next, that he wouldn't find her there, he'd taken the elevator to her floor. Finding the door unbolted, he'd cursed. The fact that she hadn't slid the bolt must mean she wasn't inside. Where had she gone, then?

In the next instant, he'd heard her.

Now Kyle appeared in the open bedroom doorway, a gun in his hand. He frowned, then cleared his expression. Deliberately, J.C. thought, as if to gain some advantage. J.C. took a step backward, his Glock ready, his mind reluctant to send the impulse to his muscles to use it.

An image of blood—and death—ran through his brain.

"Drop it, McKenzie."

Kyle didn't move. "I rather like the Mexican standoff.

So you figured me out, too, did you? Or am I interrupting another romantic interlude?''

For a long moment, J.C. stood, frozen, on the spot. The stark but obvious fact of Kyle's guilt plunged J.C. back into the Denver alley where James McKenzie had died in his arms. Swallowing, sweating, he relived the horror, then the knowledge of his own failure—despite Cameron's belief in his innocence. He fought the growing sense of panic but couldn't seem to push it away.

With his heart in his throat, he tried to see behind Kyle. If he was too late—again—if Cameron was already…

''Don't worry. I wouldn't kill her and have you miss the show. Now that you're here—''

J.C.'s tone turned deadly. ''You harm her, you won't have any worries. I'll blow you away before you can reach the door.''

''Ah, but I'm holding a gun, too. Now what, Ransom? Except brave words?''

More failure. He should have alerted the police, but about what? Cameron, disobeying his order to stay home? He hadn't known he would find Kyle here, only that Cameron was in danger. On a hunch he had called Ron, who promised to meet him here, to help him look for Cameron if she wasn't home when they arrived. Unconsciously, perhaps, that call had been his instinctive reaction to the situation he couldn't foresee. Where was Ron now?

If J.C. made the wrong move, Cameron would die.

He tightened his grip, widened his stance.

''Give it up, McKenzie. I have backup on the way.''

He smiled. ''How farsighted of you. You couldn't know I was here.''

He tried to harden his voice another notch. ''I was worried about Cameron. Turns out, with good reason. It was you who followed us yesterday, wasn't it?''

''You'd better hope that backup gets here soon. You're

shaking, Ransom.'' Kyle forced a smile. ''In a shoot-out, I wouldn't put money on your survival. Even with two hands, you can't keep that gun steady.''

''It's still a gun. With a full clip.'' He eyed Kyle's smaller .22—the double-murder weapon, he'd bet. ''You can do damage until you run out of bullets, but by then, you'll be full of holes.''

J.C. heard a small sound. He cautioned himself not to react.

It was Cameron's body that had fallen to the bedroom floor. She must be coming to now, probably considering some unwise move to help him. J.C. gritted his teeth. If they survived this, he had things to say to her...

But that would have to wait for later.

In the next breath, his panic disappeared.

He'd lost her father a year ago. And now Cameron...?

It wouldn't happen again. They would survive, J.C. promised himself.

This time, he wouldn't screw up.


IN THE SAME INSTANT, Cameron finished crawling to the bedroom doorway—and after shouting another warning to Ransom, she tackled Kyle's legs.

Taken by surprise, his eyes still on Ransom, Kyle crumpled to the floor. His gun went off and to her horror a bullet whizzed past Ransom's head, creasing his temple. He hadn't ducked quite in time.

Before Kyle could shoot again, Ransom was on him. Cameron kicked Kyle's gun out of the way but at the same time Kyle's hand chopped across Ransom's wrist—and his own gun went flying. The two men grappled on the floor, rolling and tumbling across Cameron's carpet.

''Get my gun!'' Ransom yelled, then grunted when Kyle's knee rammed into his stomach. He choked out, ''Kyle's gun, too!''

Kyle's fist slammed into his face.

Cameron's stomach rolled with nausea.

What could she do to stop them? To save Ransom and herself?

From the corner of Ransom's eye, blood now streamed from the hard right-hand punch Kyle had thrown. More blood dripped from Ransom's temple where Kyle's bullet had grazed him. She had lost her father to Kyle. She wouldn't lose Ransom now. With a strange sense of calm, Cameron placed the two guns on the mantel. She didn't even like touching them. Cold, hard steel. Murderous, their only purpose. And that did it. With a deliberate motion, she picked up the copper urn that held her father's ashes.

Still terrified, Cameron felt shaken, but her eyes had turned dark with fury and determination. Kyle had betrayed her.

First, she'd felt hurt, then sad.

Now anger was uppermost in her mind. That, and the need to help Ransom.

Silently, angling for position, she observed the struggle while Ransom fought like blazes to overcome her brother. Kyle was a strong man, too, and he obviously kept himself in shape. After months on medical leave, Ransom must have lost some of his usual strength but he was holding his own. When the next blows rained down on him, she could see him get mad.

His hands steady, he slammed Kyle onto his back. Before Ransom could straddle his body, Kyle executed a neat turn, reversing their positions. The next thing Cameron knew, Kyle was on top of him, trying to choke the life from Ransom. Cameron's fingers tightened on the urn. She still didn't have the right position from which to help. But she might not get another opportunity.

Gasping for air, his face red and blood still flowing from his temple and eye, Ransom stared up into Kyle's brown gaze. If Cameron didn't move now, Ransom would soon choke to death.

Even fighting for his life, he held Kyle's eyes. Cameron could see in her brother's expression the same flat, soulless stare that she'd seen in killers on TV. Ransom must have seen many of them himself, in person, on the job. Kyle wouldn't give up. He'd kill Ransom, he'd kill Cameron, unless—

Seizing what was probably her last chance, she lifted both arms over her head. To gain momentum, she held the copper urn high, and before she even formed the thought, she knew what she meant to do. In the next second, she brought both arms down—and brained Kyle with the urn.

The clash of metal on bone as it hit his skull rang in the otherwise silent room.

The only other sound she heard was Ransom's harsh breathing when Kyle's hands fell away from his throat. Wheezing to drag in air, Ransom slumped back onto the carpet. Kyle collapsed near him like Cameron's rag doll without its stuffing.

"Well," she said, carefully replacing the urn on the mantel. She had to clear her throat to steady her voice. She hoped her hands didn't look shaky. A light cloud of dust—or ashes—sifted through the air. "With Dad's help, I guess we've done it."

That didn't atone for her father's theft of the money, or his lie about it, but it made a decent start. Grateful to be alive, to find Ransom the same way, she fell to her knees beside him.

"I'll be okay," he managed to croak.

Her fingers gently stroked his raw throat. "He almost killed you."

A faint smile appeared. "Good thing you didn't let that happen."

"Oh, Ransom. Jordan," she corrected. "I do love—"

Kyle groaned. She wanted to say the rest, but that could wait. Right now she and Ransom had the suspect to subdue. Fighting off a wave of dizziness, she helped Ransom to his feet. "Let's turn him over," he said.

Cameron helped and then Ransom pulled a pair of handcuffs from the back of his belt. Together, they cuffed Kyle. Cameron phoned the police, and seconds later Ron arrived—not quite in the nick of time.

"Sorry. Couldn't get a cab. Christmas shoppers everywhere." He paused, then grinned. "I see you two handled everything just fine."

Ron obligingly sat on Kyle until the cops could get there.

But there was one thing missing, Cameron realized.

The money.

This had all been about the money. Well, that and her feelings for Ransom. It seemed he might return her love, but how long before he realized the same thing and asked about what he presumed to be the cash? Before he did, Ransom drew her close to kiss her.

Gratitude for his help, relief, then a surprising flash of desire swept over her.

"Just one question," he whispered into her mouth.

He'd already remembered, and Cameron's heart sank.

"I'll tell you. Later. Right now, you need the paramedics."

With Ron looking on, grinning, Ransom nuzzled her neck. "Hell, I've never felt better in my life."

Then he gave her a vital, all-out kiss she'd never forget.

# *Epilogue*

A week later, Cameron stood at the edge of a long-abandoned cornfield in western New York State. The property belonged to her mother's family, and it was here that her remains had been scattered. Now James would join her.

On this sunny but cold afternoon Cameron held the copper urn close to her body, shielding it against the wind. Her nerves felt taut. Her hair whipped out around her, and in her too-light winter coat she shivered. She really needed to go shopping.

Maybe, when this last part was finally over, that's what she would do. If she remained a free woman.

"You okay?" Ransom stood beside her. She could feel his concerned gaze on her, that deep blue of his eyes. A week ago, those beautiful eyes had looked haunted—by her father's death, Ransom's presumed failure, his post-traumatic stress disorder. And, she supposed, by his memories of his own family.

His father's crime had also been hard for him to absorb. Cameron glanced at him.

"I was wondering the same about you," she said.

Ransom nodded at the urn. His tone stayed firm. "Remember when I told you the marshals hadn't lost anyone in the program? Until then," he added. "I should have said, anyone who followed the WITSEC guidelines."

"And my father didn't."

Ransom shook his head. "Just before he died, he called me to say he'd heard from someone he knew. He was afraid. But he didn't wait for me in Denver. James met Kyle on his own. And went to his death. I followed him but I was too late."

"But how did Kyle find Dad?" Cameron felt a twinge of guilt herself. In her own need to make a normal life, had she jeopardized his safety? "I wonder if Kyle was in New York before. He may have followed me, seen a Christmas card addressed to our father last year. We had an elaborate system of communication that we thought was secure, but maybe it was my own carelessness that got him killed."

Ransom disagreed. "Kyle found him, that's all. We may never know how—unless he opens up under questioning." He looked at the ground. "I'd been fixed on Destina for so long, I couldn't see Kyle as a likely suspect. He got under my guard—but there was little I could have done to prevent James's death. Or anything about my own father, for that matter. People are what they are. All I do know is James's death wasn't my fault. Or yours." He turned to her. "How do you feel about Kyle, though? I know it's not easy to accept what he did."

Cameron shuddered again. She gripped the urn tighter.

"He's my brother. And he's a killer. I can't deny either one."

Ransom put an arm around her shoulders. "I should tell you, at his arraignment he pleaded not guilty. The feds won't plea-bargain anyway. He has nothing to give them."

Cameron stared at him, feeling her nerves begin to shred. Kyle didn't have anything, but Cameron did.

"There's plenty of evidence against him," Ransom went on. "The ballistics reports on the bullets that killed your father and Emerald...but for Kyle, that doesn't matter. Like a lot of others, including my dad, he'll try to deny responsibility.''

"On the basis that he was entitled to the money." Cameron had a hard time even now with Kyle's irrational logic. "It was he who made that one vicious call to me, Ron who made the others. Still, Kyle admitted to both crimes—Dad's murder and Emerald's.''

"He'll probably spend the rest of his life behind bars.''

"What an irony," Cameron said. "It's exactly the kind of life he tried to escape after Witness Protection." She recalled Venuto Destina's comment about her father, how he and Destina had both become prisoners. "Instead, Kyle's trapped again.''

"By his own flaws. Like my dad, Kyle will have ample opportunity to think about James and Emerald while he's doing time.'' Ransom paused, then gave her shoulders a quick squeeze. "You'll need time yourself—maybe lots of it—before you can come to grips with Kyle. Or your father.''

"You mean about his taking the missing money." A slight chill ran down her back, not just from Ransom's touch. There it was again. The money. She couldn't escape that either. Kyle had killed for it. Her father had lied. So had Cameron, by the sin of omission.

Or could she escape, at least from her own sense of guilt?

That was, unless Ransom decided that like his father, she, too, had let him down. That she was, after all, just another guilty party in the Destina case.

Warming the urn between her hands, she hesitated for another moment. Maybe, with Ransom, that was all she would have.

"You know," she said, "I was almost sorry to hear that Destina died.''

Only two days after Kyle's arrest, she and Ransom had gotten the news.

His voice turned cool. "I'm sure Tony appreciated the flowers you sent."

Cameron paused again. "I, uh, put your name on them, too."

For an instant his eyes flashed. Then darker blue met hers. And he smiled.

"Hell, why not? Destina was my cross to bear for a long time. I probably saw him—and your father—as too similar to my own dad. My personal blind spot. That's why, I suppose, I couldn't see anyone else as the killer but Destina."

"You did need quite a bit of convincing."

Ransom pulled back to study her. His eyes twinkled.

"So you're gonna gloat, are you?"

"I wasn't so much right," she said, "as more open-minded."

"You didn't want your father to turn out a thief."

Cameron's pulse lurched. She folded the urn tighter in her embrace, as if to protect James—or her own illusions about him. Kyle's explanation didn't make it simpler to accept her father's part in the case. Maybe James had hidden the money himself in her doll as "insurance" for his family. But it was still stolen goods, not his or Destina's to take. Dirty money, she thought.

And took a deep, steadying breath.

Until she disposed of it, like this, she would never be truly free.

Until she admitted that last truth to Ransom... Even if she lost him, this solution would be worth some peace of mind.

She hoped.

Before she spoke again, Ransom said, "I'm sorry about James—now that we know he did steal the money, I don't feel any satisfaction to have been right in that if not the rest. I know it makes you sad." Ransom drew her closer.

"But time will heal, Cameron, and it must feel good for now to be back to work again." His U.S. Marshals badge flashed at his belt. "I know I do."

Ransom had returned to active duty a few days ago, and she couldn't help stalling one more second to answer him.

"I'm going to be busy. I even hired Grace this morning as my assistant. You should have heard her on the phone. She's delighted. For the first time since her prison term, she feels free herself." Cameron managed a smile. "Oh, and she's already given me a number of referrals. In fact, between those and the people I've acquired through my own clients, I expect to be too busy to feel sad."

Which wasn't quite true—assuming she wasn't in a cell herself by tonight.

"And that's not all," Cameron rushed on. "Ron will join us."

"Emory?" Ransom said. "You don't need a bodyguard any longer. If you did," he added, cradling her close, "that would be me."

"I'm glad you'll be based here in New York. But Ron's giving that up. He'll keep a few clients as a personal trainer, but he's going to learn to be a chef."

"You're kidding."

"He and Grace are talking about someday owning a restaurant."

"Must have liked your cooking." Ransom's smile grew. "I'll tell you something else. Every time I see them together, Grace looks happier and so does Ron. I think they have a thing for each other." He hugged her tight. "Takes one to know one."

Oh God, Cameron thought. How could she tell him? Destroy his faith in her?

Her life had taken some strange twists, yet here she was again in the sunny cornfield where she'd played so briefly as a little girl. Except for the disappointment of her father's betrayal, Cameron couldn't feel more pleased with how things had turned out. Now, in Ransom's arms, with Christmas just around the corner, she was about to risk her entire future—her happiness—on one simple gesture.

She couldn't delay another minute. Or she'd lose her shaky nerve.

Then Ransom said, "Now that we've dispensed with Kyle, with Ron and Grace, there was something you meant to tell me."

Her heart thumped. "In a minute." Just one more. She had to do this her way.

Easing back from Ransom, she removed the lid from the copper urn then raised it over her head, as she'd done before, using it to quell Kyle a week ago, to help save Ransom's life and her own. If she couldn't do that, in a different way now...

Then Cameron stopped thinking. In one quick motion, she tipped the urn, and let its contents fly in a wide arc over the sunny field. A mist of gray—her father's remains—soared through the air, laced with sunlight. And with that, her own spirit took flight. As her father was reunited with her mother, Cameron found delight in something else. For herself, too.

When the sun glinted off myriad small, bright objects twirling almost as one in the air, bound together in their mesh pouch, she couldn't help the watery smile. *The diamonds.* She would have preferred leaving them loose, seeing them twinkle like stars then drift from the sky, one by one, to the ground, but she couldn't risk losing some in the cornfield. She needed them intact. All of them. Cameron had hidden the precious gems in her father's urn of ashes where no one, not even Kyle, had found them. Now, at last, she could bring closure to the case that had tortured her, and Ransom, for so long.

Astonished, he turned to her. For a second, their gazes

held, then Cameron looked away at the flash of light and color as the sun struck the glittering diamonds, their facets sparkling as the pouch spun toward earth, and turned them to fire. A fortune, Kyle had said. A spectacular display, Cameron thought. A symbol.

No matter what happened, she was glad she'd done this.

"That was quite a send-off," Ransom murmured. She couldn't tell from his tone of voice what he was thinking. Feeling. "But about the missing money..."

He knew, she felt sure. He just wanted to hear her say it. "Dad converted that offshore account into diamonds. He wasn't a thief in the true sense—at least he meant well—but he *was* misguided."

Giving herself one last moment before Ransom passed judgment on her, she walked away from him, deeper into the field. Bending down, she retrieved the mesh pouch of diamonds that had caused so much heartache and havoc within her family. Cameron had been wrong. She'd failed to prove her father innocent, because in the end, he was guilty. She would feel sorrowful for a long while about him, but now, she feared, she'd lost Ransom, too. He would turn the gems over to the feds—after all, he was one himself. Case closed. She felt him stop behind her.

"You knew? And didn't tell me—until now?"

Cameron cleared her throat. "A woman doesn't tell *everything* she knows."

"Especially when she's lived most of her life in Witness Protection."

His dry tone made her glance up.

He held out his hand for the pouch of stones. "You realize, you could be charged with obstruction of justice—for starters."

"I know. But I had to try, Ransom," she murmured, her throat tight. Blindly, she handed him the diamonds. "Even if I was wrong, he was my father and I loved him." When she raised her face, unexpected tears brimmed. "No matter what he was, I still do."

"That's the hard part," Ransom said. Then he pulled her to her feet.

He understood, she thought, the complexities of love. And forgiveness. Ransom, too, had loved his father. But next, Cameron expected to hear the chink of handcuffs. He was also a government agent.

Instead, Ransom drew her back into his embrace. He rested his chin on the top of her head and sighed. "For the record, I didn't see that little display of brilliance. If there are questions about this last piece of evidence, hell, I'll do what I can for you."

She could hardly speak. She had wanted him so much. He was to be the final part of her new and oh-so-normal life.

"Ransom, I'm sorry. I should have handed the diamonds to you the first time I saw them...in the beanbag doll Kyle ripped open when he trashed my apartment." She took a shaken breath. "I've mended the doll again. But I couldn't have done this any other way. I wanted to make sure my father—"

"Talk about misguided." Ransom pulled back. "I'll take care of it." He eased her chin up until Cameron looked into his eyes—and began to hope again. She saw no darkness there, except their color. Ransom's gaze looked as clear as the blue sky and all she saw in his eyes was love.

Then she saw nothing else. He dragged her close again. His head descended to hers, blocking out everything but Ransom, and just before he claimed her mouth, he smiled. "I can't have my wife in prison."

Cameron's body jolted in surprise. "Is that a proposal?"

"Official version, U.S. Marshals."

She leaned back in his arms. He was grinning, his gaze still on her mouth, but his eyes had turned a little uncertain.

She'd never seen him look boyish before, carefree yet vulnerable, and Cameron could only nod. *Yes.* Because now, she was truly free. She would never look over her shoulder again. At last, she was free of her past. But freedom, she had learned, was as much on the inside as out.

"It's a life sentence, Marshal."

"You bet."

"There's something else I need to say," she murmured, putting him on the spot this time.

"Yeah," he said, sounding wary.

"I'll marry you—for one reason." She drew his head down to whisper in his ear. "The answer is yes because I love you, Jordan."

He kissed her again.

"I love you, too. I have," he said, "for a long time."

Cameron's body conformed to his. With Ransom's love, she could move forward without fear, without having to hide. The first thing she intended to do was buy herself an early Christmas present—a new, bright red winter coat.

She could even take Destina's advice now, and forgive. From this moment, she and Ransom would create their own—normal—future. Together.

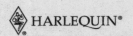

HARLEQUIN®

# INTRIGUE®

This summer, look for a Texas-sized series from three of your favorite authors...

## SHOTGUN *Sallys*

## Meting out the Texas law of the West on their own terms!

**May 2004**
**OUT FOR JUSTICE**
by *USA TODAY* bestselling author
Susan Kearney

**June 2004**
**LEGALLY BINDING**
Ann Voss Peterson

**July 2004**
**LAWFUL ENGAGEMENT**
Linda O. Johnston

*Available at your favorite retail outlet.*

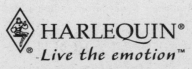

HARLEQUIN®
*Live the emotion*™

www.eHarlequin.com

HISGS

# HARLEQUIN®
# INTRIGUE®

Steamy romance and thrilling suspense
converge in the highly anticipated
next installment of Harlequin Intrigue's
bestselling series

# NEW ORLEANS
## CONFIDENTIAL

**By day these agents pursue lives of city professionals;
by night they are specialized government operatives.
Men bound by love, loyalty and the law—they've vowed
to keep their missions and identities confidential....**

A crime wave has paralyzed the Big Easy, and there is only one
network of top secret operatives tough enough to get the job done!
This newest branch of the CONFIDENTIAL agency is called into
action when a deadly designer drug hits the streets of the Big Easy—
reputed to be distributed by none other than the nefarious Cajun
mob. When one of Confidential's own gets caught in the cross fire, it's
anyone's guess who will be left standing in the shattering showdown....

**July 2004**
## UNDERCOVER ENCOUNTER BY REBECCA YORK

**August 2004**
## BULLETPROOF BILLIONAIRE BY MALLORY KANE

**September 2004**
## A FATHER'S DUTY BY JOANNA WAYNE

*Available at your favorite retail outlet.*

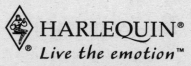

# HARLEQUIN®
*Live the emotion*™

**www.eHarlequin.com**

HINOC

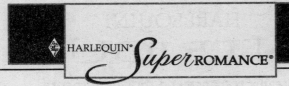

# A Full House
## by Nadia Nichols
### (Superromance #1209)

Dr. Annie Crawford's rented
an isolated saltwater farm in
northern Maine to escape
her hectic New York life and
to spend time with her
troubled teenage daughter.
But the two are not alone
for long. First comes Nelly—
the puppy Annie's ex
promised their daughter.
Then comes Lily, the elderly owner of the farm who wants
nothing more than to return home with her faithful old dog.
And finally, Lieutenant Jake Macpherson—the cop who
arrested Annie's daughter—shows up with his own little girl.
Now Annie's got a full house…and a brand-new family.

*Available in June 2004 wherever Harlequin books are sold.*

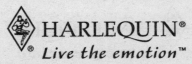

# HARLEQUIN®
## *Live the emotion*™

**www.eHarlequin.com**                    HSRCOCAFH

# eHARLEQUIN.com

Your favorite authors are just a click away
at www.eHarlequin.com!

- Take our **Sister Author Quiz** and
  we'll match you up with the author
  most like you!

- Choose from over 500
  author **profiles!**

- Chat with your favorite authors
  on our **message boards.**

- Are you an author in the making?
  Get advice from published authors
  in **The Inside Scoop!**

- Get the latest on **author appearances**
  and tours!

*Want to know more about your
favorite romance authors?*

**Choose from over 500 author profiles!**

**Learn about your favorite authors
in a fun, interactive setting—
visit www.eHarlequin.com today!**

INTAUTH

USA TODAY bestselling author

# KAREN HARPER

brings you four classic romantic-suspense
novels guaranteed to keep you
on the edge of your seat....

On sale May 2004.

"The cast of creepy characters and a smalltown
setting oozing Brady Bunch wholesomeness makes
for a haunting read."
—*Publishers Weekly* on *The Stone Forest*

www.MIRABooks.com                                    MKH2043